BIG MOUTH

GW00357351

BIG MOUTH

Blánaid
McKinney

A PHOENIX HOUSE BOOK
Weidenfeld & Nicolson

First published in Great Britain in 2000 by Phoenix House

Copyright © Blánaid McKinney 2000

'The Outfielder, the Indian-Giver' was first published in
Phoenix Irish Short Stories 1998, ed. David Marcus, and in
The Picador Book of Contemporary Irish Fiction, 1999, ed. Dermot Bolger.
'Big Mouth' was first published in the *Sunday Tribune*, Dublin.
'Please' was broadcast on RTE in 1999.

A CIP catalogue record for this book
is available from the British Library.

ISBN 1 861591 65 9 (cased)
1 861591 66 7 (trade paperback)

Typeset by Deltatype Ltd, Birkenhead, Merseyside

Printed in Great Britain by
Clays Ltd St Ives plc.

Phoenix House

Weidenfeld & Nicolson
The Orion Publishing Group Ltd
Orion House
5 Upper Saint Martin's Lane
London, WC2H 9EA

Dedicated to the memory of Audrey Beattie

I would like to thank the following:

Christine Chinchen and Diane Skakle for their technical help, creative support and friendship.
David Marcus for his unflagging enthusiasm and editorial eye for detail.
My family, and especially Douglas Law.
And finally, Mr Niven Ogg of Macduff, skipper of the *Maranatha III (U. L. 77)*, the most beautiful trawler ever to grace Scottish waters.

CONTENTS

SUB-AQUA

Even at sixty-five, I've never forgotten that I was once a student. Geology was never going to be much use, but I loved it and am reminded of it daily. This pool, for example, with its marbled floors and high, echoing ceilings, is more like a subterranean cave than a public facility, a softening place where sharp noises lose their power and human yells seem as natural as hard rain down a drainpipe. The short-sighted have a distinct advantage in this place; when I take off my glasses (the steam renders them useless anyway) and half close my eyes, the scene shifts sideways; blurred, pale bodies become like breaking stalactites, leaping, lunatic, off the edge, the speedo colours a wash of crystals. And the noise! A more relaxing din I could not imagine. My favourite position is simply floating on my back, eyes closed, immobile, allowing myself to be shunted this way and that by the movement and rippling energy of others, especially the children and the strong, grim thirty-lappers.

The architecture of this place is pleasingly old-fashioned, a very decent attempt at reproducing a Roman bath. Most people behave themselves when they come here. The young men, when they roar and shove and leap, are merely showing off. Some of them are desperately beautiful and I am reminded of my Jim when he was that age. He and his friends, they had a smart grasp of what a girl wanted. I loved watching them in their 'confederacy of leisure', as I called it;

I

driving around town in packs – elegant, loud, sometimes drunk, like puppies who knew how gorgeous they were. Down at the beach, I and my friends would lie on thick terrytowels and pose in our sunglasses, like Grace Kelly, pretending to be unimpressed by the boys' horseplay and swimming skills. But inevitably I would find myself staring, captured, almost overwhelmed by their otterish physicality, the beige perfection of their skin. And Jim, hands on hips, was the finest of them all; Jim and his poor, sweet attempts at unselfconsciousness. I suppose that's why I fell for him – he would never admit to anything.

I've been coming to this bath more and more often over the last couple of years. I enjoy being surrounded by noisy strangers, to whom I owe no debt of responsibility and who give me the soothing blanket of collective human babble – noise which does not threaten, speech to which I do not have to respond, the uncomprehending gift. When Jim stopped speaking three years ago, after the incident, I found myself trying fiercely to remember every conversation we'd had. The only thing I could recall with any degree of clarity was our last argument. We had been planning our holiday; he knew I was afraid of flying and had grown tired of it. Cajoling and encouragement merely infuriated me, so he had resorted to sneers and accusations of cowardice. It didn't work and I am still terrified at the thought of travelling by plane. Perhaps, because he had once been a pilot, he felt doubly insulted. Perhaps he thought I took pleasure in the perverse notion of a pilot, once soaring and elevated, reduced (as he imagined it) to driving a Tube train. I didn't. I was just frightened.

I have been caring for him now for three years. Not a single word has passed his lips in that time. Sometimes, at night, when he's a bit disorientated, he will lock eyes with me and seem to be on the verge of saying something. Then he sees the hope on my face, which I try to harden and hide, and his eyes fill and his face is flooded with fear. Many drivers hit a leaper. Jim just never got over it. I used to hate her, before I got so tired. What was wrong with sleeping pills? Why did she have to drag him into it?

I don't know exactly when I began to think about the city's rivers and my long-ago studies. I think it might have been when I overheard two young mothers at the pool, complaining about the fact that their minds were starved of adult conversations, adult interests. The small, pretty one said it was driving her mad. That afternoon, I went to the library. I have always been attracted to lost things, buried things, whose most valuable characteristic is their invisibility; I decided I would brush up on my geology and learn of the city's lost rivers, sweet smothered things which had been all but bludgeoned out of existence by the city's progress. It would give me something to do in the late mornings, when the nurse comes to look after Jim.

This is taking for ever. The brake's full on and we're still heading for the mouth of the exit tunnel. I didn't see anything, really, just a blue blur and cropped blonde hair. Dammit, when I get this bastard stopped, all hell is going to break loose. No, the punters aren't going to like this one little bit.

The library has an authoritative hum, which I find comforting. I'd been reading steadily for three days and it was as if I'd taken a shower that's a fraction too hot. I'd forgotten so much that remembering and being reminded hurt a little, but I was learning. Apparently the city has hundreds of miles of rivers, fed by springs and wells; some are lost to us for ever, most have been reduced to lively trickles beneath the concrete and tarmac. Their names have a beautiful, anti-quated grace – Neckinger, Falcon, Effra, Westbourne, Coun-ter's Creek, Fleet, Tyburn, Walbrook. As the city grew, villages became suburbs, rivers became streams, streams became sewers, sewers became culverts.

Last year, I dreamed that Jim spoke to me. He told me to be quiet, to please stop talking.

The Walbrook lies underneath the city, rising in Islington and heading for the Thames. Up until the thirteenth century it ran above ground through villages and meadows, providing everyone with clean, sweet, drinkable water. The dye from medieval tanneries, along with all the other human detritus, turned it into an open sewer and in 1493 a Royal Act decreed that it be vaulted and paved over.

When I got home, Jim seemed in a good mood. He doesn't move around much these days, but rather spends all day either lying in bed or sitting in the living-room, looking out of the window. When he contracted TB shortly after the incident I was vaguely ashamed. Tuberculosis. That's a disease of the poor, surely. I thought we'd cracked that one. From then on, he seemed content to be a silent invalid and I slipped uneasily into the role of nursemaid. Without children, I have had no practice in the business of having someone depend on me. Sometimes I feel like screaming at him to pull himself together, but I never do. Sometimes I am afraid I will hurt him badly.

The following week I decided to go and find the Fleet. It runs parallel to the Walbrook, rises in Hampstead, flows through Camden and King's Cross, before joining the Thames at Blackfriars Bridge. I walked for hours, following the guidebook's directions, knowing that it flowed weakly just a few yards below the pavement. The only sign of it was the occasional ghostly bubbling from a sewer outlet, but it felt good to know that I was on the right track. The traffic was deafening. I kept bumping into passers-by, because I had my gaze fixed at ankle level. I was exhausted when I got

4

home, later than usual, and Jim was anxious because I had asked the nurse if she could take on an extra two hours. He has a bedsore, but always manages to communicate his discomfort before it becomes too painful.

Back in the pool I was planning my next exploratory sojourn. I would track the Neckinger, but this time I would have proper walking shoes and some sandwiches, and I intended to set out early. It rises in a place where the Imperial War Museum now stands and passes around the back of St Thomas's Hospital. I followed it, in bright sunshine, along New Kent Road, referring to my hand-drawn diagram of its position every couple of hundred yards, arriving after a while at Abbey Street. I must have looked odd; most people trying to find their way around town assume the bobbing notion of a bird, peering at their maps, then craning upwards to find some familiar feature. But in a strange way I slipped naturally into a hunched, determined, downward pose, examining the pavements, the grimy grills, the manhole covers. I didn't even know what I was looking for, really. I just enjoyed the knowledge that the Neckinger was there, beaten, near-extinct, cowed, but still there. I followed its track to Bermondsey where, in the thirteenth century, an order of Cluniac monks built a stone bridge and two huge mills. The Neckinger looked after them and they looked after themselves. By now it was late, much too late. I had to get back. I was asked for directions by three backpackers. I couldn't help them. I've never been in this part of town before.

There was an unnecessary fuss when I got home. Three hours. The nurse used the words 'traipsing about', but she is a kind girl and meant no real criticism. Jim was in bed. The room has acquired a smell all its own over the months and years. It is not an unpleasant odour, but suggestive of things long undisturbed, a patina of inactivity, of acceptance. I sat by the bed and, after a little while, he reached out and touched my cheek with the pad of his forefinger. It was not a gesture of affection. He was checking that I still occupied the same space, but I was glad he took comfort in that.

The doctors, after nine months, had finally concluded that his illness was a long time coming, that the leaper was simply the sad little thing that nudged him over the edge. I got very angry when I heard that, because I believe it to be untrue. How do they know what went on inside his head, inside his heart, at that moment, that instant of soaring cruelty? They denied him his horror, his speechlessness. And now I can do nothing, except speak for two, like the solicitous parent of a child sensibly absorbed in other matters.

When I made as if to touch his finger, he withdrew his hand and, with the curling motion of a comfortable cat, buried himself in the blankets.

We need at least half a dozen more staff here. Passengers are just milling around, all bloody curious. They know what's happened and they'd just love to spot some gore. Well, at least the emergency services and the cutters got here quick. If we can clear the place out, then we'll see what's what. Christ, the station manager is coming over. He's shaking like a leaf. What's he shaking for? It was me who hit her. Soon as we calm this place down a bit, get everybody away, then we can get down to business. I've got pins and needles all over. My muscles hurt. God, I could do with a drink right now.

In the library I met an American student, a polite boy with a midwestern accent, which made him seem thirty years older. He called me 'ma'am' and we talked about his home state, Colorado. I was reading about the damming of the Colorado river, the diversion of an obstreperous Midwest monster to the artificial, dainty oasis of Los Angeles. Everyone is interested in water. And this handsome child knew his stuff.

6

He told me, whispering, that Roman Polanski was spot on. It isn't gold, it isn't oil, it's water. Water is life. And the taming of the Colorado shifted life to the West Coast, and turned groundwater aquifers into dry, depleted caves within two decades. The same thing happened to the Ogallala, a massive hydrographic beauty running from South Dakota to West Texas, that over forty years was drained, centrifugally pumped, ruined and sucked almost dry, so that the Lone Star State could became the wealthiest farming region in the world. The water will run out in less than twenty years.

I was fascinated. I tried to imagine the Colorado as Lewis and Clark would have seen it, a roaring, house-high, humbling creature, and then I thought of the Neckinger and I laughed aloud. The librarian frowned at me, slightly, and the young American changed the subject. His beautiful girlfriend sat nearby reading about Raoul Wallenberg, while he told me of his father's suffering in Vietnam.

It was the first proper conversation I had had in months. My throat hurt from whispering.

At home I phoned my younger brother. He has lived in America for thirty years and I love the way his accent has slid, rather than changed. We spoke for a long time, because I had not contacted him in over two years. He is a graceful man and a silky talker. Afterwards I kept Jim company. Sometimes I imagine that he is secretly developing a sign language all his own, a nerveless, dumb ritual, which he can rely upon me to understand. I don't know. I know that I understand his flinching needs, that the clean interview of our communication actually works, that in my exhaustion lies a victory of sorts. Jim was never the type simply to crack. His response to what happened was the reaction of a sane man. And I cannot forgive him that act of ultimate common sense. Whereas I must continue in a groove of ordinary moroseness, he has clung to that tidy, mad grudge. But I cannot ask him to let go. I can't insult him like that. He

sighed long and deep, then reached out his hand, his face still
buried in the pillow. And because I was afraid to do more, I
touched the pad of his forefinger with mine.

I knew that I wasn't covering my tracks, but I couldn't help
it. I phoned Jim's brother and asked him to stay with Jim for
the weekend, just to give me a break. I told him I was visiting
my old friend in Wales. I could be found out with one idle
phone call, but I felt adventurous and determined too. That
night, in my spartan bed-and-breakfast in Belsize Avenue, I
laid out on the bed my windcheater, my flask, my sandwiches, my walking boots, and my maps and diagrams. I had
fifteen pounds in my purse, for soft drinks and sundries and,
in case I was defeated, bus fare. On the Saturday, I rose early
to look for my first river, the Tyburn, also known as the
King's Scholar's Pond. I followed its eastern source, in warm
sunshine, from Haverstock Hill, across Adelaide Road to
Norfolk Road. I am not unfit, but my back began to hurt after
a little while, so I sat in a doorway and had a sandwich.
Passers-by looked at me as if I was a displaced person,
although I was respectably dressed. Without meaning to, I
dropped my gaze and concentrated on their ankles as they
strode past, and finished my sandwiches very quickly.

Two hours later, I found myself at the US ambassador's
residence, under which the Tyburn runs south through
Regent's Park. At the lake it was quiet. My ears were ringing
from the noise of the traffic and my nose stung from the
fumes. I took off my boots and walked about on the grass for
a little while, just to relieve the pain in my heels. In the soft,
cautious quietude of our house I have never felt old, but out
here, in the overland velocity of the city – and a city I have
never seen – I began to feel very tired. The anonymity of the
noise, the smells, intimidated me. But after a few minutes I
remembered the stream, put on my boots and headed for
Oxford Street, which the Tyburn crosses before cutting

beneath Berkeley Square and reaching the Thames. I stopped for another sandwich, then caught a bus to Earls Court. It was late afternoon and I was in search of Counter's Creek, which rises near Kensal Green Cemetery, flows south under the Grand Union Canal and Shepherd's Bush roundabout, crossing Fulham Road and King's Road, before heading for the river.

By now I was very tired and very hot. I had no idea the city, taken in one bite, could be so exhausting. I looked up at the buildings and wondered if there was such a thing as an architecture that is literally capable of driving us insane. An architecture that hits us with precisely the right lines and angles, the perfect combination of shadows and overhang, in precisely the wrong ways, until we silently, collectively, agree that we can't stand it any more, and that we would rather be blind and without hands, *anything*, just so long as we didn't have to squash ourselves around, and into, these beautiful stone details. Above ground, we see ourselves only by reflection, only in plate-glass and shop windows. I think it must have been while I was admiring a gaggle of stylish teenagers on King's Road, all loose-spined and effortlessly gorgeous, that I fainted.

Sometimes I think I am going mad.

When I came to, a young man was holding my hand and looking at me with a worried expression. He was very dishevelled and his hair hung in thick black braids. With the late-evening sun streaming into my eyes, I realised that I had passed him, begging in a doorway, a few hundred yards ago. He offered me a cup of tea from his flask but I couldn't stomach anything. People passing by took no notice. I wanted to continue my journey. I wanted to find and follow the Effra from Norwood to Brixton, and especially the Wandle, one of the few streams with water open and visible, but I felt tired and nauseous and, in the doorway, beside the braided lad and his ridiculous, aged terrier, I felt safe. He gripped my hand and told me everything was all right, in a warm Northern burr, until my head almost stopped swimming. He talked and talked about his homelessness and about his home, and he smiled so much, for my poor sake, that I thought I would cry for his. In the sun's mottled dying I realised I would never see the water visible, that I was an old woman with no energy left, who did not even understand this child's tatty, gentle fun. I knew, vaguely, that I could catch a bus from here to somewhere near Belsize and my room, but I chose to rest for a short time. In the doorway I sat watching the day's light buckling and half closed my eyes against it. Shifting again, the pastel of concrete and car, and thumping passer-by, lost its power before my tired heart and, from nowhere, or perhaps everywhere, arose a different scene. I was so tired and wobbly, but I imagined a rising up of big, useful rivers; the tarmac for a small moment was green and yellow, and softly humming; I saw expansive meadows and the bellowing city as a tiny optimistic village, the brazen streets as smoked lavender, with no songs of praise and velocity, but simple stasis, and nothing happening but habit. I was so exhausted, but the young man kept hold of my hand until I felt a little stronger and ready to catch my bus to Belsize. In the countryside the sky gets up to all sorts of wideboy tricks. Here it is a static, constant thing and doesn't do anything interesting at all.

On the road back to my room I thought of pain's career, its route through that lad and his elderly, scruffy companion. Sometimes I really am very afraid that I am going mad, and my head is filled with thoughts of medieval tanneries, whorehouses and taverns – noisy and without the modern digest of damage, crazy with life. And I think of all the streams and rivers I will never find, because tomorrow I have to go home for good. That night I dreamed of America and of Vietnam, of New York's mole people, their Barrio spirit and shifty heroism, and of the Cu Chi Tunnels, and in the dream Jim walked with me and talked of anaemic alligators in sewers. In the dream he held my face in his hands and laughed out loud.

The following morning, Sunday, I sat on my bed for a long time, listening to the Sabbath sounds outside. I was going home but there was something I had to attend to first.

I stood hovering at the maw of the underground station; I hadn't travelled by Tube since the incident and everything had changed. New machines, new barriers, new voices on the tannoy. Eventually, a young woman helped me to buy a ticket for where I wanted to go and I began to walk towards the trains. My legs still hurt from the day before and I was grateful for the easy concrete decline. On the platform I remembered the gentle rush of air before the roar and got a seat near the door. This was easy. I knew exactly what to do. The rhythm was so familiar and comforting. People moved like gently flung marbles – together, unbumping, directed. I did not alight at my station but stayed, deciding to complete the loop. I had plenty of time. I closed my eyes and thought of the 'dead' stations, where no one would ever alight again. Brompton Road, closed after the war, still beautiful in its dusty Art Deco tiling and green ticket hall, its stern wartime posters and wrought-iron baluster. Pristine. Inexplicable. Dead.

We think we are alone down here and everything encourages us to believe that. But we are surrounded. Surrounded by a web of industry, a silent, frantic circus. Above us, and all around us, lies a couching net of pipes and tinny messages. Eight thousand miles of water pipes, gas pipes, the Post Office's ghostly, unmanned twenty-three miles of electric track, Brunel's Tunnel. I had a sudden, soon-subsided moment of panic when I saw in my mind's eye the earth beneath the city as a honeycombed, fragile thing, just waiting for the Thames to burst in – ferocious, possessive – and drown us all. The thought made me laugh aloud and I didn't need to open my eyes to know that my fellow passengers were looking at me, and that I had, again, reached my stop. I got off very slowly and made my way to the northbound platform.

It was very quiet. Only two other people were waiting. I stood at the edge of the platform and looked into the black mouth of the tunnel. So this was where it happened. This was where she gathered herself and jumped, and took with her all her distress. This was the very spot where ours began, mine and Jim's. The genesis of our lives. I was frozen in that place for a long, long time, staring down at the rails. Tiny, black, mutant mice darted noiselessly about and I had a sudden urge to throw crumbs to them, to help them to live, like I used to do with the birds in the park. The night-ladies – the 'fluffers' who keep the lines clean – were they asked to clean the station rails that day?

Nothing like this has ever happened to me. I don't want to see. We've got the carriage backed off a few yards so that we can see what we're at. Two medics, a fireman and I are on our hands and knees, peering underneath. No one will look me in the eye. I can see her. My God, I don't believe it. There isn't a mark on her. She's perfect. She could be asleep. She's lying on her side between the rails, one hand almost touching her cheek. She's perfect, there isn't a mark on her. Just then, one of the firemen reaches in with a hooked rod and pulls at her beltstrap. Her legs fall sideways while her upper body remains still and that's when I see that she has been cut in half, perfectly sliced in two, and her torso ends in a hideous, red, round slab. I can barely hear the groans of the others because I am retching and vomiting and crying and running. The station manager is gripping me by the shoulders and saying something but I can't hear him. I can't stop shaking, I can't stop crying. I just can't stop. How will I tell

Hazel what happened? How will I speak of this? How will I speak of this?

Jim's brother shouted at me for half an hour and called me crazy. He'd phoned my friend's house to find out if I'd arrived safely and of course she didn't know what he was talking about. I just let him shout. I didn't tell him. I didn't say anything. Then he looked as if he was about to cry and I realised he had been frantic with worry. I still didn't say anything but climbed the stairs to be with Jim for the night.

The nurse's busy presence was manifest in the slow-motioned billowing of the curtain. She was a great believer in fresh air and stimulating noises. Jim was asleep, motionless. He coughed occasionally. Apart from that, and his soft breathing, there was no sound in the room. I took his hand in mine and was glad when he didn't wake or flinch. Sleep was his salvation and his silence was embedded so deep in his head that, even then, he never said a word. I had to admire that. I don't usually dwell on the past – it's pointless – but tonight I could think of little else. My God, he was so beautiful and, in a way, still is. Even in his sixties he still had that svelte, curvy grace one sees more often in a man half his age. We went to Blackpool once, for a week, and he spent most of his time on the beach doing cartwheels until he felt sick. He was forty-three then. How did this happen? How did he fall away from us so easily? What thing was it that seeped around the frock of his heart and sealed him up and took him away? As a teenager on the beach, he possessed such a cavalier, wet arrogance. He was so good at the kind of exceptional tomfoolery that made me want to canter up and bite his throat, at least to grab a handful of hair. It has been so long since he touched me. In our fractured domesticity I have, of necessity, become expert at the discipline of saying nothing well, at negotiating the angular airpockets of a lined language. Perhaps he hated me for that.

Perhaps he is implacable and without forgiveness, and rightly so. He cannot forgive himself and I cannot forgive her, but I know one thing for certain: in the ruined froth and dusty amalgam that is our life together I know that he is fearfully content, and I know that he will never speak to me again. Our incendiary past is gone and will never return. I remember the one occasion, years ago, when he frightened me. We were arguing. He balled his fist, raised his arm and, for one exhilarating, artificial moment, I thought he was going to punch me. Then we both looked at his fist and I shall never forget the expression of crumpled and utter guilt that invaded his face. For a moment he looked like a different person, like the man whose face he now inhabits, a man who owns injured dreams and a terrible, golden damage.

I sat, dribbling tears and listening to my own scalded heartbeat, for most of the night. A lack of faith is by no means fatal, but I have sought too long for love where love no longer rests and I am so very, very tired. As I got up from the chair, his fingers left my palm in a near-carnal brush. Telltale warmth, full of clues, is not enough any more.

That was two weeks ago. Today, I am floating in the pool, drenched in the delicacy of its steam, eyes closed, thinking about a wildlife documentary I once saw. David Attenborough was crawling around a termite mound and the camerawork made it seem as if we were actually inside the mound, with its myriad caverns and tunnels, and I remember thinking how simple the insect world is. Eating, reproducing, killing and dying. That's it. And I remember the feeling of strangeness that came over me. This was so bizarre, so far removed from normal life. I found it tremendously cheering. Then I watched Oprah Winfrey talking to a convicted serial killer about his three wives and his hopes for reincarnation, and exactly the same sensation came over me. I laugh, floating, because I can't help it and I swallow water. I'm coughing slightly when I see the young, well-mannered American boy and his pretty girlfriend. They look worried, but I wave, smiling. I'm okay. They are a very handsome, gleaming couple and strong, splashy swimmers.

In the library this morning I was reading about the strange things that get left behind on the underground and the conscientious, interested people at Baker Street who deal with them. A stuffed eagle, a divan bed, two hundredweight of raisins and sultanas, a carton of bull's sperm, breast implants. Some 25,000 objects, all Lost Property, all unclaimed. Or unwanted. All lost underground. I could laugh again but I don't because I am still floating and thinking of the ticket in my locker. An airline ticket to Arizona, to my brother's home. And I am so frightened at the thought of flying, but even more frightened at the thought of staying. I never thought of myself as cruel. I don't know. There are few things as cold as loyalty. Perhaps I am dreadfully wrong, but I know that I cannot go on. I cannot continue with this agony. I can't. Oh, God, Jim, I am sorry for this bloodless mutiny. I am so sorry. I am so sorry. I am so sorry ...

The Langbourne is a lost river. The geography of myth holds that it ran from Fenchurch Street across Gracechurch Street, and held a lively and businesslike course down Shorebourne Lane before homing in on the Thames. But that is merely its story. No one really knows for sure.

THE GOLD OF TOLOSA

Robert punched the intercom and said, 'Okay, Linda, how about this? One shot each of dark rum, white rum, pineapple juice and a touch of soda, with lots of crushed ice, in a nice, fat, chunky glass.'

'It's been done. It's either a Bahama Mama, or something bloody close. Anyway, it sounds horrible. Listen, I've been thinking about whiskies. There was one on the market about ten years ago with *real* gold flake in it. We could concoct something around that. I keep trying to remember the name of that Roman consul, the one who stole all the gold from some temple or other in France. Donkey's years ago. Who the hell was he? Anyway, we could name it after him. Real gold flake. Pretty flash, eh?'

Robert laughed. Last week it was famous Canadians, this week it was the creation of a new cocktail, next week it would probably be her collection of Tex Avery cartoons, edited together for the staff during lunch hour. Robert's personal favourite was her scale outline of the US Starship *Enterprise* 1710–D, superimposed over an OS 1:2500 map of the city. The damn thing covered most of Crouch End.

He liked Linda. He liked her clever enthusiasms and had never comfortably regarded her as his secretary, especially as she held a first class degree, had travelled a great deal. Yet she embraced her clerical job in the Environmental Health Department with the same unselfconscious, kind energy with which, he had come to learn, she approached everything. She didn't make him feel unsophisticated and he was grateful for that. Still, he was surprised at what appeared to be her genuine disappointment when she had asked him to come to her thirtieth birthday party and he had declined. Most people had stopped asking him years ago.

'Oh, Bob, listen, by the way – are you free this afternoon for a site visit? Graham just called in. His pumping station meeting is overrunning and there's no way he'll make it back before five.'

'A site visit? Linda, the reason I like my desk job is that I don't have to go out and meet the great unwashable. Jesus – I'm kidding. Okay, okay. Who and where?'

'It's an old lady in Cecile Park, not very mobile. She just wants some advice about clearing out old furniture and whatnot. Big house. Been there for years, so God knows what she's collected. Come on, you heartless sod, go and say hello to a little old lady.'

They both knew that something so simple could be sorted out by phone, or delegated, but Linda liked to force him out of the office every so often and he liked to let her.

'I'll drop by on my way home, okay?'

'Hurray for Mother Teresa. Oh – and the garage called. They've finished the service, but there are a few bits and bobs needing done. That'll be another couple of hundred quid, eh?'

'Thank you, Linda.'

'You're welcome, Robert. Have a think about the whisky.'

It was raining gently. On the bus, he sat behind a black girl in a bright African dress who'd hauled herself noisily up the steps. Her hair was webbed by thousands of tiny raindroplets, which sparkled dully in the electric light. Robert stared at the back of her head and thought about his mother, and about how much better it would have been if someone had turned up in a mourning colour other than black; the deep blue of ancient Rome, the bright yellow of Egypt and Burma, Iranian beige, Korean white, the mad scarlet of Celts and gypsies.

His throat tightened slightly. He concentrated hard on the damp halo in front of him, its amiable bounce, on the two boys in front, all denim and elbows, on the blundering sparrows outside in the dusk.

The house was late Victorian and had a slovenly look of historical sneakiness to it, as if the builders had changed their minds halfway through. Robert liked the pale, warm brickwork, though, and the frozen calligraphy around the door. He had trained briefly as an architect before giving up when the money ran out, and he still took an interest. When walking around town he tended to look like a confident tourist, his gaze always fixed at a point above the shopfronts. He loved the tatty snobbery of some buildings, the injured hooliganism of others, the ones that looked like a collapsed scrum, where there was barely enough time before the developers moved in to find out which neck had been broken, which Georgian or Edwardian urban harpy had been ruined, or scalped beyond saving.

He laid his left palm against the pearl brick and pressed the doorbell. A few moments later the door opened a couple of inches. She was in her early seventies with surprising, arctic-blue eyes and the pale, soft skin of an elderly woman.

'Mrs O'Sullivan? My name is Robert Beck, I'm from the Environmental Health Department.' He held up his card. 'You called recently, saying you needed help in disposing of some rubbish?'

'Ah, yes, please come in.'

Her voice was brisk and strong. Still, he was surprised that she showed none of the frail, doorstep suspicion, a look worn by many women who lived alone.

'Sorry about the mess.'

'Mess' wasn't exactly the word Robert would have used. The place was like a bomb-site. Hulking pieces of ancient furniture lay everywhere, some upended. Paintings, candle-sticks, footstools, lamps were stacked in a careless heap in the middle of the high-ceilinged room. Where the paintings had been, the wallpaper sported clean, naked rectangles of all sizes, like the work of a bad-tempered Cubist.

'Well, Mrs O'Sullivan, you've certainly got quite a lot of ... stuff. Are you certain you want it removed? I'm sure some of it could go to charity shops.'

'No. Most of it's rotting anyway. I want it pulverised, destroyed, all of it. My hideous nephew and his disgusting wife have decided that I'm to go into a residential home. I don't want them or anyone else using it. Swine. Just because I fell down the bloody stairs.'

Robert suppressed a smile. His head was beginning to hurt. She had a faint Anglo-Irish accent, slightly aristocratic, and she talked as she grasped his sleeve and led him around the other rooms, three of them with piles of 'stuff' in the centre of the carpet or on the beds. In one room, however, the walls were festooned with very old enamel and metal Underground and street signs. 'Stroud Green Road', 'Panton Street', 'St Augustine's Avenue', 'King's Cross' – dozens, perhaps hundreds of them, from all parts of the city. They were in pristine condition. Probably worth a fortune, thought Robert. Probably stolen, too. The rest of the room was bare, apart from three enormous five-foot-tall potted plants in the centre of the floor. Robert stared at them. They were marijuana plants.

'Very attractive ferns, aren't they? My grandson gave them to me. Would you like a cutting?'

'Ah. No. Thanks all the same.'

Her grandson. Right.

Mrs O'Sullivan had moved back into the main living space and was nibbling energetically at the lumber, hauling objects into the centre of the room, poking in drawers, talking. 'As I was saying, I don't know how we managed to accumulate so much, especially since my husband's job took us all over Europe. We moved here in 1971 and he just filled the place right up. He was American. He died four months ago.'

'Oh. I'm sorry.'

Four months ago.

Mrs O'Sullivan gazed directly at him. She said nothing.

Robert searched for something else to say but it was as if the dim claustrophobia of the house had begun to slow his mind to a crawl. The air seemed to have become thicker and he found himself gazing stupidly at the dust falling slowly through the shafts of light from the blinds, disappearing silently into her white hair.

'Would you like a cup of tea? You can do an inventory, or whatever, and work out how long it will take your men to move all of this.'

'Yes, I would like a cup. Thank you.'

He wanted to sit down. His headache was getting worse. She disappeared into the kitchen. She can't wait to get rid of it, he thought. He walked slowly around the room, touching the furniture. A job where he could use his hands. Yes. He remembered how, as a boy, he'd wanted to be the best pickpocket ever. He would always have given the wallets back, of course. Or someone who makes children's pop-up books. A skill.

'No ambition, that's your problem,' his mother had said, with authentic bitterness.

There was a muted crash from the kitchen, followed by a laugh and the sound of broken crockery being kicked across the floor. Mrs O'Sullivan appeared, carrying a tea tray. 'One less thing to carry out,' she said cheerfully.

As he sipped his tea, Robert noticed a photograph on top of the pile. It was a picture of a good-looking young man, probably taken in the 1940s, judging by his suit. 'Your husband?'

'Yes.'

'And you're throwing it out?'

'Yes.'

There was no inflection in her voice. Robert's wallet was stuffed with photographs of aunts, uncles, friends, his father and, now, his mother. Striking. Unforgiving. Gone.

Mrs O'Sullivan smiled at him. 'Have you ever lived in Mexico?' she said unexpectedly.

'Um, no. North London, born and bred. I'm afraid I'm not the adventurous sort.'

'Well, Jack, my husband, was and I've lived in quite a few places. Mexico was my favourite. On the first of November every year they celebrate the Day of the Dead. The *chilangos* dress up as skeletons, get blazing drunk and the souls of the dead walk the earth. They embrace death. They don't run away from it. I don't need a photograph. It's all just clutter.'

He thought of the roomful of signs. King's Cross. The man whose body was never identified, never claimed, even after computer enhancement and the pathologists' patient detective work. When she was younger, his Catholic mother and her sisters had made an occasional novena for the repose of the dead. All Souls' Day. He had loved the blind, logical decency of that; the living carrying out the work, the reparation, the charitable acts, which the dead had had neither the time nor the heart to undertake while they still lived. Robert hadn't prayed in years. He had never been religious, but as a boy he had loved, smugly, the almost architectural exaggerations of the Creed, the Gloria, the Act of Confession. He could wrap himself in luxurious and absolute forgiveness for his heroic sins, disappear completely inside his own lovely, plastic devotion.

'At my age, clutter is the last thing I need, young man.'

Young man. He was forty-seven. Robert stared at his cup. Inertia was getting the better of him. First thing Monday he'd write a memo and delegate the whole bloody house. Graham was going to kill him.

He struggled to bring his mind back to the job. 'I can probably arrange something for late next week.' He glanced around. 'It'll take three or four hours. Will you be here in the mornings?' he added helplessly.

She wasn't listening. 'Jack was a couple of years younger than me,' she murmured. 'He was a collector, I was a scavenger. There's a big difference, but we got along fine in Dublin. I was studying Classics at Trinity, but I was dying to go to New York with him. He had some strange jobs before Exxon took him on in the Fifties. He even worked at a TV station, as a scorekeeper on a quiz show. But they fired him.'

'What happened?' Robert found himself asking.

'He got plastered one night and racked up 250 points for the biggest moron the show had ever seen. The studio audience damn near lynched him.' She laughed. 'But the moron took us both out for a fine dinner.'

Robert smiled. 'You seem to have had fun together.'

'Yes, a lot of fun.'

She talked a little more about her Jack, jobs he'd had, places they had lived. Her voice had a svelte, otterish quality, with traces of different accents surfacing and receding as she spoke.

'We once got arrested for dancing on McCarthy's grave.'

Robert blinked in confusion. 'The puppet?'

'Ha! No, the patriot, or at least that's what he called himself.'

Robert had always wanted to go to America. Mainly to look at the buildings, but he was also fascinated by the idea of a people whose sense of space was so different from his own. To drive across the mid-West for hundreds of miles and see nothing but horizon. And to hear only the graceful patois of the Plains. He knew it was all rubbish. He knew that the unimaginable spaces were becoming imaginable and manageable, filled with features that, in dot-to-dot fashion, would slowly chase away the loneliness of such places. He knew that the middling drawl of Kansas, after three weeks, probably bounced off the ear no more attractively than the glottal stops of South London. He knew that he wanted to have it both ways, so he had never gone.

For the first time that day, he thought about his wife.

He wanted to ask the old lady about the signs in the other room.

'Do you miss him?' He couldn't believe he'd asked her that. 'I'm sorry, I didn't mean to pry. Sorry.'

There was something about her vagrant yarns, the casual tetch and shrewdness of her voice, about this scruffy house, its livid squares, its doomed heaps, something that made him want to know more about her.

'Who, Senator McCarthy?'

'Eh? No, no, Jack, your husband.'

'No. I don't miss him.' She waggled a translucent, mesmerising knuckle at him. Her voice was utterly level.

'Oh, don't misunderstand me, I loved him dearly. We were together a long time, but after three heart attacks, the fun and the dog-dancing and the *shine* on things just doesn't come back. Besides, he wasn't in pain. I'd say he had a very reasonable death. I've never been lonely or bored in my life.'

A reasonable death.

'And my grandson visits me occasionally, takes me for a drive, prunes the plants. He says he'll take them back when I move out. I've already given him all the books. His girlfriend wanted a lot of my clothes, strangely enough. Some sort of "chanteuse", I gather.'

Outside, a few starlings were settling down for the night. Robert thought of the Fridays when he hadn't wanted to go straight home, but had gone instead to Leicester Square, just to watch the thousands of starlings on top of every building, to listen at dusk to the hysterical, sociable racket. They were almost a tourist attraction. Sometimes the noise was so great that dozens of people would stop strolling and just stand there, looking up, eating ice cream, holding hands. The itinerant compassion of anonymity.

On a recent Friday, watching the sleek inaccuracy of young birds, as they shot across the neon, he'd had a moment of utter panic as he realised that he might never again want to go home. That the only thing he really wished to do was to withdraw and watch the others get on with it.

These thoughts had wandered through his head as he stood and watched a rare litter whirlpool on the ground, a tiny vortex of leaves and sweet wrappers; he caught a tourist watching it too. They'd given each other a raised eyebrow and a shy smile of recognition.

No ambition.

That was fine with him.

'Are you sure you wouldn't like a cutting?' Mrs O'Sullivan was looking at him again with that steady, interested expression. 'It grows like wildfire and just needs lots of sunlight.'

He had a sudden impulse to laugh and tell her that if the cops ever stumbled across this place, between the plants and the roomful of – what? Public property? – she could be in trouble. Maybe she knew. Maybe she didn't give a damn. As a gesture of respect, he tried to hold her gaze. 'Yes. In fact, I think I would like a cutting. It's very pretty. Thank you.'

'Fine.'

She left the room and Robert tried to think of what to tell Graham to do with the signs. Storage, maybe. He really had to go.

She reappeared with a small, clear plastic bag, with greenery inside. 'I think it's an annual, so there are a few roots in there as well. Lots of sunlight.'

'Thank you. Well, if you're here, say, Wednesday morning of next week, we should have the place cleared in a few hours, okay?'

'Noon would be better. I'm not an early riser. I'm moving

to the home on Saturday, so that means only three nights with my nephew. And his wife. The Trojan Mare.' She looked around the room. '"*Bahalla na*" – what the hell.'

As they headed for the door a thought struck Robert. 'You were a Classics scholar?'

'Many, *many* years ago. I did enjoy it, though.'

'I don't suppose you know anything about the story of a Roman consul who stole gold from a temple in France, apparently? It's for a quiz at work.'

He felt suddenly ridiculous, asking her that.

Her expression changed slightly and the pale blue of her eyes reflected a colour that came from a long way away, from centuries ago, as she struggled to remember. Her voice echoed a soft classroom mantra. 'The Gold of Toulouse. Caepio. Caepio and Maximus. 106BC. Their army desecrated the temple of the Celtic Apollo. They stripped it of its gold, its jewels. And they mocked the gods. But the Apollo of the Celts exacted a terrible revenge and placed the howling Cimbrians in their path. One hundred thousand men died on that battlefield. They all died. Caepio and Maximus. 106BC. The Gold of Tolosa.'

She blinked. 'Ill-gotten gains never prosper, I suppose.' She sighed. 'The ultimate security is to possess nothing worth stealing.'

Robert stared at her.

He felt his headache lifting. He paused, with his fingers touching the door handle, ready to go, wanting to stay. He wanted to hear another anonymous story from this woman and then another. About people who had nothing to do with him, about places he would never comfortably visit, and to let her voice act as a door, opening and closing, keeping him safe, allowing him a glimpse of danger. 'Thank you, Mrs O'Sullivan,' he said softly.

'Goodbye.'

She smiled and closed the door behind him. As he walked

from the house, he thought he heard music coming from an upstairs room. It sounded like Louisiana cajun.

The rain dribbled slowly down the bus window, melting the orange street lamps beyond. Robert knew that in a city lights that threw no shadows were necessary, but he hated them; if a migraine could have a shape it would be like that – a chic, bright wound.

The bus was filling up with the Friday night pussycats. That's how he thought of them, the urban environmentalists, in their lunatic colours and perilous hairstyles. Robert wore navy or brown, but he enjoyed having something interesting to look at. One couple looked nice. The boy, a handsome Indian lad with letters shaved into the side of his head (Robert couldn't make them out), wore a magnificently sloppy red T-shirt with the Silver Surfer on the front, cycling shorts and huge chunky boots. His girlfriend looked like an oriental Clara Bow, a diminished, soiled little ghost in grey lace, pale make-up and spectacular South American earrings. As they got up to leave, the boy turned, taking her elbow in a delicate, gentlemanly way, and Robert saw that his hair said 'SKUNK'.

Others took their place. A serene, beautiful teenage boy with one fingernail painted gold. A collection of girls, quite drunk, shrieking and finishing each other's sentences, with roars and muscular whoops and magazines of laughter. Just past Finsbury Park a weary man in a navy suit climbed heavily into a seat and for half an hour stared at the back of Robert's head.

The desiccated cyphers of North London streamed wetly past, in elongated cameos. Robert wondered where exactly Mrs O'Sullivan was moving. He'd forgotten to ask. What had she meant by describing herself as a scavenger? A young woman got on with two children. She had a look of sad, fierce thrift about her. Robert noticed her lean, muscled forearms, as if she worked out. Like Madonna, he thought. Her children were very well behaved, and chatted to each other in scorched, prayer-like whispers while she stared distantly out of the window, trailing the odd dreaming finger across their heads.

Robert had lived here all his life, yet had rarely failed to be overwhelmed by something as basic as a bus ride. The fact that it all worked. So many miracles of purpose. The million tiny crimes, the sticks-and-stones civility, the palpable intelligence in the city's spine. The fact that it can't possibly work, yet did.

His mother had always wanted to return to the countryside where she was born. She hated the city and, when his father retired, they'd moved to Abingdon, fifty miles away. The countryside made Robert uncomfortable. Several years ago he'd taken his wife skiing in the Cairngorms. Well, she skied. He'd spent most of his time reading Raymond Chandler in the hotel bar. He didn't dislike the vastness, or the desolation of the place. He merely disliked being surrounded by people who felt it necessary to climb into their Volvos and travel 800 miles just to feel humbled. Besides, in the countryside he was surrounded by creatures eating each other, silently. No, greenery made him nervous.

He fingered the plastic bag in his pocket and wondered if it would grow on the bathroom windowsill.

Everyone had said she was brave, towards the end. Perhaps she was. Robert didn't understand the process whereby disease transformed an embattled, clever, snobbish, substantially ordinary woman into a saint. He suspected that it was for the benefit of others, that few people are authentically courageous, but we must convince ourselves that they are. Besides, he hadn't been involved. Not really. There had sprung up legions of people, mostly women, to look after her, to organise everything. His sister, his wife – it was as if the job of coping, the business of unfussy practicalities had fallen to them as naturally as rain. His male colleagues, his younger brother, Robert himself – they had gradually and, over the months, helplessly, assumed the demeanour of listless squaddies standing around a bomb-site, watching the disposal experts, waiting for something to detonate, hoping it wouldn't. He had welcomed casual exclusion, when it happened, all his life. What use would he have been? He was no good at the warm, tawdry engagement of the whole business. But he resented the way in which everyone assumed that he was so happily preoccupied that he didn't care. But he was forty-seven. Everyone dies. This was absurd. He was forty-seven, for Christ's sake. He'd just tried to maintain a cool allowance for most things.

At the dinner table four months ago his wife had begun to weep and complain about the enforced cheerfulness of the whole thing. The cheerfulness that does not cheer. And she was tired. And she wasn't even sure she'd liked the bloody woman. And why hadn't he taken any days off work? It wasn't a crime to grieve properly. No one was forcing him to rush from catastrophe to instant forbearance, the way bereaved parents of murdered children look on television. He hadn't planned it like that. He hadn't meant to be stoically frozen; he simply was unsure as to how he was supposed to behave. In a small way he resented those who showed off the luxury of their – what? Self-indulgence? No. He was just tired of being the villain of the piece, the walking icebox in which they all stored their irritating melodramas. Robert was a good watcher. He had seen a little of the damage done by people who loudly and continually mistook their instincts for common sense, their emotions for evangelical gospel, and then accused him of being cold-hearted. He knew he was not cold. At least he hoped he wasn't. He didn't know what kind of comparison to make. He didn't know whether he would go twelve rounds, because he'd never gone near the ring. Very slowly, very slowly, as he stared at the violent hairdo of the girl in front of him, it occurred to Robert that his mother had perhaps meant, not ambition, but something else. Something requiring a little colour and arrogance and effort from his ignorant heart.

It occurred to him that, all his life, his mother had been calling him a coward.

His wife was not there when he got home. He'd actually forgotten. She was staying for the weekend with her younger sister in Reading. He suspected she preferred that household, with its noise, with the teenage sons' absurd horseplay. She always came back with an apologetic air and a plastic bag full of CDs. She would tape most of them and return them on the next trip. The latest ones she played in the mornings, very quietly, as if parading her nephews' musical tastes and now, magpie-like, hers, would insult him. Robert felt like shouting at her that hardcore techno wasn't supposed to be played as a reverential background hush and that if she was so bloody touchy about it, all she had to do was wait until he left the house, then turn the volume up to maximum and to hell with the neighbours. Until it occurred to him that she probably did.

He dug out the smallest plant pot he could find, filled it with a little earth and, as gently as he could, patted the slightly crushed cutting and roots into place, until it stood more or less upright. It was a pathetic scrap, but he put it on the windowsill anyway, checked for draughts and turned off the bathroom light.

Then he turned the light on again, went into the kitchen and fixed himself a large whisky.

He stood beside the back-porch light, on his third drink, eyeing the stupidity of moths, holding his glass up to the light, and tried to imagine gold flake floating, darting like gypsy shoals, like bog rain, like the glittering stony follicles

of granite buildings that, after a wet spell, made parts of the
city twinkle.

What if she decided she never wanted to come home? Her
weekends away were becoming more frequent and she had an
excited look about her when she came back, laden down like
a June bee (as his mother would have put it) with plastic bags
and T-shirts and, once, a new haircut.

When she'd cried, four months ago, he'd tried to comfort
her by appearing to be affected in a manner people seemed to
find more acceptable, by sort of moving down a gear. But she
saw through his solemn, shy tableau after a couple of days
and he ended up feeling like an unconsenting donor. He tried
a consoling brand of romance, only to be depressed by the
careless impoverishment of the language. Flowers, dinner,
candles.

The most romantic thing Robert had ever seen was the
shabby, lichen-covered grave of a seventeenth-century Aberdeen butcher, with a skull and crossbones carved on the table
stone, accompanied by grotesque, worn reliefs of the tools of
the man's trade – axe, cleaver, knife and the stern message,
'Memento Mori'.

Okay, then – a holiday. He suggested going to the January
ice-sculpture contest in Finland. Something unusual and
beautiful. And skilled. To spend a long weekend watching a
bunch of huge, bearded Rodins creating astounding structures with pickaxes and blowtorches and chainsaws.

She didn't say no. She just stared at him.

Dinner it was, then, in a nice restaurant. And a fragile,
injured night it was. She was looking so pretty, so much
younger. When she smiled and said in a fake Brooklyn accent
that she was just going to 'fix her face', he'd asked her if she
knew the origins of lipstick. She said no and her face set in a
slightly preparatory way. Lipstick, he told her, in what he
thought was a joking tone, was used by prostitutes on the
streets of ancient Rome to indicate a willingness (for extra

denarii, of course) to perform fellatio. Her expression didn't change. She just stared at him. Thanks, Bob, she had said in a voice that raked his heart and raised his neck hairs. He didn't know. He had no idea she was feeling so hurt. And then she'd lowered her eyes and actually blushed.

They had been married for eleven years.

He shivered on the porch, went back inside and poured himself another drink.

The phone rang. It was his wife. She was staying the week. Yes, she had his mobile number. She would call him on Wednesday. He was pretty drunk. He swayed upstairs to bed and dreamed of sodium lamps, of seagulls' guff and of eighty-foot black obelisks standing guard over a radioactive land-scape; warning markers that had to last for 10,000 years.

Robert stayed in bed for most of the weekend, watching television and drinking beer. Outside, the city fumed greyly, working up a layer of crisp, talkative frost.

On Monday he picked up his car and drove to work. Two hundred and fifteen quid and the damn thing was still going like a pig on stilts. What the hell.

'Hiya, sexy!'

Even Monday mornings couldn't get the better of Linda. 'Good weekend?'

'Oh, so-so. You?'

'Brilliant! I jumped out of an aeroplane and you owe me fifteen smackers.'

Christ, the sponsored parachute jump. He couldn't believe she'd actually done it. He took a twenty out of his wallet, shaking his head. 'Keep the change. You deserve it.'

He suddenly felt like laughing. At his desk he ploughed through eight internal memos, four Committee reports, wrote Graham's instructions for Wednesday, and called the Transport Museum and invited them to send someone along. You never know. They might recognise something valuable.

Around noon he went out to Linda's desk. 'By the way, I found that cocktail for you. Red vermouth, gold flake whisky and a dash of bitters. It's basically a Rob Roy but with the gold, and an orange slice, you could call it the Gold of Tolosa, or a Toulouse Special. Your consul's name was Caepio. He ransacked Apollo's temple at Toulouse. Around 106 BC,' he added airily.

Linda stared at him, then laughed. 'Well done! Been to the library, have we?'

'The old lady in Cecile Park. On Friday. She used to study the Classics.'

'I wonder if they still make the gold flake whisky?' murmured Linda.

'Anyway, listen.' Robert studied his nails. 'I'm sorry I can't make the party, but would you let me buy you lunch on Wednesday as a birthday present?'

'Bloody right, you can, I could murder a plateful of chicken tagliatelle!'

She seemed genuinely pleased and the whiff of a tiny victory hung around her.

He watched her eat and thought how unlike most women, most people, she was. The other women in the restaurant ate delicately, hardly at all, with small gestures and a pained, wilted air about them. He sometimes watched the way the girls in the office behaved when a man entered the room. There was a perceptible shrinkage, a sense of puncture, of implosion. Linda waved a fork at him, her mouth full, and carried on, telling him why she hated dogs.

'I've got nothing against your average individual mutt, okay? I just dislike them as a species. No, I don't. I dislike what we've done to them. I mean, my Pete's got some kind of heavy-breed lurcher. Now this is a big, powerful bloody dog. This brute could quite easily walk off with your leg between its jaws for a snack: and it just sits there, looking up at him, the "lurrve" just pouring out of its eyes. Jesus. I hate the fact that we make them do all our dirty work – and what do they do? They adore the ground we walk on. Yuck. Hey, if you're not going to finish that, I'll have it.'

They drank a bottle of white wine, and laughed quite a lot and toasted dead Romans, and killer dogs and Mrs O'Sullivan's agile girlhood. He could fix it. He knew he could make it better, make it like . . . make it better. They walked back, casually late. He had always thought the sound of high heels on paving slabs a cowering noise, the nervous tic of vulnerability, and if he found himself walking behind a woman at night he tried to hang back decently, or cross the road. From Linda's heels, in the sunlight, it was a military tattoo, a sonic gauntlet. The louder the better. She didn't care.

Something was wrong. Graham had called in during lunch. No, he wouldn't normally barge in and anyway, he didn't *barge* in. After ringing three times, he'd tried the handle and the door wasn't locked and it had opened part of the way so he shoved it the rest of the way and she was behind it, at the foot of the stairs, dead as a doornail. He wasn't made of stone, y'know? He'd called the police and they came and hung around for a while, and then they went away to contact the nephew, and the morgue boys had taken her away already and it really, really wasn't pretty, y'know? He didn't get paid for this kind of shit. These old houses were bloody death traps and why the hell was she living all by herself anyway? At her age.

And then he'd begun to cry over the phone. The lady in clerical told him, kindly, to have a cup of tea and take himself off home. Just go home, pet. She would talk to Robert. Robert would take care of it. Go home.

Robert pulled up outside the house. There was a young policewoman leaning against the bulging wall who raised her eyebrows expectantly at him as he got out of the car. She was waiting for the deceased's nephew who was coming to collect the keys and, well, have a look around, sort things out, whatever. His wife worked nearby. She'd gone with the body. The policewoman looked closely at his card. Well, since his boys had been here earlier, sure, he could have a look around.

Inside, Robert took off his coat. He folded it and placed it across a chair. The antimacassar had been sewn on. There was nothing for him to take care of. Everything had been taken care of already. The room was perfectly still. Sturdy parallel bars of afternoon daylight sliced the airless gloom. He turned, satellite-like, in a slow, imbecilic circle, then went to one of the bedrooms. His shoulders and neck hurt, as if a malevolent weight was crushing him. The signs were there but, on the floorboards where the plants had been, there were three large, dust-free circles. Robert stared at the wall until the places and streets, the roads and stations, became a wash of colour before his eyes. He blinked and sighed hard, then walked over and took one of the smaller signs off the wall. After a moment's hesitation he slid it into his briefcase.

In the bathroom there was a tiny rectangular wooden frame, propped up by the sink, with a quotation in Spanish and underneath a translation – 'Que los yerros de amores, dignos son de perdonar.'

Faults of love deserve to be forgiven.

A feeling of something like misery rose in his chest and subsided, and he forgot for a moment to breathe. He moved to the kitchen in a kind of dreamy march. There was a half-bottle of gin on top of the fridge. He poured himself a medium-sized one, walked to the living-room and sat down heavily on the floor beside the window, his briefcase on his knees. He felt as if he was disappearing, as if the room was slowly, sponge-like, drawing the energy from him. His chest felt crushed, his throat paralysed. He wished he'd told a few glossy lies in his life. He closed his eyes and saw his wife's damaged expression, his mother's dead countenance; glamorous, totemic, and then the grieving criminal germs of memory crept up on him. She'd been afraid to die and she didn't hide her fury at first. But the silent, desperate need for heroism broke her; the weakness of the embarrassed, the healthy, the solicitous, was too much for her. She was not permitted to behave badly. She was afraid to die but that was okay. She wasn't afraid to live. Robert remembered the time she'd disappeared for three days. He was just a child but his father had reeked of anxiety and had cried hysterical tears when she'd finally strolled, mad-eyed, in the front door, carrying a bottle of expensive perfume, her handbag jangling with French francs. She never ran away again. The years made her polite. Maybe she died of good manners. There must be sins greater than cowardice, but the constant insult of her disreputable courage had stung him all his life. It was not coldness that had battened down the hatches. It was bad manners. Robert made as if to laugh and it emerged as a desolate, dirty sob. He lowered his head into his hands and cried in utter silence like an exhausted, famished child. The grief rose up and battered at him for several minutes.

Gradually, his breathing returned to normal. He gripped his briefcase and blinked at the opposite wall in genuine surprise. He didn't know whether he felt better or worse. There was an almost imperceptible scratching noise from the attic. Robert looked up. A mouse, probably. He let his mind wander. He couldn't be bothered any more. He thought about the genetically engineered Oncomouse in America, a poor creature whose only function was to develop tumours for laboratory examination and then die, but not before reproducing similarly cursed offspring. Had it been patented? He couldn't remember. He was very tired.

He took the enamel sign out of his briefcase and ran his palm over its cold surface. It was his beloved Frank Pick's Underground 'bull's-eye' motif. He would put it in the bathroom, the way students used to put stolen traffic cones in their bedrooms. Maybe his wife would like it. Maybe the plant would actually take. What had the old lady called her husband, whom she loved dearly? – '*illustre sconosciuto*' – an illustrious nobody.

Fine.

Robert sat there, sensing the world recede from him, letting go, waiting.

He felt as if he was standing on a cliff edge.

It was Wednesday. His wife had said she would call on Wednesday.

He sat with his mobile in one hand and the bull's-eye in the other. Waiting for the nephew. Waiting for her call.

Waiting to be interrupted.

PLEASE

Now this thing had its beginning in the car park. He was a young man, around twenty-four, distressingly handsome, and he sat in his car loading his gun. This was new to him, and awkward. He had none of the authentic bloodlessness of a man who is comfortable handling a gun. It felt like a melon in his hands, which were calloused. The black dirt, or perhaps oil, under his fingernails, had a true, terminal kind of blackness. He looked like a man who could fix things. Loaded, the gun was too heavy. He removed the bullets and shook them from his fist into the glove compartment, then he put the gun in his jacket pocket and got out of the car, stooping, as if he carried the weight of the world. He began to walk slowly towards the hospital entrance. He had a nice walk, a slightly rolling gait, but his bowed head gave him the look of a man with elderly heels and a broken heart, a man with some antique injury.

At the entrance, he gripped the railing and looked up at the hospital's structure, shielding his eyes from the glare. It was a beautiful, white, Modern Movement building, a cool, redemptive place he had been to so often that its smells had become as familiar as those of his own kitchen. A decent, optimistically menacing place, where he had stayed overnight many times. He hauled himself up the dozen steps or so and walked inside. In his pocket, it seemed to weigh a ton.

The Reception was a noisy, brazen place and he loved it.

Cascades of nurses stalking about with important pieces of paper; white coats and metallic tannoy voices, and the diffident wounded, the shy, injured patients just waiting around, bored and grateful at the same time – this slovenly place was his sanctuary and his bedroom, and it teemed with shuddering, rough people, each intent on his or her own purpose. He recognised most of the staff as he walked slowly through the lobby; he wobbled slightly and thought that perhaps their nerveless calm, the sheer velocity of their vocation, as they helped people, and healed and soothed and murmured, might shame him from his own purpose, might cause him to turn round and walk back to his car, dropping the gun in a litter bin as he walked. He caught sight of himself in a mirror. He was twenty-four and he looked like an old man. He had dark circles under his eyes and the guilty frown of someone who had only one small thing left to lose. He looked into those eyes and then, because he was afraid that he might cry, right there in the reception, he shook himself and headed for Paediatrics.

There was a blonde nurse, young and very beautiful, who looked after the day-to-day running of the unit. Sometimes she felt more like an electrician, or a plumber, than a nurse. They were so tiny, so ugly. She believed with a terrifying fierceness, but once in a while they made her flinch, and occasionally she disliked the softly implosive delicacy with which they had to be handled, and the brightness of the place. She worked off her energy in the gym, and escaped the bullet beams in bars where darkness and mystery had not yet been made casualties. She was tending to one baby on life support. The baby was two months old and had not been expected to last as long as that. Her veins were still visible. She was hooked up to a plastic forest of tubes and electrical wires. She was utterly still, apart from the small, sucking, fluttering of her heart, which made the waxy skin on her chest shine and anxiously recede.

The doctor came in and leaned over the incubator with her. He came by several times a day, every day, just to look at the nurse, and the baby, and listen to the quiet hum of the unit. Time, it seemed to him, slowed down here. There was no real activity. It was just a matter of watching and waiting and being careful. He was thirty-two and sometimes the tiredness made him want to curl up and die. It was the carelessness that got to him more than anything. The unkind word that could so easily be bravely ignored, but led instead to a glamorous knife wound, the husband whose wife's evening class on assertiveness drove him so crazy with a rage he didn't even understand, and could only deal with by using his fists, the uncomprehending drunks, the thoughtful revenges, the blurred Chaplinesque gang fights, the little ladies who thought that varicose veins for fifteen years was nothing serious and besides, they were busy living their lives, bringing up families ... Sometimes he just liked to come here and feast his eyes on the beautiful nurse's pale face and watch the babies hanging on like grim myths, for dear life, and listen to their faint, faint breath. This child in particular. There was no hope. She shouldn't even be here. Another week. Two at the most. It had arrived with her and they couldn't fix it. He was irritated by that. And he was irritated by the fact that she still had a presence in this place, a pained, struggling insult.

He climbed the second flight, his hand in his pocket. Even without the bullets, it still weighed him down on one side. He was walking so slowly now. He would have welcomed a hand slapped on his shoulder, a stern, authoritarian face asking him where he thought he was going and what was that in his pocket. A soft capture, an easy end to this, that was all he wanted. He passed the janitor cleaning the stairs.

The janitor had been working at the hospital for twenty years. He really had been there, done that, bought the T-shirt and he wasn't fearing a damn thing. Even when his wife got cancer, all it did was set up a grainy, adrenal response in his heart and he just got on with it. That's all you can do. Sure, there were times when the things he saw in this place almost took his breath away, with their horror and cruelty, but he had a daughter who was smart and ambitious, and when he got too old to do this any more, she would look after him. He smacked his broom as noisily as he could against the underside of the wall radiator, sending up dust like a swarm of fruit flies, and smiled at the pale gent passing him on the stairs, his fists bunched in his pockets.

This murderous climb might beat him yet. He felt as weak as a kitten and his heart was pounding. His life seemed to be flashing in front of his eyes, fleshed out by the worn progress of his heels. He kept thinking of the future that would not be. Daughters in swarms of glee, talking nonsense, swatting his face with their small, complicated fingers. He had had the future whipped into shape. And then the viscous tragedy of her birth had damn near killed them both. Two apprehensive months, at best. He'd had a mental picture of her as an infant in the polite grasses of their garden, knees buckled, collapsed in padded safety, arms hovering, the dog not quite knowing what to make of this creature. Right now, he envied its ignorance. He felt as if one more flight would be more than he was capable of. The relatives were the worst part of this nightmare. Their distilled, flabby sorrow did not help. It made it worse. He knew it wasn't his fault, it wasn't some sneaky, disreputable gene of his. He knew it wasn't any-body's fault. He just hadn't wanted to be in the glare of their overheated sympathy. He wanted cool, quiet, charitable shadows, where he could think this thing through. And he had. And he had come to a decision that would end nobody's suffering. But it would give their suffering a kinder colour. He wanted a witchcraft solution. This was the best he could do.

The doctor looked at the nurse while she checked the

feeds. She was roughly tactile in what she did, as if she was checking fresh vegetables in a supermarket. He liked that. All the nurses scared him with the businesslike hardness of their charity. Sentimentality had no place here, so the hell with it. If you crumble with what used to be called 'fellowfeel', then you're no use to anyone. No place for it in a place like this. But he had never acquired the knack of being genuinely, usefully detached. He just acted that way. He hadn't felt involved with a patient for years, he was too tired for that. But some guilty impulse in the back of his mind and in the back of his heart injected his voice with an elaborate, persuasive concern that his patients knew was false. They were more comfortable with the nurses.

The janitor worked his way slowly up the stairs towards Paediatrics. He would stop by and talk to the beautiful nurse with the pale skin, and see if that dying rag of a baby was still there. Pausing, he took out a Kleenex. He spat on it and cleaned his glasses, humming to himself. He was in a good mood. He felt strong today. He felt like he could sweep all day. He was going to retire soon and, on that day, he would begin to live for ever.

The doctor and the nurse were still leaning over the cot when he approached, like two friends in a bar on their third drink. She turned and saw his face, and smiled. He had been here so many times and she had grown to like his looks. Her smile became a redundant, frozen thing and slowly faded as she stared at the gun that was pointing directly at her heart. The doctor, hearing her gasp, turned and saw the young father he'd got to know quite well. His face was grey and exhausted, and the gun trembled in his hand. His whole arm shook as he gestured them to move away from the child. No one spoke. They stared silently at the gun, fear freezing their lungs, and they forgot to breathe. Then the doctor moved dreamily to one side and pulled the nurse gently with him, still staring at the young father with the pining eyes and the gun in his hand. He felt the resistance in her body. She didn't want to leave the child. She knew what he was going to do. She knew what he was going to do. They moved to the far side of the room.

Still pointing the gun at them, the father began with his left hand delicately to pluck the tubes and wires and the mask from his daughter's mottled body. It was so hushed in here. The nurse began to sob quietly. The doctor's throat hurt and tears scalded his eyes. When the young man had removed all the life-support feeds and monitors, he slid his palm under her spine and scooped her to his chest in one movement. She wasn't much bigger than his hand and hardly weighed anything. He walked the couple of steps to the wall and sat down heavily in a chair beside them. He bent his head silently and wanted to crush the child to his chest, he loved her so, but he was afraid she would break. The gun was pointing at no one in particular and his face had the look of a blind man. All he had to do was wait. The nurse cried in distress and begged him, with a bruised, wet sign language, not to do this terrible thing, not to commit this sin. She pleaded with her eyes and said one word, over and over again – 'Please'. He could barely hear her. He felt as if he was very far away, as if his spirit had floated away from this hugely nervous place, and was alone and far away, in some vast reservoir of solitude.

He did not understand this thing, he could not get a smart enough grasp on the vocabulary of our ascent, how one life avoids catastrophe for ever while another crashes hopelessly at a sigh. He knew every colossal detail of this tiny bundle in his hand and he could feel the burden of breathing begin to fall away from her. And under his jewelled scrutiny she died.

The janitor opened the stairwell door and strolled towards the unit. A small semicircle of people had gathered around the door and were murmuring quietly to each other. A young man was sitting beside the wall, holding his dead child, weeping bitterly. And the janitor saw that the young doctor and the pretty nurse were staring, vacant and red-eyed at the dead child, as if they couldn't quite believe any of this. The gun was lying on the floor and the young man was clutching the child's body with both arms. Thin, terrifying curses rose in the janitor's heart but he said nothing. He strode forward and picked up the gun. He didn't have to check to know that it wasn't loaded. He knew enough about guns. He looked around him at the doctor and the nurse, and the few others, a brood bereft of purpose, and he looked at the broken youngster. For a moment he felt that he might strike him. He raised his hand and his rage made him the strongest man on earth. But there was nothing to be done. There was nothing to be done. To repair this thing, to patch decently would be next to enough. He lowered his hand and stroked the young man's trembling head, and made soothing noises and wiped his tears, the way he would comfort a wounded animal.

Somebody called the police.

THE KLONDYKER AND THE SILVER DARLINGS

John stood on the doorstep, hands on hips, head thrown back, eyes closed. 'I can't cut your grass,' he wailed. 'My heart's just broken! She threw me out, I've got a broken heart and I can't do your garden. Aw, fuck, what am I going to do? Pardon the language, Mrs Buchan.'

Diane stared at him for an embarrassed moment. She hardly knew the guy. He cut her grass, and did a little weeding now and again. He stood there, miserable, and probably a little drunk, so she felt obliged to say something kind, or at least vaguely soothing. 'Ah, God, John, I'm sorry to hear that. Is it definitely over? I mean, did she seem serious about it? Forget about the garden. Never mind about that – just go for a pint or something. You poor thing . . .' Christ, she was beginning to sound like Claire Rayner.

He wasn't even listening. Taking an enormous breath, with his hands on top of his head, he blathered on for five minutes about his cracked heart and the woman he loved, and his neglected begonias, while Diane leaned against the door frame, adding an occasional 'aw' of sympathy, secretly enjoying his gruff threnody. So it wasn't just her, then. Plenty of people, even her tough, broad-shouldered gardener, found comfort in the accidental, near-anonymous ear, the almost bureaucratic privacy afforded by a stranger. Not that Diane told anyone; she took a polite pride in being the shoulder that everyone else cried on. Peripheral intimacy, the kind of support that the wailers knew incurred no debt – Diane was good at that. So she held his hand (without inviting him in for a cup of tea) and patted him on the arm and, eventually, he wore himself out with talk and tears, and shambled off down the road.

'I'm going to have a talk with her tonight and if she doesn't thump me, I might feel up to tackling that crazy paving you were after,' he shouted over his shoulder.

'Don't worry about that,' called Diane. 'Just look after yourself, okay?'

When he'd disappeared, Diane went to the back door and stared at the garden for a long time. It was a mess. It was almost winter but the garden had more than the quiet bareness of hibernation about it; it was as if nothing had ever lived, ever grown in it. She'd lost count of the number of bulbs and seeds she'd planted. Nothing ever grew. Perhaps it was the soil – too acidic? Too alkaline? Or perhaps it was too stony, too rocky. The only things that ever seemed to grow were weeds. When John came to cut the grass and do the weeding it was almost an embarrassment to her, because there was nothing else for him to do; nothing to look after, or separate, or repot, or even just stand back and admire. No colourful show-offs, just sneaky bloody weeds. Diane swore silently, marched over to the redundant flower bed and began savagely to tear up whatever weeds she could find, flinging them over her shoulder on to the ruined, twig-strewn lawn. She drove her bare fingers into the afflicted earth, churning up newly planted bulbs and showers of pixie seeds, and she didn't care. She recognised the sterile, scruffy things as she tore them up – Polyanthus (Hybrid Crescendo: Mixed), Aster Alpinus (Trimix), Anemone-de-Caen (Mixed), Alpine Pink, Pasque Flower, Freesia (Double Mixed), Stonecrop – she destroyed them all, sniffing stupidly to herself, perched brittly over the beds, arms flailing. The only seeds she'd really had any hope for, Snow-in-Summer, were too small to be seen, a microscopic, pebbledash dust, so she scooped up handfuls of earth and threw them over the wall, just to be sure.

When she had finished, she sat tamely on the lousy grass and nibbled miserably at the dirt packed hard under her fingernails. Her husband, Douglas, was going to be at sea for another two weeks. Something had to happen.

Doug had taken delivery of his new boat a month ago. After the maiden voyage and a few coastal trips, just so that she could get some catching time under her belt, he had decided to take her out for a fortnight's deep-water fishing. More and more skippers, realising that cod and haddock stocks were never going to recover completely, had taken to deep-water fishing off the east coast, and the market nowadays saw ever-increasing landings of alternative species such as grenadier, black scabbard, blue ling, forkbeard and orange roughy. It also meant that the crews spent much longer at sea. Diane knew she was going to be spending even more time alone in the house.

He had been as excited as a child when his newly built boat, *Maranatha IV*, arrived at the harbour. It certainly was a beautiful vessel, and Doug gave Diane the full tour, with a running commentary: an 85-foot stern trawler of all-welded steel, she had a 995 horsepower Caterpillar engine, a bridge-deck and wheelhouse of marine-grade aluminium, two Promac ice-making machines, and trawl winches with a core pull of 20 tonnes and a capacity for 1250 fathoms. She didn't understand half of it, but she was amazed at the sheer luxury of the boat. The crew of nine had a galley almost as nice as her own kitchen, comfy bunks, TV, video, computer games. It was a wonder they got any fishing done at all. In the wheelhouse Diane watched her husband as he rambled on cheerfully about the electronics.

49

'See this?' he said, pointing to a frighteningly hi-tech computer screen with various add-ons. 'This is a Decca Fishmaster FM202 plotter – it doesn't just find the bastards, it knows their names and addresses!'

'Fascinating, pet,' said Diane drily.

'And *this*! This is a Racal Bridgemaster radar C251/6 auto-track and *this* is a Philips AP-MK4 Decca Navigator. We'll never got lost again, that's for sure.' He leaned over and gave her a hug. He had been so happy.

Never get lost again. Diane sighed heavily, hauled herself off the grass and went inside to clean her fingernails. Discovering that he had been unfaithful had been bad enough, but what made it worse was that the crew probably knew. She didn't care about what the women thought, but the notion of all those men knowing and saying nothing, that rough, exclusive conspiracy of silence, drove her crazy. She hadn't confronted him. She knew he would've stood there like a stranded puppy, denying nothing, leaving her with nowhere to go. It had always been that way around here. The men left to go fishing, or travelling, or selling, or simply because they could not bear to stay, and the women kept house and waited for them to come home. The men always left and the women always stayed. He had fallen in love with her because of a 1931 Stutz Bearcat; he had a vast collection of model cars and when she correctly identified the Bearcat he'd decided that this was the lassie for him. Any woman who could appreciate a handsome piece of technology was definitely the one. The following Saturday they'd gone to the beach, dropped some acid and watched the sunset, swapping five different pairs of tinted sunglasses, whooping to each other with amazement at the colours. He was fun to be with, she had to grant him that. They were married six months later and in eight years she never dreamed he could hurt her. And now he was off again on his beautiful boat, happy and excited, and she was alone, ready to explode with a percussive misery she barely understood. Two weeks. Something had to happen.

The following afternoon her mother phoned. 'The Klondykers are here!'

'Yeah I know. Two massive ones arrived yesterday. Poor bastards.'

'Well, myself and a few of the girls are doing the usual boxes for them. Want to give me a hand?'

'Okay. I'll be over in a while.'

The Klondykers were huge Russian factory ships that moored off the harbour for a couple of months every year. Local skippers returning from a trip would sell part of their catch to them, which they processed on board before freezing. It was a good arrangement; the Russians had access to supplies they had difficulty obtaining in home waters and local fishers were able partially to get round the quota rules. The only drawback was that the Klondykers constituted the most monstrous offshore eyesore for three months of the year; they were ancient, hulking rustbuckets, barely seaworthy and crewed by a sorry collection of badly fed, badly paid, reluctant seamen. On the rare occasions they were allowed onshore, they spent their time swapping vodka for food, selling army uniforms and caviar at knock-down prices, and cleaning out the Oxfam shop. The locals usually took pity on them and Diane's mother, a widow with time on her hands, always organised 'necessity boxes': soap, toilet paper, canned food, cigarettes and the like. It made everybody feel pretty good.

On her way over to her mother's house, Diane took a walk around the harbour and past the fish market. The industry had made this town and kept it alive: 16,000 jobs in the north-east alone. The fishing was everything. The harbour was over 400 years old and a miracle of construction, its intricate, horizontal, lattice brickwork as tight and solid as when it was built. Diane loved the harbour, its sweet, ancient density, and she loved the market. Sometimes she would rise early when Doug was away and just hang around in the starving dawn while the selling was going on. The 4000 boxes, the amazing array of fish entranced her, the fatty carnality of their colours and shapes, the mellifluous mantra of their names – saithe, megrim, dabs, witches, monkfish, baby codling, brill, lythe, coley, roker. But it was more than that. The fishing had allowed her to make her own money before she married. With a secretarial course under her belt, Diane had worked for a marine engineering firm and, after that, a boatbuilder's, then a net-making company and, when the catches were up, on the gutting floor in a whitefish processing business. The market made her feel connected, even though she hadn't worked in years. The bruising vaudeville of the auction was fun to watch, with the fishers and the processors bickering about prices, roaring down their mobile phones, poking the product and scattering cigarette ash all over the place. Most of the sales were hooked up by computer to international auction houses. The place was a brittle combination of the ancient and the modern, traditional catchers with their arctic roughness and skilful scars, colliding with the sellers' technological creed. When she went there, Diane always stayed at the back. To have a woman on a fishing boat was considered bad luck; to have one hanging around the market, just watching, was a little unnerving. Sometimes she thought that what she was really trying to do was to find a way of climbing inside Doug's world. And this was the closest she could get. Just hanging around, grieving, waiting for things to change, and never believing that time and patience were the only things that mattered, never knowing that the frivolous pathology of her pain was no match for a man who could leave any time he wanted.

When she arrived at her mother's house, the rest of the family was already there, energetically stuffing boxes with various household items and sealing them with yards of sellotape. Her two older brothers, David and Sandy, were downing beers and talking about how to control the seagull population.

'Poison, that's the only way.'

'Nah. All you need is a couple of dozen folk out on the cliff during the breeding season, puncturing the eggs.'

'Maybe. Or how about some kind of sonic alarm set-up? Ah shit, why don't we just shoot them?'

'Has it occurred to either of you,' said Diane, 'that seagulls are a protected species?'

They both looked at her.

'That can't be right,' said David. 'There's millions of the bastards! My God, when I'm on the phone with customers – sometimes I can't hear myself *think* for that squawking bloody racket going on outside.'

'Well, they are, so tough.'

Diane liked the seagulls; they were obstreperous buggers who had the good sense to know that the town's rooftops and chimney pots were an infinitely safer place to roost than the cliffs nearby, but in their thousands they were becoming a bit of a problem and everyone was dreaming up ways for the Council to kill them.

'I like Grandad's idea best!' David laughed.

'That wasn't population control, that was pure sadism,' said Diane. Their grandad once told them that, as a kid, he and his friends would amuse themselves by stuffing an old carbide battery inside a small herring, and then flinging it to the gulls. Since the bird can't expel gas, the poor creature would get no more than ten yards off the ground before exploding in a shower of guts and feathers. David and Sandy thought it was hysterical.

'"Gulls can't fart!" Great name for a band!'

David was head supervisor at a local pelagic fish company. Sandy ran his own game processing firm. Diane's younger sister, Lilian, worked for a timber company. Their uncle ran a smoked salmon operation in Peterhead. As she settled down on the carpet to help with the packing, it occurred to Diane that all of them relied so much for a living on slaughter, on the death of other creatures. She had absolutely no problem with that at all. Last year David, a vocal member of the local fish processors' association, was calling for a seal cull off North Uist to help conserve fish stocks. There are 200,000 of them and each damn creature ate around two and a half tonnes of fish every year. That's about £2000. But the previous month, he had been out on the freezing rocks at 3 a.m. with the local wildlife trust, helping to rescue and clean a couple of dozen grey seals caught in a minor oil spill. Diane had never been able to figure him out. And Sandy ran a harbour security business on the side. Youngsters kept breaking into the boats' medical kits, looking for drugs. Morphine, mainly. All in all, her brothers did okay for themselves. Resourceful boys, both. Diane had always been slightly intimidated by their coltish invention, their energy, their swaggering tetch. Just like Douglas. She thought of his carnival gait as he bounced on to the deck two days ago, like some kind of smelly, slack Diaghilev, before chugging skilfully out of the harbour on his deep-water adventure. So happy. So happy.

David and Sandy and her mother were all watching her carefully as she slammed tins of beans, toothpaste and kitchen roll into the boxes with an antic violence that wasn't exactly necessary. 'You okay, pet?' asked her mother gently.

'I'm fine. Why? *Why*?'

At 8.30 the next morning the Russians were down at the harbour, six of them, to take delivery of the dozen or so boxes. They were from the *Vazgorsk* out of Murmansk. Most of them were burly creatures, bundled up in their donkey jackets against the wind, unshaven and chain-smoking. They had no sense of embarrassment in accepting the towns-people's charity. It had become something of a tradition and, as they began to recognise some local faces from last year, the atmosphere lightened. Backs were slapped and guttural yells of greeting in halting English floated around the harbour, as the two delegations mixed and milled in the chilly air. One of the Russians stood slightly apart from the others, by the hydraulic storm gate, and Diane found herself staring at him. He had very sallow skin, high cheekbones and close-cropped, jet-black hair. In his late thirties, his bearing was almost aristocratic, as he stood looking up at the skeletal shaduf of the ice-making company's crane.

Diane strolled over to say hello. 'Welcome to Fraserburgh.'

He turned to look at her.

He didn't smile. That was one thing that had struck Diane about the Russians, they rarely smiled but when they did, by God they meant it. We, on the other hand, smile all the time, chimp-like, and hardly ever mean it.

'Thank you. This is a magnificent harbour. Is it sixteenth century?'

Diane was stunned. His English was almost faultless.

'Yes. Round about 1545, I think. You should see it in the summer, during the Fish Festival, when every single boat comes home. You could walk from one side to the other without getting your feet wet.'

He smiled and Diane relaxed a little. There was something about this man that suggested a hinterland, a quiet, whisper-ing conviction, a core that no one could touch. 'Where are you from, anyway?' she asked.

'Well, I was born in Siberia, on the shores of Lake Baikal. But I've moved around a little.'

'Lake Baikal! Oh, wow! I've read all about it. It's the most beautiful thing I've ever seen, or rather, never seen.'

He laughed and they began to chat more easily, ignoring the rest of the party who had cracked open a bottle of vodka and were having a noisy, alfresco breakfast on the slipway. He told her about Baikal, the oldest and deepest lake in the world; seven times the size of the Grand Canyon, over 1700 metres deep, with 2000 aquatic species, most of them unique to Baikal.

'I read somewhere', said Diane, 'that it's so clean and so deep, if you look over the side of a boat you get vertigo.'

A look of sadness crossed his face. 'When I was a child, yes, but not any more. It's being polluted by waste from dozens of timber companies. It's not so clean any more.'

'Oh.'

He looked at her in silence for a moment. Diane felt herself blushing. She'd been flirting with him and he knew it. Suddenly she felt angry. Why shouldn't she? Everyone else was enjoying themselves. She looked across the slipway where her mother, whose system wasn't designed to cope with vodka at nine o'clock in the morning, was hugging the Russian skipper and telling him filthy limericks.

'Do you like smoked salmon?' she asked suddenly.

'I'm sorry?' he said, confused.

'My uncle produces the best smoked salmon in the country. I'd like you to see his place. It's only half an hour's drive away. What's your name, anyway?'

'Vadim Shuljenko. I'll have to ask the skipper first.'

He went over and chatted briefly to the skipper, who glanced at Diane and raised an eyebrow, then sniggered unpleasantly. Her mother threw her a very hard look.

Diane stared back. She didn't care. She had to get away from here, just get in the car and drive and keep driving. And she liked the way this Vadim looked at her. 'For God's sake, Mum, I'm just taking him over to show him Uncle Peter's smoke house. It's historical. He'll like it. Relax.'

On the road to Peterhead, Vadim told her a little of his background. He'd trained as a marine biologist and had worked for twelve years at Sovrybflot, the fisheries ministry in Moscow, specialising in the control of caviar production, but after the break-up of the USSR the lab technicians didn't get paid for six months and then he was fired. Klondyking was the only job he could get. One hundred and fifty dollars a month. He hated it. Diane thought of Douglas's undentable cheeriness as he pottered about his three-million-pound streamlined beauty. The last thing he'd said before sailing was, 'Hake and monkfish. Next month! West Coast of Namibia. Big money there, pet!' Diane gripped the steering wheel and tried to banish from her mind the thought that when he got home she was going to kill him.

As they drove, Vadim marvelled at the countryside, the sheer treeless expanse that was the north-east coast. It was a murderously beautiful landscape, one that Diane hadn't looked at properly in years. But as he gazed towards the sea and the astonishing brutal cliffs, and gave periodical low whistles, she began to look with him and appreciate what he saw. His appreciation, as they drove, was quiet and cool – unlike the countless yelping tourists she'd taken for a spin – but when he pointed out the corrosive, almost plastic sheen of the frost on the cliff-edge fields, Diane found herself braking slightly to get a better look.

'This reminds me of home, it's so beautiful,' he said quietly.

'Oh, don't be ridiculous! Nothing could be as beautiful as Baikal,' Diane snorted and instantly regretted it. She sounded as if she hated her life in this place. Vadim said nothing, but pointed to a velvet gash in the cliffs where the late-morning shadows ran shivering up the hill from the water's lace-edge. The whiteness of the sky almost blinded her as she drove, and when Vadim rested his fingertips on her shoulder while reaching for the cigarette lighter she wanted suddenly to stop the car and amble to the cliff and look at the sea, and keep looking at the sea until it did something extraordinary. Until it brought Douglas back, or made her feel brave enough to leave. Seeming to sense her tension, Vadim just folded his arms and stared out of the window at the hayfields, still with their prettily spaced patterns of round bales, and at the spooked, witless crows spiralling across the road. The wind caught the car on a turn, and she had to fight to control the lightweight Nova. Vadim wasn't bothered. He'd felt every kind of weather on land and at sea, and every kind of wind – arctic, anatole, hesperie, cryere, mesembrine – he'd had the zephyr almost tear off his ears four miles out of port, he'd felt the sensual tickle of the galerne and the sirocco on the back of his neck in the Caspian, the stabbing parched swoop of the besch and garbino during that ragged-arsed summer off Norway. At times like that, everybody stayed below, no work got done and the boat became simply a crèche for lovely nightmares. Redundancy and no fish. At least when they came to Fraserburgh they got to go ashore, they got the chance to make some money, to meet people . . .

He looked across at Diane's profile as she gunned the car up to sixty. Without meaning to, he patted her hand on the wheel. Her jaw muscles bunched, but she didn't say anything. She didn't tell him not to.

Uncle Peter greeted her at the front door of the smoke house, reeking of fish and apologising to Vadim for not being able to shake hands. He was covered in grease and scales, and small, bloody Band-aids.

'I just wanted to show our guest how you operate,' said Diane.

'No problem – come on in. He can have some to take away with him.'

The building itself was extraordinary, a 500-year-old, tiny, low-ceilinged, irregular block of granite perched solidly at the shallow cliff-edge, just yards from the Ythan river. Most of Peter's stock was farmed, but now and again he bought in some wild salmon and he was keen to show Vadim his methods. He loved to show off.

'Look at this monster here!' he said, slapping a three-foot wild salmon laid out on the slab beside its netted kin. It was a beauty, with gleaming skin and muscle as hard as stone. He showed them how to skin the beast and fillet it, then the brining tanks, where the flesh is salted for twenty-four hours. The process fascinated Diane and she never got tired of watching it. Vadim helped Peter lay out two dozen fillets on steel racks in the ancient, cupboard-like smokery. Peter lit the wood chips below and closed the door. Chips from oak whisky barrels were best.

'And that's it. Leave it for twenty-eight to thirty-two hours and they'll be perfect.'

'Just time and patience,' murmured Vadim.

With a here's-one-I-made-earlier flourish, Peter showed them a smoked fillet he'd just finished slicing by hand. Held up to the light, the slices were perfect – pale, fleshy prisms as thin as gauze. He slapped them between two branded labels and slid them through the vacuum packing machine – his only concession to technology – then handed the 12 oz pack to Vadim. He loved his work and he was proud of it.

'Right, who's for a nip?'

Sipping Edradour whisky and nibbling salmon, Peter and Vadim got on well, discussing the trade, the salmon, the sturgeon, while Diane wandered about the dark, pungent room, touching the wooden beams. Everything about this place was so old, still, warm. Time and patience. The cautious craft of Peter's work seemed to slow down time itself, and the functional sensuality of the rows of dead flesh made her feel strangely safe. She'd loved this place since she was a girl. She glanced over at Vadim, at the nape of his neck, where the black hair disappeared. He turned and held her eye for a moment, and smiled.

As she dropped him off at the deserted harbour to return to the *Vazgorsk*, he rummaged around in his holdall for a moment, then produced a tin of caviar and a cassette tape.

'Thank you for a nice afternoon. I enjoyed it. These are for you,' he said.

Diane studied the tin. This was Beluga, the real McCoy. Even a small tin like this was worth about £120. 'Are you sure about this?' She didn't feel like arguing with him.

'Please. And you might enjoy the music. It's Alexander Zeltkin, one of our most famous folk singers.'

'Thank you.'

They stood in silence for a moment, then Vadim extended his hand.

Diane took it. 'Come to my house for lunch tomorrow.'

Christ, she couldn't believe she'd said that. He hesitated, then smiled and said, 'If I can get permission, yes I would like that.'

Suddenly embarrassed, Diane said, a little curtly, 'Hey, maybe you can help me out with my garden. It's like a bomb-site at the moment, because my gardener's got a broken heart, his girlfriend left him, you see, and by all accounts she's a bit of a stroppy cow, not that I would . . .' Now she was just babbling.

'It would be my pleasure,' he said.

She gave him the address, they said goodbye and Diane drove home very fast.

That night, alone in the house, she drank vodka and tasted the caviar, and danced slowly around the room to the sweet, sad Russian folk music, without understanding a word. As she drifted off to sleep, she wondered if Douglas was safe. Poor Douglas, whose sense of continuity and history was as fragile as a small animal's breath in winter, whose intangible folly had trailed him, sniffing and stupid, into another's bed. She hoped, drowsily, that he was safe and dry, but everything had changed and now she was prowling the outskirts of their marriage. Wounded, she didn't know what else to do. Poor, bed-swerving Douglas, who behaved as if he were going to die tomorrow, because he simply didn't realise that we must act as if we are going to live for ever.

Vadim arrived at noon and started on the flower beds straight away while Diane prepared lunch. He dug and weeded until sweat poured down his face. The grass was going to have to wait until John was feeling a little better, because he brought his own mower and Diane didn't possess one. Just before he came in for lunch, Diane put on the one Tchaikovsky CD she possessed.

'Is that to make me feel at home?' He laughed, standing sweating in the doorway.

'Sort of. Do you like it?'

'I prefer Ennio Morricone, to tell you the truth. Bruno Battisto D'amrio – big hero of mine.'

'Who on earth is that?' she asked.

'At the end of *The Good, the Bad and the Ugly* – where Clint Eastwood, Lee Van Cleef and Eli Wallach are squaring up for the big gunfight?'

'Yeah. So?'

'Well, the big, thudding guitar on the soundtrack – that's Bruno Battisto D'amrio.' He beamed at her.

Diane stared back at him. 'How did you get to be so knowledgeable about American movies?'

'Oh, all that stuff is very popular at home. My brother was very keen on American architecture and artists. He was training in automotive design when he got drafted. Harley Earl. Genius.'

'Who?' Diane was beginning to feel out of her depth.

'Harley Earl. He was General Motors' main designer in the 1950s. All those classic Cadillacs and Chevrolets, with the chrome and the fins – that was Harley Earl. Beautiful. Beautiful.'

Diane was impressed. He seemed to know more about the vagaries and incidentals of her world than she could ever know about his. She'd read about Lake Baikal somewhere and that was it. She didn't even know where Siberia was, exactly.

He dried himself off with a towel and, over lunch, they chatted about his home and how tough things had become since the break-up; the disappearance of government subsidies for the fleet, high taxes, rising fuel prices. Diane felt slightly embarrassed by the relative opulence of her home, but he gave no hint that he was envious. Instead, he was coolly appreciative as he wandered around the living-room, touching the furnishings, the snazzy ornaments. As he stroked a painting with his fingertips, it occurred to her that this was the calmest man she had ever met. Standing with his hands on his hips, surveying the garden, everything about him spoke of a soothing economy, as if he didn't care that he was clever and impoverished, as if the *Vazgorsk* were a palace and he still didn't care, as if his own heart's curriculum vitae had nothing to do with him. As she watched him, Diane felt for a terrifying instant that she wouldn't be able to stop herself from going up behind him and putting her arms round his waist, tightly, so tightly. She took a deep breath and made coffee.

As he left, a thought occurred to her. 'Your brother – what's he doing now?'

Vadim was silent for a few moments. 'He was killed in Chechnya five years ago.'

'Oh, Christ, I'm sorry.' She didn't know where Chechnya was either. She took his hand in both of hers and, for a moment, he looked as if he never wanted to leave.

He touched her face with his forefinger. 'I haven't nearly finished in the garden. I can come tomorrow, if you like,' he said and there was no trace of guile in his voice or in his face.

So he came back the following day with his own seeds and bulbs, and the day after that, and for seven days in a row. Working in the garden, eating his lunch, talking. Diane's mother phoned a couple of times, and made a few pointed remarks about the neighbours and the fact that Douglas was due back in three days, and that most of these Communists would sell their own grandmother, never mind what Lenin said. Diane listened patiently and made polite noises, but she gave nothing away, because she wasn't afraid any more. Something was happening. She knew from the way he leaned towards her when he spoke and his voice took on a sweetly conspiratorial tone. It was now or never.

When she walked into the garden and asked him to come to dinner next evening she knew he would get in trouble for it. The crew weren't allowed ashore at night. He didn't hesitate.

She arrived back from the shops the following afternoon to find that half the lawn had been cut. The front half. John must be feeling a bit better, she thought. Either his woman had taken him back, or maybe he'd just got over it. Or perhaps they'd had a civilised chat and she said she'd think about it . . . whatever. Diane had a lot to do before Vadim arrived. Christ, she was nervous.

Her dress was perfect and Zeltkin was playing in the background. As she waited for the doorbell, Diane stared across the calm sea for a long time. The sun had almost set and the sky was a riot of colour. Sturdy slabs of vermilion cloud scudded towards the west and the sea twinkled blindingly. It all looked so peaceful, but she had heard enough fishing horror stories to know that the sea was a widow-maker.

'What's the point in learning to swim?' Doug would say. 'If I go over, I want to drown right away, not hang around for two hours until the cold gets me.' Most of the crew couldn't swim. The sea was tough, and it bred hard men and strong women. As she watched the vagrant, brittle shadows deepen over the fields to the north, Diane remembered how her grandfather had told her, with no sense of embarrassment, that in the old days, when they went to sea in small, open boats, the women would actually carry the men out to the boats so that they wouldn't get wet; once on board, if you were wet, there was no way to get dry. So that's what they did.

She thought about her working days on the gutting floor, with the rest of the girls. It was boring, chilly, repetitive work, but the camaraderie and cheeky antics of her friends made it fun. It took two or three showers to banish the corporeal odour of fish from her body afterwards, but since everybody smelled the same, no one noticed. Sometimes on a Friday night the pub smelled faintly like the market. Back then, as a teenager, she had the pesky spirit of a guttersnipe and was fearless. And then she fell in love. Doug hadn't meant to, but his energy and menacing optimism had just, somehow, magicked the fearlessness from her, leaving her solid and dependable and cautious. Like a dead religion, a static creed, her heart no longer pounced on invigorating heresies, or on anything that sparkled and was different. She had loved his persuasive breeziness and, God knows, she still loved him, but over the years she had begun to realise that she was actually jealous of him. Jealous of his freedom, his bouncy independence, jealous of the fact that he was always leaving. Always going somewhere else. Always bloody leaving. She didn't mind being alone. She just wanted to go somewhere else too.

The sun had just disappeared in a vivid barrage of pinks and pale blues when the doorbell rang. Vadim was there.

'Are you in trouble?' she asked.

'No, it's okay. The skipper's drunk. He won't notice. Here.' From behind his back he gave her a rose. 'Not very original, I know, but at least it's stolen. From your neighbour's garden,' he said levelly.

Diane studied him for a second, then laughed. He probably did steal it too, poor sod.

She poured them both a couple of vodkas and asked him to translate the lyrics of the song still playing in the background. His voice took on a formally poetic tone as he told her of the rejected lover's pleas to his woman, how he would stand below her window and wait until she took him once again in her arms, into her heart. Diane closed her eyes.

'"I will stay here until I grow roots in the stony ground," he's saying, "until I have become like an oak tree. My body will perish but my love will never die" . . .' Vadim stopped. 'Actually, at home this song is regarded as pretty – what's the word? – corny?'

Diane smiled, thinking of poor John, and went into the kitchen to get dinner ready. While she pottered around, she was acutely conscious of him watching her. Pouring himself another drink, he brushed past her and laid his hand on her shoulder with a feathery, gentle touch that made her turn round and look directly into his eyes. He said one troubled word in Russian and stroked her hair, before moving away. She poured herself another nervous drink and heard him in the living-room begin to hum gently along with the music.

'It's lobster thermidor, by the way. I thought I'd try something different,' she called.

'Lobster thermidor! I haven't had anything as nice as that in a very long time. Although when I worked in the lab they were my favourite creatures. They're perfect. They're like sharks. They haven't evolved in a million years. Because they haven't had to. Perfect hunting, killing machines. Miraculous creatures,' he said as he walked into the kitchen.

He found Diane a picture of distraught elegance, standing over a pan of boiling water, holding a three-pound live lobster in her left hand. She looked at the lobster, then at the boiling water, then back at the lobster. It waved its antennae at her and flailed feebly. She looked at Vadim, who was suppressing a smile. This was ridiculous, she thought. She and her family had been killing things for food all their lives, and *now* she was squeamish? Vadim began to laugh silently. Diane started to laugh too. They laughed until tears streamed down their faces.

'I'm sorry, Vadim, I can't do it.' She giggled, as she dropped the creature back into the saline bucket where it scuttled huffily into a corner. My God, she thought, this is like that Woody Allen movie. Wiping his eyes, Vadim gave her a hug and poured himself another drink, still laughing. After that, Diane felt calm and relaxed. She lightly kissed his palm and fetched a vegetable lasagne from the freezer. Tonight, she thought. Tonight, things will start to change.

Over dinner they talked for hours. He told her about his time with Sovrybflot, his trips to the Caspian to monitor the sturgeon fishing for the government, the longevity and size and sheer ugliness of the beast – the Sevruga (Acipenser stellatus), the Oscietra (Acipenser gueldestaedti), the Beluga (Huso huso). The Iranians produced the best caviar on the southern shore anyway, and after the break-up, the newly-independent Azerbaijan, Turkmenistan and Kazakhstan on the northern shore couldn't agree on a damn thing, so – quality went down, smuggling went up, breeding grounds became polluted, the Mafia stepped in and he got fired. Diane could tell from his voice that he had loved his job, his work – this exotic, beautiful man who had lost most of what he valued and whose dark, near-shaven head she could scarcely believe she was stroking. He gripped her hand and kissed it and sighed heavily, as if the pessimism of home was something for which he would again be destined.

'At least you have travelled,' she said quietly. 'I've never been anywhere. Sometimes I wish I'd been born a hundred years ago.'

He looked at her quizzically. She seemed to be struggling to remember something.

'The Silver Darlings. The Silver Darlings. That's what they called the herring. A hundred years ago the women travelled too. The herring lassies, the fisher girls. By God, they moved around. All year round they moved from port to port, hundreds of them, thousands of them, following the migration of the herring.'

Vadim watched her carefully. Her eyes shone as she thought about all those women, constantly on the move, gutting, salting, packing, selling, then leaving. Leaving. Moving on.

'They would start in the Western Isles in May, then move to Shetland in June and July, down to East Anglia in October and end up at Dover for November. Two pounds a week and everything they owned in a single trunk!'

Diane laughed a quiet, breathless laugh, then she stopped and put her head in her hands. She thought of that singing, noisy, knitting, mobile horde, long since dead, with their gutting knives and their hand ulcers and their one good dress, who weren't afraid to go on strike when the mood took them, and she felt like weeping. She'd never been anywhere, and she wanted this man because he was quiet and handsome, and because through him and his wanderings she could finally say that she was tired of waiting at home for fine, faithless Doug, that she'd finally been somewhere. Even if it was a lie. She blindly reached out her hand and Vadim took her in his arms.

The expression on his olive face was distressed, anxious. '*Goremika*, Diane? Are you sad? *Nyet*,' he said, hugging her fiercely, while she fought back tears, her breath ragged. He wiped her eyes and said '*Klad*' – 'my treasure' – again and again. Diane stopped crying and sat back a little and looked at him, at his fine, troubled face, and made up her mind. She leaned forward carefully, took that face between her hands and kissed him. It was a kiss that lasted a long, long time, that sent acute tremors shivering down her limbs and had them grasping savagely at each other's skin. And then, after a time, she began to feel the bite of trembling resistance in his muscles, a slow, shaming inertia in his hands as they lost their urgency and gently caressed only her shoulders. Very, very slowly Vadim pushed her away and sat, head bowed, breathing heavily, a million miles away from her.

They remained silent for a little while. She stared at him, stunned. This man hadn't see a woman for four months, for Chrissakes. What was wrong with him? Or was it her? She sat quietly, mesmerised with shame and embarrassment.

Vadim didn't look at her. He reached for his wallet with the weariness of an old man and, still staring at the floor, handed her a photograph. 'Listen to me,' he said. 'Listen to me,' as Diane stared dumbly at the picture of a pretty strawberry-blonde, clasping to her chest two small children with high cheekbones and olive skin. 'We separated soon after I lost my job. They live with her parents in Moscow,' he said in a dreamy, hopeless whisper. 'If I can go home to a better job, I can try to get them back.' His voice was now firmer and tinged with fear. He looked at Diane directly. 'I *must* get them back. I must. I am sorry.'

And he meant it. He really was sorry. Diane stared at him, trying not to let this impossible humiliation overwhelm her. And in that moment of rejection she realised, dimly, that she might be in love with him. She had sought him out, to ease her betrayal, only to find that he could not betray, that in the diaspora of men abroad in the world a scrap of something like nobility existed.

He took her hand and squeezed it, almost apologetically. '*Goremika, klad*?' he said gently.

'*Nyet*.' Diane let out a huge sigh and sadly smiled. 'I just wanted something to change, Vadim. I just wanted something to happen. And Douglas, well . . .'

He stroked her knuckles. 'Listen to me, Diane. Time and

patience, that's all there is. He will come back to you, I promise.'

Diane looked at him sharply. She hadn't mentioned Douglas's other woman.

'He will come back. Everything that is valuable takes a long time and is difficult. To be brave is difficult, to be decent is difficult. He will come back and someday I will go home. But we must wait. I won't be coming onshore again. I'm sorry.'

He'd probably seen enough of worried women and their hopeless husbands, she thought, as she rested her head on his shoulder and felt the shame fall away from her. Tomorrow he would leave, as men always do, and Douglas would come home and she would begin again to pray for bravery, for the courage to speak his language, to pick up the mundane grammar of his love for her and see where it took her, to try to forget the emotional hieroglyphics that had led her so close to this clever man, who now stroked her head and told her that all that mattered was time and patience and bravery. As the damaged evening ended, he told her that he would go home some day and set up his own company producing Siberian sturgeon (Acipenser baeri). She knew, they both knew, that he stood no chance of getting his wife and children back, but as Diane looked into those dark eyes they both also realised that he must behave as if he did. There was no other way to live.

Before he left he led her to the back door and pointed into the blackness at the flower beds. 'Those bulbs will take a few months to show.'

'Nothing grows in that garden, Vadim. Nothing.'

'The sturgeon takes eighteen years to mature,' he said quietly.

My God, thought Diane – she was standing there with her heart broken in about ten different places and he was talking about fish. She didn't know whether to laugh or weep, so instead she put her arms around him and they held each other for a long time. For one disfigured moment, something almost rare inhabited that space.

And then he was gone.

Diane had one more drink and went to bed. In the place between wakefulness and sleep she thought about the sea, and about bravery. She hazily remembered a television news story from years ago, from when she was a girl, a story that had haunted and inspired her ever since. The Man in the Water. Flight 90, Air Florida. The Potomac River. January 1982. Five crash survivors clung to an ice floe in the storm and when the helicopter lowered the rope, one man grabbed it – and passed it to the woman next to him and she was lifted to safety. And he did that three more times. It was night, they were freezing to death and if you went into the water you died in minutes. When the chopper came back for him he was gone. He must have known. He *must* have known that if he kept passing the rope along he would die. He watched the world move away from him and he deliberately let it happen. Diane was only a child but she remembered being horrified by his courage, thinking to herself – is that what I have to live up to when I grow up? Even now, as a grown woman, that old epiphany, that sedge of history crept up on her when she was alone and sleepy, and worried about Douglas, out at sea, out on the water.

She rose just past noon, with a hangover, in a bad mood. She looked out of the window and saw that not only had the back lawn been perfectly cut, but John had also started on the crazy paving. His woman must have taken him back. Well, thought Diane bitterly, at least someone's happy. Doug phoned from a few miles offshore and said he'd be home around three. He sounded tired and subdued. Her mother arrived soon afterwards and pottered about, making tea. She managed to stop herself from mentioning the Russians.

Diane wasn't in the mood to chat and sat sullenly at the kitchen table, staring at her fingers.

Nervously, her mother said, 'Did you hear about Valerie? Valerie Anderson?'

Diane stiffened. She had never spoken to her about it, but her mother knew. Pretty much everybody knew.

'She's leaving. Yeah – got herself a job with an export consultancy firm in the Borders.'

'Well, good for her,' said Diane through gritted teeth, but inside, a tiny, ludicrous sense of hope sprang up. She decided to walk down to the harbour to see the *Maranatha* come home.

When she got there, the harbour was quiet; the market had closed hours ago and the landings that morning had been small. She sat on the granite, dangling her legs over the end of the south breakwater and looked out at the *Vazgorsk*. A very light, cool breeze blew from the east and the sea was perfectly calm.

Eventually, Doug's boat appeared on the horizon and grew larger, sailing smoothly past the filthy Klondyker and into the harbour. Doug let the rest of the crew finish mooring procedures, bounded up the steps and threw his arms around her. 'Hiya, sweetheart! Miss me?'

'Of course, pet. Was it a good trip?' She did her best to smile brightly at him.

'Pretty good, yeah. We were all over the shop – got a few good hauls of haddock and codling in Viking and Bergen, and Fair Isle wasn't too bad either. Picked up some quality groundfish. I'll tell you, the weather was an absolute bitch, but this beauty was just perfect!'

He beamed with pride at the *Maranatha*, which bobbed gently in the water and still gleamed. The crew scuttled about the deck, tying everything down and generally tidying up, like drones ministering to a queen bee. He hugged her again and, over his shoulder, Diane stared at the *Vazgorsk*.

The wind began to pick up a little. Doug shivered, uncharacteristically, and held her much too tightly.

That evening she cooked him dinner. She put the lobster in the freezer for a couple of hours until it lost consciousness, then dropped it into the boiling water without a qualm.

During dinner he was strangely subdued and once or twice she caught him looking at her with an odd expression on his face. Then he took her hand, still silent, and for an instant Diane was terrified that he was going to confess. She didn't want that. That was the last thing she wanted. 'You know, pet,' he said slowly, 'I'm not so sure about these deep-water trips. I mean, I've been talking to a few buyers in London who want the stuff, if I can get it. You know, Southern seas stuff, like redfin and snapper and albacore, and shad and bonito, and fusilier and streaker and pomfrey' – on his lips it was like a religious chant offered up to auspicious, watery deities – 'but, well, I just don't know if it's worth it. I mean, Jesus, *Namibia* for Chrissakes!'

He tightened his grip on her hand slightly, eyes still cast downwards. Diane said nothing. 'I'd like to spend more time at home, I suppose,' he said quietly.

Diane studied his frowning face for a moment. He looked lost and unhappy, and when he buried his face in her shoulder in silent plea, she knew that she had no choice. Vadim was gone and he was here, like a sorry, punctured schoolboy who was no good at being sly and no good at coming clean. His skinny credentials as a good husband were gone and it scared the hell out of him. He wanted forgiveness without hurting her more by asking for it. So neither of them said anything for a while, but they simply held each other in a kind of miserable, wholesome breach, suspended between truth-telling and moving on. Diane knew he was sorry and that she would be no good at dishing out the kind of thumping purgatory many wounded women angrily relish.

This decent man, with his muscular cowardice and gypsy

blood, this sophisticated hillbilly really did love her more than his own life, and this was the closest to forgiveness he was ever going to get.

She hugged him fiercely, and stroked the stubble on his chin and told him she was pleased. They both knew it would never be spoken of openly.

'If we just look after the cod stocks and the herring stocks the boat will still pay for itself. If we just look after them, they'll look after us, yeah?' He sounded close to tears.

Yes, thought Diane, eyes closed. Yes. If we just look after the Silver Darlings . . .

A few months later, in the spring, John arrived to cut the grass and was amazed to find a profusion of blossoms in the flower beds, a panic of gorgeous first editions – bluebells, crimson Welsh poppies, hysterical lemon-yellow narcissi, assertive hyacinths in pale pink.

John was impressed. 'Did you do this?' he asked Diane as she wandered outside, his tone almost accusatory.

'I had some help,' she said.

Vadim's colours. In this sterile soil they were a miracle.

John wandered over to the far corner, whistling happily to himself. He was going to become a father in the autumn and his bliss was ironclad. 'Mind you,' he said, pointing at a small mutilated patch of white, dying blossoms, 'that's the mess-iest fucking arrangements of snowdrops I've ever seen. Sorry. Pardon the language, Mrs Buchan.'

Diane strolled over to look. And then she began to stare at the snowdrops. They formed a pattern. They formed a word. A word in Cyrillic script:

ЛЮбВÓЬ

'Do you want me to dig them up?' said John.

Diane stared at the snowdrops for a long, long time. When

she'd bought herself a Russian dictionary, that had been the very first word she'd looked up. She stood there, staring and quietly paralysed, her heart shattering all over again. She took a deep, deep breath.

'Yes. Dig them up.'

GUNSEL'S HAND

I've got his arm twisted up behind his back and I'm thinking about the knife in my pocket. He's pretty scrawny and he's got all the weight of a feathery teenage girl, but he's beginning to annoy me. It's like trying to pin down a plastic bag full of snakes. No, I decide, he's not worth the hassle and ram his face against the wall, making sure I get a good handful of hair. It's surprisingly clean, it even smells of coconut conditioner, or jojoba. Well, he cracks his front teeth and goes down, crying and spitting.

Behave yourself, okay? I tell him. He just sits there, all crumpled and bloody, and cries. He's about sixteen. I walk away. That was nice and straightforward. He gives Hashim grief, I give him grief. That's what the punters pay for and, once in a while, it's nice to earn it. And I love Indian food.

I check into the bars between six and seven. Everything's fine, everything's smooth. I like being manager of two places. They run themselves. I just have to show up regularly, check the books, report to Mr Kennedy. He tries to get me to call him David, or Dave, but it doesn't feel right. Maybe in a few months, when I've run rings around those other clowns he's got working for him, maybe then I'll start calling him David. He's a worried man. He thought he had everything sewn up and the other things too, but Pearse is a busy man. We've all heard a few things about Pearse, mainly how he killed one of his girls by shooting her in the throat. Now, most people thought that was uncalled for, but me – well, it gave us something in common. I like his reputation. I haven't run into him yet but, in my books, a man with a few murders under his belt has got Brownie points already.

Around midnight, I drive over to the club for the card game. That's another nice thing about this job. I don't have to get up early and go to some nine-to-five office job, I make my own hours. I'm pretty much my own man. That's where loyalty and efficiency get you.

The boys are there already. Jesus, they are the ugliest bunch of people I've ever had the misfortune to sit around a table with. Beer bellies, bad skin, shabby suits – why don't they tidy themselves up once in a while? Or read a book once in a while? I don't mind their looks as much as I mind their conversation. I like to look smart and I like to read. I'm thirty-four. I try to improve myself. At least I make an effort. But they lose money without a fuss, so I keep showing up.

Mick cuts the deck. He's a red-faced guy in his fifties, with surprisingly long fingers. He likes to make a big show of shuffling and dealing. He thinks he's in Reno, the moron. Nobody ever notices his beautiful hands, they're too busy looking at that disfiguring scar across his lips. Well, I haven't got a mark on me and I will keep it that way.

Stan opens. He's probably got two Jacks. I never open unless I have two Kings or better. But that's Stan. Maurice stays. He's maybe trying to finish a three-card straight. He'll never make that hand. I raise on my two Aces and Stan, who always makes the mistake of thinking that the money in the pot still belongs to him, follows me up and calls. At the draw, Mick folds, I've still got my two Aces, Stan has his two Jacks and Maurice has a fat nothing. Forty quid. Nice for openers.

Stan deals and says, Hear about that guy on Monday?

Yeah, he was bit of a mess by all accounts, says Maurice. He's sweating and squinting at his cards up close. I hate it when he does that, he looks like a fucking retard when he does that. Well, says Mick, throwing in three cards and frowning at his draws, I heard a thing that didn't get into the papers. I heard they castrated him first.

Well, that makes the boys go very quiet for a few seconds. I raise on Jacks Up, Maurice stays put and says, Well, was it Pearse's or wasn't it?

Stan and Mick could be on a pair each. I'm not certain but bet on my Jacks anyway.

Of course it was Pearse, snaps Stan and calls, with Nines Up. Now that was a poor move. He should've guessed when I took only one card.

Castrated? says Stan. I'd say that was Pearce, wouldn't you?

I'm saying nothing. Seventy-five quid. That's okay. That's all right. I'm thinking about the kind of loyalty that makes a man useful. These three have the loyalty of dogs. Except Stan, maybe. He's smarter than the others. He's the only one who can tell, very occasionally, when I'm bluffing and when I've got a solid hand.

Poe said, 'It is merely an identification of the reasoner's intellect with that of his opponent.'

I wonder if Stan has been thinking about loyalty? It might not be a bad idea to let a few other people know just how helpful I can be. And I look good. Sometimes Mr Kennedy doesn't seem to grasp the facts. With him it's an old-fashioned family thing and anyone who isn't family has to act as if they are. I'm full of good ideas but they won't see the light of day. He likes to think he's part of some fucking Medellín dynasty or something, coming out with Spanish quotes like '*Palo, Plomo, Plata*' – meaning a stick for waverers, lead for enemies and silver for friends. Sometimes he's an impressive man and I learn from him. Mostly he's an embarrassment. But he is the boss and I have made myself indispensable.

Maurice deals. I am on three Fours. He folds on a bust. Mick draws three. I draw two and bet on my three Fours. Stan takes a swig from his glass and calls. On three Deuces. I never drink when I play cards and, win or lose, I neither brag nor whine. Since I almost always win, there's no mileage in annoying them.

Mr Kennedy's getting really pissed off, says Stan. I just hope he doesn't ask me to get involved in this. I collect the rent – that's what I'm good at.

Mick shuffles the cards and looks at the ceiling and says, I heard he's got an arsenal. All the latest kit. Money no object. He's even hired people, so they say.

Guns aren't really Mr Kennedy's style. He thinks a reputation and a good thumping are enough to bump things along. Reputation is a funny thing. Mr Kennedy has more money coming down now, from the girls and the restaurants and the videos and the other stuff, than he ever did, and he's got the nine of us. And yet, it's as if the word just shifted a little, the tone changed and suddenly his reputation isn't quite what it was. Funny that. I don't use guns, but I sort of like them. I could be proficient, if the opportunity presented itself.

Frankly, Pearse scares the shit out of me, says Stan, drawing two, and I hope to Christ I never run into him.

I deal and pick up a bust. Mick opens. Stan and Maurice fold, Mick stays. I raise on the bust and look at him. He's wondering.

Sometimes I don't like the way Mick looks at me, when he's trying to figure out if I'm bluffing. It's as if he's not just puzzled, but also afraid. As if he would wave the cash goodbye if it meant he didn't have to look me in the eye. What does he think I'm going to do? Stab him? It's that reputation thing again. Mick wants to be hard. Mick wants us all to be like me. Stan is more civilised about it. He pretends we're all greengrocers.

Mick sweats some more. He has this habit of scraping the upper edge of the cards down his forehead. If we're playing for a few hours, the whole pack ends up sticky. Jesus. I'm betting on a bust. If he has any sense he won't call.

He doesn't. He had three Kings.

I'm good at this game. Not the best, but efficient. I can usually figure everybody out, eventually. When they're holding nothing, their eyes will become a shade too nonchalant, or there will be a shift in their chair. When Stan is holding a beauty he becomes left-handed all of a sudden.

We play a few more games. I lose £50, but I'm still about £220 ahead. That's okay. There's a nice suit I've got my eye on.

It's just before dawn so I drive to the City. I love this part of town at dawn when it's completely empty. Crammed with people, it's invisible, ruined, polluted, but early in the morning I get the whole place to myself. I took Grace down here once. She's a whore I pick up once in a while. She's okay. We don't have sex that much. I just like to listen to her talk. But it was all wrong. You're supposed to be quiet down here and she wouldn't stop talking. Not loudly, but in the half-light, her voice echoed all over the piazzas and bounced from pearl building to pink building, until I wanted to strangle the bitch just to shut her up. I let her walk home that morning.

Stan is always talking about his family. His family and football. I have no family, and I stopped being interested in football in the mid-Seventies, when I followed Leeds United. Bruce Lee and Leeds United. That was it. I loved that team – Bremner, Madeley, Giles, Harvey, Gray, Clarke, Lorimer, Yorath. And I liked the fact that they played all in white, with no advertising plastered all over them. I found out as I got older that they had actually been regarded as a fairly dirty team, but by then I didn't care any more.

The man I killed had a football tattoo on his forearm. It said 'Arsenal FC' and it was quite fresh. They always look good when they're new and this one had clean, true colours, not the mucky navy and black of years ago. He struggled a bit, but when I got the knife a good four or five inches in, into his heart I think, he slowed down. His eyes stayed open and I think he said a name, and then he wasn't anything at all, he was just a lump, a heap. You'd be amazed at how little it bothered me.

A few years ago, when I was repossessing stuff for a firm, I went to the house of a very stupid man who owed the clothes he was standing up in. His wife was lying across the kitchen table with her brains on the floor and he was hanging from a door upstairs. Now that did annoy me. People get themselves into trouble because they're inept and careless, and then they upset everybody else. My fellow died innocent and pure because he didn't have a choice in the matter. It wasn't his fault. It was my decision. Not like the hanging man. Not like Hashim.

Two weeks later. I'm parked outside Hashim's, reading the paper, before I go in to have a chat with him. He's been getting cheeky. He's only handed over seventy-five per cent of the usual amount for the last three weeks. Says he can't afford it. Well, that's bullshit for a start. He's driving around in a Saab. In the paper, I'm reading about a Japanese man named Seiichi Kawaguchi, who sent letters vaguely threatening blackmail to 4000 total strangers. He got 130 replies and 5,000,000 yen. That's around £20,000. Now that's pretty funny. I tear it out and put it in my pocket. Everybody's got a little secret something to feel bad about.

I go in by the kitchen door. It's steamy and hot in here. And noisy too. Hashim's wife is clattering pots and pans in the sink. He's got his back to me so I go up to him, tap him on the shoulder and, when he turns around, I ask him politely when he thinks we'll get our twenty-five per cent. His eyes widen. He's not supposed to throw a punch at me but he does. Now that really surprises me, because I've known Hashim for quite a while and eaten in his fine restaurant many times, so I hit him hard on the cheekbone. I really put my shoulder into that punch and his whole face breaks under its weight. He falls by the cooking range and his tiny wife steps between us. I am not enjoying this. She is small and fragile, and she starts screaming at me in Urdu or Hindi, and beating at me with her fists. I would laugh but this is annoying. I've seen her standing outside the pub, asking strangers passing by to go in and call Hashim out. He's not supposed to drink and she was too good a woman to darken the doorstep of a public house. She knew he was in there, drinking whisky, but everyone lies for him. Hashim? they would say innocently. No, we haven't seen him. And here she is protecting him. Now why would that be? I grip her wrist and, by squeezing, break it. She screams and I don't understand the language, but I don't think she's calling for help, or wailing from the pain. I think perhaps she's calling down upon my head every magnificent curse her grandparents taught her. I let her drop in a faint beside her careless husband. I think about the scrawny kid who was smashing their windows every day. That's the business. I did not expect them to be grateful then and I do not expect them to be outraged now. That's how it works. And if people just took a little time and made a little effort it would work just fine.

I hear a noise behind me and turn. There are two of them, my build, wearing suits. I know they're from Pearse. I kick the first one in the groin and he's trying to double up even as he falls backwards. The second one ducks to avoid a left hook then slips inside and catches me, full on the jaw, with a roundhouse right. I counter mechanically. I'll be damned if I'm going down. We circle each other breathing heavily. My jaw feels like a balloon. The first guy is still on the ground, moaning and clutching his balls. As I circle, I bring my left heel down, real hard, on his face, never taking my eyes off the other guy. He stops moaning. The other guy's expression changes slightly, he lowers his hands an inch or so and I see an opportunity. I drop my fists to my sides and stand up straight. You're Pearse's aren't you? I ask.

He nods, surprised. This isn't exactly his patch, I say. Is that what he's up to? gesturing towards Hashim. He nods again. It's not an expression of fear on his face, it's something else, something weird. I can't exactly read the guy. Well, I say, pressing my advantage, if that's the best he can send, he's going to need someone with a little more finesse and a little local knowledge. He doesn't say anything, but looks a little sneaky suddenly, as if he knows something I would soon find out. I don't like that look. His pal is still out cold. Suddenly he relaxes and looks at me coolly.

Looking for a letter of introduction are we? he says with a smile that was only slightly unpleasant.

I'm a talented boy, I say, and I'm tired of playing Happy Families. You can walk out with your baggage here and deliver the message or we can start this thing up again, right now. I raise my fists.

Forget it. He smiles a genuine smile this time. His pal shows signs of coming to, so he hauls him up and they leave. Good, I'm thinking to myself. Good.

Hashim and his wife are lying crumpled against the cooker. I look at them for a while. Hashim's nosebleed has splashed all over his clothes. She fell with her arms almost folded, as if she was taking a nap, her head almost leaning on his shoulder. A bruise is beginning to form around the tiny bones on her wrist. In repose, her soft, brown face is still wearing a trace of the fury it wore when she pounced and it bothers the hell out of me. He's a bad husband, he's a sloppy man, yet she leaped to his defence. That doesn't make sense at all. I'm twice her size and she didn't care. Breaking her wrist was so easy. I remember now that it didn't feel so great. Before I leave, I turn and look at them again. They look horrible. My jaw hurts, badly.

A week later I'm making a small delivery for Mr Kennedy. The pub owner takes me into the back room, and we chat about this and that before getting to the point – it doesn't hurt to be civil – then I see his expression change and I hear a noise behind me.

When I wake up, I can't move my left arm. It is tied to the floor with wire. I am lying on bare floorboards. My skull is pounding and my feet are cold. I raise my head with difficulty; my shoes and socks are gone. There are five men standing over me. Oh, God. No. Make it quick. I can't think of anything else. Just make it quick. I want to die well, if I must die. My skin is shrivelling with fear. They all just look at me, as if they are watching interesting bacteria under a microscope. Or a snowflake. I remember that from science lessons at school. Snow from the classroom windowsill. I am trying very hard to be quiet and still, and they just stare at me. The one in the middle is boyish and handsome. He laughs gently, and the others relax and smile. Hello there, sleepyhead, he says. My name's Gary Pearse. I know who you are. I gather you've expressed an interest in contributing your services. The others laugh a little. Out of the corner of my eye I recognise the two from Hashim's. One has an ugly, bruised cut down one side of his face. Good, you bastard, at least I did that, you bastard. I want to kill him. I wish I'd killed him then. But even he is smiling. I begin to feel the kind of fear I haven't felt in a long, long time.

Pearse gestures and all but two of them leave. One of them holds my left arm straight and flat against the floorboards and forces my fingers down, palm upwards. I try to struggle but I have no strength. My head doesn't hurt that much, but I can find no energy.

You think I'm going to kill you, Pearse says flatly. There is no trace of a smile in his voice and he suddenly looks much older. He nods at the second man, and I see that this man has a masonry hammer and a six-inch spike. I feel its point tickle my palm then he raises the hammer and with one blow drives it through my hand into the floor beneath.

I don't know how long I scream. The pain tears me to shreds. I'm reaching for my bloody palm with my free hand, screaming, but every move I make wrenches my impaled hand and makes the pain worse. I feel the world going black and my voice gives out. I can't scream any more. My head hits the floorboards and I'm just sobbing, sobbing. My eyes are filled with tears and I can't see.

The three of them watch me for a little while. I try to breathe properly and I concentrate on the agony in my hand. It's like a bad, bad toothache, I tell myself. Don't try to distract yourself. That doesn't work. Concentrate on it, focus on it. After a while it will stop being just pain and will become something else instead. Focus. Give it due care and attention and you will tame it, turn it into something other than a nail through your hand. Something interesting. They're still watching me.

Pearse nods again and the other two leave the room. I don't know where I am. It looks like part of an old church. I'm trying to breathe properly. I'm making a God-awful, ragged noise, but the pain isn't as unbearable now. I can't lift my head.

Pearse moves towards me, until he's standing directly above me. He looks fifty feet tall. I wipe my eyes with my free hand. He kneels down beside me and brings his face very close to mine, and stares into my eyes and begins to speak to me. I can smell coconut off him.

How many people do you think I've killed? One? Three? Five? I know that you've killed. I know all about you. I know everything. You're good with your fists. You're a lovely fighter, but you'll use a knife if the mood takes you and you're good with a knife too. How many people do you think I've killed? Seven? Nine? Eleven? The problem is – you're scum. You make my skin crawl.

I don't get this. I thought there were possibilities.

He glances at my red, spiked hand and frowns. The problem is, there's only one kind of language scum like you understands. And I have to employ that language to get scum like you off my back. How many people do you think I've killed? How many?

He's really asking me.

I don't know. In spite of the pain, I need to know this thing. I need to know, how many. I try to hold his gaze and I ask him, How many? My voice is almost gone.

None.

None, he says and he doesn't blink, not once. He just looks at me as if I am the most wondrous, bizarre, hideous thing in all creation. It's that reputation thing again.

I have this theory, he says and his voice penetrates the pain in my head and my hand like a razor, a soft hiss. I have this theory. People say that if a man has killed once, it becomes easy, and there's no difference between one and one hundred. It's true. But not because it's easy. It's because, once you've done it for the first time, that's it. That's it. You have committed the ultimate sin and you can never, never atone for it. You are damned for all eternity. And there really is no difference between one and one hundred.

His voice is a priestly monotone. His face is so sad and I try to move but there is no point any more.

You disgust me, he says, and his voice is worse than the wound in my hand. Do you know what judges say to prisoners after they've sentenced them to death?

Then he gets up and walks out, leaving me alone.

It's so quiet. I can't feel my hand any more. Something is terribly wrong, but it's not my hand. I can't quite get a fix on it. Someone will show up, sooner or later. I've lost some blood and my head is beginning to swim. I thought I had this thing down. I would be perfect. We had something in common. I thought we had something in common. The fear has gone now and has been replaced by something else. I have done that thing and he has not. I was the novice, he was the expert and I was going to come home, and it hasn't turned out that way at all. The fear has gone away and been replaced by something else. I was wrong.

I understand what he does not. I understand what it feels like to kill. I was on the winning side. All I can see is an Arsenal FC tattoo, and all I can feel is the soft weight of a dead man and I have never been so lonely in my life.

I can hear a music coming from somewhere. I think I'm going to faint. It's a country song. I know this song. It's called, 'She's Acting Single and I'm Drinking Doubles'.

I'll just lie here. Stan will come and get me. I know what judges say. Stan's okay. Stan's a damn fine lad. I remember the time I went with him to the morgue for an ID. His son was supposed to have been in a car crash. And Stan looked at this crushed corpse and it wasn't his son, and we both burst out laughing, right there in the morgue. May the Lord have mercy on your soul, that's what they say. Stan will come. Please. Oh, God, I think I'm going to pass out soon. Can a man die from being only half-crucified? The pain is coming back. Somebody will find me soon. Will I play poker with a hand like this? A Royal Flush sweeps into my head. I was eleven years old. I'd convinced myself that it was possible to play two hands of poker, by myself. Just put yourself in the other guy's shoes and forget your own cards for the moment. It was totally, beautifully random. The first sweep of cards, I dealt myself a Royal Flush.

There was no one there to see it.
That's a million to one shot.

AMONG THE GĀDJÉ

'No, Mum – you *can't* change your name to Barbra Streisand.'

'Why not?'

'Well, I don't know – Barbra's probably got copyright on it. And you'd be a bigger embarrassment than you are now, okay? Besides, you'd be a bit of a let-down on karaoke night, wouldn't you, eh?'

'How about Rita Hayworth? How about somebody dead? Maybe the copyright's run out. I'm fed up being called Dolores Moonie. Or Veronica Lake! I liked her. She was always getting poor little Alan Ladd into trouble. Did you know he had to stand on a –'

'*Mum!*'

She dragged a couple of strands of white hair over one eye and looked at him with a squint. 'You do know how to whistle, don't you, Steve?'

'You look ridiculous. And anyway that was Lauren Bacall.'

Dolores sighed. 'Jesus, getting sued by Barbra Streisand would at least liven things up around here. Christ, Rory, I'm bored.'

'I noticed. I thought you were helping Clare with all that ... dress ... business.'

They looked at each other. His daughter had announced two weeks ago that she was getting married. To James. He was an estate agent and a decent lad. Solid type. Reliable. Rory hated him. The wedding was next Sunday.

'Besides, it's Saturday, haven't you got your classes to go to?'

'We finished Native American Art last week. I've signed up for Scholastic Philosophy, but that doesn't start for another fortnight.'

'Scholastic Philosophy? You mean, people like Nietzsche and that?'

'Don't know. Haven't looked at the syllabus yet. Could be.' She sighed again. 'Laughing Fred. Your favourite comedian and mine.'

Dolores had been going to evening classes on and off for years. Pretty much since her Jude had died fifteen years ago. It was something to do and she'd learned a lot; archaeology, Middle English literature, ceramics, yoga – she'd tried a couple of science-orientated subjects but they generally gave her a nosebleed. Still, over the years she'd ploughed her way through most of the curriculum. She had shied away from the course on Romany Culture for a long time. She hadn't wanted to know what the Gorgio academics thought of her own people, the gypsies. But it was more than that. She and Jude had settled in 1955, when she was nineteen, when they married. They got a council house near Stourbridge and that had been that. Accusations of *marime* – defilement – had flown at them from all the family, far and near, but Jude had dug in his heels. He wasn't moving, and he'd protected his pregnant bride from the slurs and the shameful rows. And eventually the family had packed up and, businesslike, moved back to Ireland. Her brothers and uncles loved a good feud; Jude's decision to settle was for them just an excuse, just something else to fight about. That's what he'd always told her, but sometimes, in the early days, she'd felt strange and twice-exiled in her clean council house on the estate.

Sometimes, during the day, especially when Rory was crying, she'd wanted to pick him up, take off her shoes and walk to the nearest open field, and just keep walking. But there were no roads of painless dust and sand, just tarmac, and the nearest open field was a football pitch. Eventually she'd got used to it and stopped dreaming about the din of dogs and motorists, caravans and the way children's voices seemed to carry for miles in the open air. Jude had found himself a job as a labourer with a local builder and she concentrated ferociously on Rory. She was proud of him. He was a handsome boy – clever, politicised, with the same magpie interests as his mother. He'd married at nineteen, too, like her. Marion was a loud, brave, South London woman who ran a tiny café and crafts centre next to the house. She was trying to get a grant from the local TEC, to set up an Internet Service Providers Site in the café, like the ones springing up in London. Half the time Dolores didn't understand what the hell Marion was talking about, but she liked her anyway, and her steadiness usefully balanced Rory's intensity and occasional dark moods. He was a features journalist on the local paper and lectured now and again in Media Studies at the university.

When she'd finally plucked up the courage to try the Romany Culture course (and only then because it was going to be dropped, permanently, in favour of Aromatherapy) she was both relieved and disappointed. It was all terribly rarified, concentrating on such topics as 'Economic Adaptation', 'Kin-Group Competition', 'Mànus Belief Systems', 'Bilateral Kinship', 'Gādjé-Gypsy Relationships', 'Rom Population Movement', 'Environment and Ecology', 'Shantytown Ethnicity of the Boyash' and 'Distribution and Inter-Group Conflict'. After a while, that gave her a nosebleed too. Sometimes she felt like an old house that, after fifty years, was still settling. Creaking and softly thudding, and settling.

'Hey, what about Marion Morrison? He's dead.'

Christ, thought Rory. '*Two* Marions about the place . . .?'

he said patiently, with visions of his mother in a cowboy hat, on a horse.

'Oh. Right. Fair enough.'

'What's wrong with Dolores anyway? It means "Lady of Sorrows". I think it's a beautiful name.'

'The hell it is,' she said in her best Western drawl. Rory laughed. She'd christened him Ruaidhri, the Red King, after her Irish father, but he'd anglicised it at university. It was too much like hard work. It bounced harshly off uncomprehending English ears and the spelling meant that he was called everything from Rudder to Roadie to Rudeboy. Besides, he felt that it was almost slightly antisocial, having a name no one could use, rather like refusing to look someone in the eye when they were speaking to you. So he'd changed it, informally. That had stung a little. Names were one of the few things we could call our own. Our bodies, our names and some form of . . . belief, maybe? Still, when Jude had been dead a couple of years, she'd gone back to using her own maiden name. It had just been one of Rory's ways of telling her, gently, that he wasn't her baby boy any more.

Neither wanted to talk about the wedding, so they were still bickering about names and movies, and were in the middle of a sub-Ritz Brothers routine when the door opened and Stephen glided in. Stephen was Rory's best friend. They'd gone through university together and had stayed best friends ever since. He was a computers expert and ran his own small training and consultancy company in town. They both just looked at him for a second. Neither Rory nor Dolores had ever got used to the sight of Stephen. It wasn't simply his relaxed, shoulder-rolling gait or his nicely arrogant, proprietorial air. It was just that Stephen was the most astonishingly beautiful man either of them had ever seen or was ever likely to see. They'd never got used to it. Every time he showed up, it was like the visual treat of the week. He had that effect on everybody. Shopkeepers would fiddle about with change and engage him in idle chit-chat just so they could look at him for a while.

Today he had a tiny cut above his left eyebrow.

'Hiya, Toots,' said Dolores. 'How's the portrait in the attic coming along?'

Stephen smiled. When he smiled, it was like the sun coming out. Dolores had been teasing him for years. 'Never mind that, kiddies,' he said. 'How're the wedding plans coming along?'

Neither of them spoke.

Stephen sat down and stared at them. 'Jesus, Dolores, are you going to give her away or just leave her out the back for the binmen? I don't like it any more than you do, y'know.'

'Okay, then, cards on the table,' said Rory. 'Why don't you like it?'

'Because it's a hideous, patriarchal institution, designed for the exchange of property among men. Chattel, that's what Clare is, goods and chattel.' The three of them burst out laughing.

'All right, all right, what's *your* problem then? What's wrong with James?'

'Nothing. Everything. I don't know,' Rory said, frowning. 'Mum?'

Dolores stared at the table, smiling faintly. 'He's a nice boy. Very . . . trustworthy.' They burst out laughing again.

'I mean it! He works hard, he's ambitious. And he'll be good to Clare. That's the main thing,' she added lamely. 'I just wish he wasn't so . . . flat.'

'He reminds me of one of those big, static caravans, the kind on concrete blocks, with running water and gas cylinders,' said Rory.

Dolores shot him a sharp look. Was that a dig at her?

'Pretending it's a house and not going anywhere,' he continued absently.

'I don't know the lad that well,' said Stephen. 'He tried to explain endowment mortgages to me last Sunday. You know the kind of calligraphy in the Book of Kells?'

They both looked at him.

'The letter "*S*"? Where it's usually a snake coiling round and round until it eats its own tail? Trying to talk to Jimmy boy is a bit like that. He gave me a headache after a while, but I can't actually pin down anything about him that I would call unpleasant.'

'Yeah.' They looked at the table.

'Maybe he's a Tory!' Rory said hopefully. 'Maybe we could clobber her around the lugs with something like that, eh?'

'Would she care?' said Dolores drily. 'She cares about two things, that girl – fish and James. Christ Almighty, marine biology – you'd think someone who was studying marine biology would have a more finely developed sense of how to find a mate slightly higher up the food chain than James.'

'A great white shark maybe,' said Stephen.

'I was thinking more along the lines of Flipper.'

'Poppa, I think Flipper's tryin' ta tell us somethin'!' giggled Rory with mock-American urgency – 'What is it boy? Has Clare fallen down a well?'

'It's worse,' intoned Stephen, joining in. 'The building societies are raising interest rates a quarter per cent!' They laughed.

'Oh, come on, he's all right, is James,' said Dolores.

'No he's not,' they both snorted.

'Well, okay, he's not. But it's her life. And there's nothing we can do about it.' Rory and Stephen glanced at each other.

Stephen looked thoughtful for a moment, then said, 'You know, since it's in a good cause, I could sort of test the old Jacobite waters here. I could perhaps have a go at trying to –'

'NO!' shouted Dolores and Rory, laughing.

'All right, all right! It was just a thought. Anything to help out.'

Deciding to change the subject, Dolores reached over and

very gently touched the small cut above Stephen's eyebrow. He flinched slightly, but held her eye. The flaw simply made him look more beautiful. It had stopped bleeding only recently.

'Another car park, pet?' she said softly.

'Afraid so.'

'And the other guy?'

'I think I broke his nose At least I hope I did.'

Rory, smiling faintly, studied his coffee cup intently and said nothing.

Stephen glanced at him, then winked at Dolores. 'Just as well I didn't have the shock troops with me, or the poor bastard would've had a hell of a lot more than a broken nose.'

'I worry about you,' said Dolores.

'And it's much appreciated, but I can look after myself, okay?'

She looked at him. He did enjoy a good brawl, so long as it was in a good cause. And he always won and would come over the following day, glowing and exuberant, with tiny marks on his face, or on his knuckles.

'How's John anyway?' Dolores said.

Stephen looked slightly distracted for a moment. John was his partner. 'Um, he's fine. He went off yesterday to Aberdeen for the week. He's doing the sound for Loudon Wainwright. He'll probably take in a couple of days on the north-east coast.'

He sighed. 'He seemed very keen to go. Maybe he'll be back for the wedding. I'm not sure. He knows it's important.'

Stephen yawned and stood up, stretching extravagantly, his loose, six-foot frame filled the room. He worked out every day and it showed.

Just then Marion, and her fifteen-year-old son Gene, came in. She kissed Stephen on the top of his head. 'Well, Ugly – have you come to sort out the PCs for me, get me hooked up? What the hell happened to your face? Oh, don't tell me. I'm not interested. What about lamb pasanda for lunch? I found this great recipe on the library's computer – an on-line Recipes Forum! It's pretty cool.'

'Sounds great,' said Stephen.

'Sweetheart, you have something like sixty cookbooks already,' said Rory.

'I know!' Marion laughed. 'But for some reason a recipe seems to acquire the significance of the Rosetta Stone when you know that it's travelled all the way downline from a university in Michigan or something.'

'It's like phones,' said Dolores. 'People still talk about long-distance phone calls as if they had to walk every bloody inch of the way. Go on, pet, give Marion a hand.'

While Marion and Rory prepared lunch, Gene polished his violin and educated Stephen and Dolores on what was cool in the local music stores.

Dolores went into her senile old judge routine. 'Sven Vath? Sounds like a particularly dangerous Scandinavian dentist. And the Aphex Twin? What's that? – two cockroaches on a keyboard?'

Gene giggled. He'd actually taped some of his stuff for her and had bought her a Walkman for her last birthday. Sometimes she would take it along if she was going for a long walk. Most of it baffled her, some of it frightened the hell out of her, but he was a sweet grandson and he liked the idea of having a grandmother who could listen to music without any lyrics. And wasn't classical. And she'd done evening classes in Ecology, so he could brag about her to his friends, no problem.

'There's this other group, combo, whatever, I forget what they're called, and they use just the sounds of waterfalls and jungles and birds and stuff. It's frigging brilliant!'

'Don't swear, pet.'

'That's not frigging swearing. This is fucking swearing!'

Stephen cuffed him lightly on the back of the head. 'Do as your gran says, you.'

'Okay, sorry,' said Gene. Everybody knew that, when the mood took her, Dolores could swear in a way that had dockers running for cover. Gene adored Stephen. He was thin and bony and, at fifteen, didn't seem to be getting any bigger. Stephen had promised to teach him a little basic self-defence. And there was that time, a year ago, when a few of the older lads had ganged up on him outside the takeaway. He'd been with his girlfriend and, as the insults mounted, he'd thought he was going to throw up from embarrassment and shame and fear. Then Stephen had come strolling round the corner. He just smiled at them and, quietly, almost apologetically, told them that if they didn't run along home and tidy their rooms, like good little boys, he would have to break their legs. And he'd said it up close, as if he was just having a pleasant, blokey chat with a couple of friends. His girlfriend didn't hear, but Gene heard. 'Personally, I think fighting is overrated myself,' Stephen had told him later. 'I just happen to be very good at it.'

'How come?'

'I've had a lot of practice,' he'd answered in a tone that had an edge of weariness to it.

'*Noli me tangere.*'

'What?'

'Never mind.'

Over lunch they all sat and chatted and drank wine, including Gene. Rory wasn't a strict father. In a way, he liked it when Gene got into trouble, especially as it didn't happen that often.

'Here, kid, have some red,' said Rory, glancing at Dolores.

His mother was a one-off, a sharp, wandering blade. He'd been settled all his life. But sometimes he felt as if he was the bottleneck. As if all the sweet, fictional travels and yarns, and stories of travels had stopped with him. And it was his fault, the responsibility his crime. His daughter. Christ. Clare was embracing the settled life with open arms. She wanted a mortgage and a holiday in Tenerife. Dolores had made her choice, but at least she'd had a life to learn with, before she'd stayed put. The vagrant clues, the tiny histories, only came down to him much later, after Jude died. He'd grown into his thirties with the envy and pride building in his blood. He was settled, but he'd never known anything else. Clare knew, she'd always known, and she was still happy to do it. To marry, to engage herself with these shrivelled, joyless days as kindly as she could. He knew Clare hadn't given up. He just wanted her to play a little, to take on board some of his mother's churlish idealism. He knew he wasn't being fair on her, but right now he didn't care.

Marion and Stephen were stuffing down pasanda and bickering about who was better, Astaire or Kelly. Okay, okay, Stephen conceded, Astaire was technically a better dancer, but he was perfectly plastic somehow; Kelly *bled*, you know? In his routines, he was a flesh and blood, hurting human being. Dolores said she liked Michael Jackson's dancing and then announced that from now on she was to be called Latoya, and to hell with the lawsuits. Stephen had been rubbing his eyes and that started the cut bleeding again. Dolores and Gene both ran to get a plaster. When she wiped the blood away and carefully applied the plaster it seemed to Dolores that Stephen was close to tears.

'Poor baby. It's such a small cut, but very deep – how did that happen?' she asked him.

'Well, he got me with his left and he was wearing a particularly vulgar wedding ring. Maybe that's what did it.' Stephen smiled sadly.

'Christ, I need an hour's kip, at least,' he said. 'Are you coming to the pub later?'

'Yeah! Course.' Rory leaned over and unexpectedly stroked

his head. 'Now piss off and stop bleeding all over my kitchen.'

As he left, Stephen felt glad that Rory hadn't been in the pub with him last night. Rory didn't understand the rules. Stephen didn't fight to kill. He fought to win. And if he could win without fighting at all, that was better than anything.

Later, in the pub, Rory got the drinks in. Marion had gone into town with Clare to have a wander around the shops. Looking for some kind of headgear for Sunday. Marion loved the whole idea. She positively wanted to be a grandmother at forty-one. She and Clare had been best friends for the last three weeks. It wasn't going to be an expensive wedding, and James's parents had graciously offered to pay for most of the food and drink. Just as well, thought Rory. He and Marion couldn't have afforded it.

Dolores announced that some of her relatives were coming over from Mayo especially for it.

Rory was thrilled. 'I hope they all get blazing drunk and trash the church before the bloody service starts!' he said gleefully.

'Stop that. They'll be perfectly well behaved. I think.'

'Oh, well then,' Rory said to Stephen, 'we'll just have to think of something else, won't we?'

Stephen swallowed half his pint in a few seconds. 'Well, I did offer to help. Eh, Dolores?' Dolores laughed and smacked him on the cheek lightly. Rory looked at him. Sometimes he couldn't take his eyes off that amazing face, the slightly rough skin, the mesmerising green eyes, the slow, slow smile.

They'd had a hell of a time at Manchester University in the Seventies. Rory could barely remember any of the details. It seemed a blur of parties and music and demos. He'd met Marion at a demo. He couldn't even remember what it was for. Or against. But he remembered the first time they'd made love, in a tiny bed-and-breakfast in Eyam, the plague village. She'd talked to him all night, telling him about how the heroic villagers had, through their self-imposed quarantine in the 1660s, prevented the plague from spreading, and how most of them had died. And in the half-light as she talked, she seemed genuinely upset at their extinct, faraway courage, and he adored her for that. They married at the beginning of their third term in Political Science and Clare was born less than a year later.

God knows how they managed to graduate. Stephen was always there to help out. He was best friend to both of them. The way he looked, he attracted women like a magnet. Sometimes, on an infrequent night out, Rory would find himself watching the girls watching Stephen and would feel a tiny pang of jealousy. Married with a kid at nineteen. Christ. And here was Stephen, decorated with girls. Mostly, though, it made him feel absurdly proud and he liked the way his friend didn't brag about his conquests.

One Sunday, in their final year, they went to the Free Trade Hall to hear a concert. In between the second and third movements of Bruch's First Violin Concerto, Stephen leaned across slightly and, staring straight ahead, told Rory very quietly that he was gay. Rory turned his head to look at his friend's perfect profile, his black lashes, the sheen of tears in his eyes. He stared at that profile for a long moment, then stood up and walked out. He found himself trembling more and more with every step. When he reached the door, he threw up on the steps and didn't speak to Stephen for two years.

It was the deception, he told Marion, that's all.

'You pathetic liar,' she said. 'You guys just can't stand the thought of it, can you? It's fine as long as it stays on the page as a handy ideological club, but when it sits down and has a cup of tea in your living-room you run like a fucking rabbit.'

She was genuinely angry and went for drinks with Stephen regularly. Partly, Rory thought, to annoy him. For a long time, he was sick at heart and couldn't apologise. Then, one night, Marion came back drunk and laughing, and talking about the time Clare, as a flailing, bad-tempered ten-month-old, had given Stephen a black eye. Rory lowered his head into his hands. 'It's very simple,' she said loudly. 'You *miss* him, you stupid bastard.'

The following Friday he phoned Stephen and asked him if he'd like to go for a drink. Stephen was calm and gracious all evening. Rory was a bag of nerves but, by eleven o'clock he was feeling a little more comfortable. On the way home, they turned a corner and found themselves facing a skinny teenager with a nine-inch knife. He held the tip of it just under Stephen's chin. Rory backed off. Stephen didn't move. He didn't even take his hands out of his pockets. He just stood there, looking calmly into the mugger's eyes. My God, thought Rory, he's smiling. The kid stared at him. Stared, mesmerised, at Stephen's face. For a stretched, greedy moment there was complete silence and then, having forgotten to breathe, the kid gulped a lungful of air and, very slowly, backed off.

When he was gone, Stephen and Rory looked at each other and burst out laughing.

Rory whooped and threw his arms round him. 'What the hell was that?' he gasped.

Stephen hugged him fiercely for a moment, then released him and said, with no trace of vanity, 'Art lover, probably.'

Rory laughed until his chest hurt. Saved by sheer beauty. Maybe the kid and Stephen knew each other, maybe they'd been lovers, maybe there was some other agenda. He didn't care any more. He'd been forgiven, redeemed and saved by beauty. That was the version he liked and he was sticking to it. Later on, when he and Marion said goodnight, finally, he kissed Stephen briefly on the mouth and apologised properly.

'So, how're we gonna nobble this wedding then?' said Dolores. She was on her fourth gin and tonic and felt damn fine. She was sitting in her favourite seat, beside the wall, which the owner, Gerry, had, over a quarter of a century, completely covered with pub matchbooks from all over the world. Every country was represented, every ratty den, every spit-and-sawdust dump, every palatial cocktail lounge and foreign hotel. She liked to think that that wall suited her. She liked to think of herself as a mobile collection of foreign matchbooks. Especially when she'd had a few gins.

Rory and Stephen were on their sixth pint and decided to concentrate on the priest.

'He's a soft sod,' said Stephen. 'I can scare the shit out of him, no worries. That bit where he asks if anyone objects? Me and twenty of Dolores's mad relatives can stand up and "object" to the point where he'll pee himself. Hah!'

'There's no such part in Catholic weddings,' said Dolores, 'at least not nowadays, anyway. There are only three things than can put a spanner in the works as far as the clergy is concerned – Consanguinity, Affinity and Spiritual Relations.' It fairly rattled off the tongue.

'What does that mean?' said Stephen.

'It means don't go marrying your first cousin, your dead wife's sister, or your godmother. Mind you, it's easy to get dispensations these days,' she added absently.

Rory warbled something about Stephen claiming *droit de seigneur* and the pair of them collapsed in giggles, and Dolores just let her mind wander. She didn't mind it so much.

Yes she did.

She hated this wedding with a ferocity that would've terrified them. This thing was hitting Dolores where she lived and she hated herself for it.

'Tell you what,' said Rory. 'We'll get Carol from across the road to stand up and declare that she's pregnant. Ah, no, wait a minute, didn't she have her tubes tied . . . ?'

After the initial shock of Jude's death – he was only forty-eight – she'd picked herself up and carried on. And it dawned on her as the years went by that from the moment he lit that last non-filtertip in the pub, then dropped like a stone, she'd become more and more content. Surrounded by young people, she'd helped to bring up her grandchildren, almost as much as Rory and Marion, and she realised that she felt free and safe, and happier than at any time in her life. As Romany men go, Jude was one of the best and when she remembered the early times, when he'd thumped her, usually for answering back, usually when he was drunk . . . well, she'd been too young and stupid to get really angry about it then, so there was no point in letting it annoy her now that she was in her sixties.

'How's about we get in early, sabotage the plumbing and flood the church?'
    'Or better yet, burn it to the ground! Bomb it!'
    Now Rory and Stephen were just being silly. Couldn't hold their drink, either of them. But there was something about Stephen this weekend. As if he were biting down on some piece of misery and would be damned if he'd let it go.

God, life on the road seemed like a million years ago. All she could remember about her girlhood in Ireland were the bright, summer things. The details of outdoor noises. The buzzes and murmurings of summer evenings. There must have been cold, cursed winters, but they were gone. The chordless tunes she could still grasp, or wanted to, were of the crushing, high-smelling horse fairs in Ballinasloe, Killorglin and the biggest of them all, the Cahirimee Horse Fair in County Cork, with its acres of strangers and twitching horseflesh. And the mantra of the patterned routes around the six churches of Athenry, Glendalough, Lough Derg, St Christopher, St Clement, St Dunstan, and the Whitsun and Croagh Patrick Festivals.

Those times always brought feuding families together and once, when she was eight or nine, she'd watched from behind a bread van, as two glorious families brought the entire town of Fermoy to a standstill with their drinking and fighting. There were a thousand families in Ireland in the late Forties, a blackened web of motion and industry, of disorganised necessity and making do. Of sneakiness and genius, the mark of a people who still had to deal with Section 3 of the Vagrancy (Ireland) Act, 1847. They were all grubby swans; serenely, exotically indifferent on the surface and, underneath, working frantically to keep body and soul together.

Her family, and Jude's, had moved to the West Midlands when she was eleven. There was no sense of permanence in that, or of shame – it could have been the Far East, it could have been the next parish. The men went where the work was and there was a need for informal, gap-filling metal workers, and coopers and knife grinders. They paved footpaths and roofed houses, whitewashed sheds, picked the turnips and thinned the beets, sold cars, painted fences, told fortunes, traded horses and did just about anything else that came along.

There were often six or seven children in a family. A traditional blessing was 'I wish you the wealth of Joy – May you have many children'. The weddings were noisy and hysterical, and the funerals were even better. When her grandfather had died, sixty or seventy families had come, and they'd laid him out in his best rig and opened all the shutters on the caravan so that his soul could see and bless (or spit on) everyone he passed on his way down the Long Acre of Widows Green, pulled by two tired, heavy horses. Her father sold the old man's caravan and the animals too. He didn't want bad spirits or feckless memories hanging around. And he needed the money. In the old days it would've been burned, along with every item the old man had ever owned.

The night of her grandfather's funeral Jude had become very drunk. He was upset about the old man but it was more than that. She was pregnant with Rory. She hadn't told him yet but he knew. He'd made as if to strike her and for the first and last time in her life she defied him. She did more than that. She picked up a heavy frying pan and brained him with it. He swayed a little and dropped. After a few moments of lying on the caravan floor in the dark, he began to laugh and hauled himself up, and she looked at him, laughing and drunk and bleeding, and realised she was stuck with him.

It could've been worse.

'Hell,' slurred Stephen on his eighth pint, 'let's go the whole hog. You bomb the church, I'll seduce the groom and we'll both cripple the priest, okay?' He looked as if he was itching for a fight.

Poor baby, thought Dolores. *Fighting every bloody inch of the way.* Another thought struck her, something from the evening class, about the Sinté – the Romanian Boyash gypsies. The word came from 'Sind', meaning 'from Hindustan'. They claimed descendancy from Northern India. Maybe they were right. The Romany language had about five thousand words and most of them were corrupt Sanskrit. The Boyash legend held that their people were condemned to wander the earth because they had refused help and shelter to the Virgin and Child on their flight to Egypt.

Well, sod *the gādjé Virgin, and her sodding Child*, thought Dolores.

I wish you the wealth of joy.

Many children.

She dragged her mind back to the present and looked at Rory. Her only child, who bawled louder than any other baby on the estate. She felt like a laboratory scientist who'd robbed a bird of its strategic feathers, just to find out whether, when winter came, it would attempt the journey on foot. She'd given him the two halves of two lives and he had to live with it. And now he was taking it out on Clare. All the poor girl had wanted was her own house. That's what Dolores had wanted in 1955. She believed in threads, in continuity, in the silent strength of what the years got up to, the tricks they pulled. Maybe she was just the last rags of an old romance.

'*Mockadi*'.

'*Marime*'.

Defiled.

She thought of the day her father caught her with a book and wondered with a ludicrous shame if her bad, clever blood had gone ahead of her.

Stephen was watching her carefully. She was miles away. It was midnight and the pub was emptying. 'Come on, Dolores, let's go home.'

They drained their glasses and headed for the door.

A group of four young men sat nearby. One of them, a dark-haired lad with heavy stubble, had been glancing at Stephen all night. It hadn't gone unnoticed.

As he passed their table the lad hissed, 'Fucking faggot.'

Oh, Christ, no, thought Rory. *Not with Dolores here.*

Stephen stopped dead and turned round, squaring his shoulders slightly.

'Leave it,' said Rory quietly. 'Come on, kid, leave it.'

Stephen didn't hear him. He was staring at the dark lad. 'What did you call me?' His voice was soft and vicious.

The lad stood up. He was tall and sturdily built. 'I said you're a fucking poof, a dirty shirtlifter. Faggot.'

Stephen sized him up. He could break both this guy's legs without working up a sweat.

'Stephen, please. Not tonight.'

Dolores was beside him, speaking very softly. She put a hand on his arm. He felt like a bomb buried in granite. If he didn't smash this idiot's face, he thought he might explode. The two men stood, squaring up to each other. The tension was unbearable.

Stephen was tired of this. He was sick of winning but even more scared of losing. He was so tired of having to do this. And John was gone. He just knew it. John, his gentle, best-ever hope, who couldn't put up with the bravado any more, would meet some nice Aberdonian lighting engineer with an attractive brogue and that would be that. 'You're the only man who's turned "standing your ground" into a bloody psychosis!' he'd snapped before he left.

Stephen stood transfixed, staring at the boy, fists clenches by his side. He was miserable and he didn't know whether to weep or kill.

The boy began to look a little afraid. His friends were very quiet.

'Please, pet, come on.'

Dolores knew Stephen better than anyone. Her voice glided over him, like a fever breaking. He looked at her. All he wanted to do was stand his ground. All she wanted to do was run. He couldn't hurt Dolores.

He took a very deep breath and relaxed. He smiled brightly at the boy. 'Faggot? Listen, pal, only my best friends are allowed to call me faggot. Isn't that right, Rory?'

Rory went red and coughed. 'Um. Yeah. Right.'

'Besides,' continued Stephen in a chatty, seductive tone, 'I'm a bit surprised at your attitude. The way you've been giving me the glad eye all night, I thought we'd – well frankly, I thought we'd shared a moment back there, you know?'

The boy looked thunderstruck. 'What? I never bloody did, you bastard!' One of his friends suppressed a smile.

'Hey, don't worry about it,' said Stephen kindly, hooking

his thumbs into his belt. 'You're just a little confused, aren't you? You don't know whether you want to fight me or fuck me, eh?'

'I bloody didn't. I never did!'

He was beginning to repeat himself. One of his friends sniggered. Stephen threw him his sweetest, loveliest smile. 'Well, I wish you'd make up your mind. It's confusing for me too, you know.' Hands on hips, he added in a purring falsetto, 'Goodness, I don't know whether to raise my fists or drop my pants!'

The boy blinked and opened his mouth. Then he closed it again. He realised he no longer had a patch on which to fight. And the barman was giving him a very hard look. 'Piss off, queer,' he snapped and sat down.

'Good boy. Right, kids, let's go.'

'Thanks, pet,' whispered Dolores.

Stephen draped his arms over her and Rory, and they took the door as one. The triumvirate. The boy could hear them laughing as they marched off down the street. Well, he wasn't going to get himself barred from his local, just because of some queer, was he?

Two of Dolores's nephews, the twins, had come over by ferry and were spending a couple of nights in a guest house in town. Most of the old family was either dead or settled now. Apart from her brother. He was still moving on, still shifting. Around County Mayo mainly. She'd only seen the twins when they were babies and once or twice since, when her brother came over. She'd never gone back. She couldn't have borne the scrutiny. But they were polite, handsome men, her two nephews. In their thirties and dark like their father, with his extravagant taste in loud shirts. She just hoped they didn't have his taste for fighting. Not with Stephen around. He loved hearing about the town-stopping brawls in the old days and his interest could have been more than academic.

The week disappeared. Stephen stayed away from the house until Friday. When they'd staggered back from the pub that night, he'd ended up crying like a baby in Dolores's arms, begging Rory to drive him to Aberdeen at three o'clock in the morning and threatening to thump him if he didn't. Not surprisingly, he was feeling a tiny bit embarrassed with himself.

The day before the wedding the priest dropped by. He sat sipping his tea, chatting to Dolores, Marion and Clare, and wondering nervously why Rory and another handsome chappie were glaring at him from the scullery, making growling noises in his direction and giggling like madmen.

After he'd gone, Dolores decided to have it out with them and ordered them outside into the garden. 'Right, you two, that's enough. Just leave it alone, okay?'

She surprised herself with the anger in her voice. Rory and Stephen looked at her.

'What's changed your mind?'

'I haven't changed my mind. It's just not . . . *fair* on the girl. Come *on*. No more snide remarks about James, no more bad moods, no more estate agent jokes – and stop trying to put a hex on the bloody *priest*! Poor Clare's miserable. We should be . . . happy for her.' Christ, that sounded so lame.

She had been feeling bad all week and now she was taking it out on the boys. But they just didn't get it. They could fling careless remarks and rant woundingly, because in the end Rory knew his own daughter and he had the good sense to accept the world the way it was. For Dolores it was different and it scared her. Clare's embrace of James's world was like both a slap in the face and a reminder of her own weakness. Had she really wanted to settle? She wanted Clare to have it all, to travel a little because she had travelled a lot. But she'd turned her back on it in 1955 and now she was angry with the girl for doing the same thing.

Dolores was Tchinga'ni. Romany. And it was driving her

mad with pride and shame. If she was honest, she knew that she'd never had a choice. She wasn't a traveller, she was baggage. Her father had dragged her around the landscape from the day she was born and in 1955 her husband had put her in storage. That hurt. But right now she was ashamed of herself. She was behaving like a Victorian bourgeoise, sniffing vindictively over a daughter's bad marriage. She sighed to herself and rubbed Rory's head. 'It's Clare's life. Just knock it off, okay?'

Rory studied her face for a moment. She was serious. He made as if to say something, then didn't. Clare was his shining glory, his daughter, for God's sake. Did Dolores seriously think he was trying to hurt her? 'Okay,' he said and gave her a hug.

There were tears in her eyes. Now that was a rarity. 'I'm sorry for acting like some hysterical old bat.'

'That's okay,' said Stephen. 'You're good at it.'

They were just going to have to deal with it. And that's all there was to it.

The house was quiet, dark. Everyone was asleep. The odd, soft thump of a timber found an echo in the collie's tail against the kitchen sideboard as he recognised Clare gliding noiselessly out of the back door, carrying her shoes. She'd passed Stephen, snoring on the sofa, without waking him. And he slept like a nervous cat. Outside, she put on her shoes and ran through the streets towards James's flat.

The night air was cool, fresh and, in the beige blur of 3 a.m., the houses and trees had lost their outlines, their very shapes. The fields and gardens and the town itself had merged with a bad-tempered, beguiling sky, and the only things that were real in the universe were her legs and her lungs, and the cold key in her fist as she swooped along the alleys, sweating, precise, muscular. All the lopsided ferocities of the past month fell away; the crushing, cavalier kindnesses of family and friends, their terrible gifts of sympathy, their breezy interference. She loved their desperation and vicarious little snobberies, but she felt as if she was made of steel. As she ran, faster, through the park leading to his home, her heart was undismayed, her heels nerveless. She ran like the wind. Everything fell away as she pounded up his steps and inside, and then he scooped her up in his arms and held her so tightly, and swivelled quietly around the room, laughing, not allowing her feet to touch the floor. If he couldn't see the bride the night before the wedding he would starve to death and he would die of thirst. He would, he honestly would. He worshipped her with every ounce of energy he possessed; his arms and face and voice were desperate, inadequate to the task of communicating to her how she dissolved and remade him. She held on to him and kissed, savagely, his solemn face. Her fingertips picked his clothes from him and stroked his sore, still-healing tattoo, and as they sank to the floor, they never stopped murmuring and talking and whispering. He worshipped her. Sometimes that was enough.

Dolores heard her sneaking back in at 6 a.m. She knew the girl's tread like she knew the inside of her own mouth. For a second she lay there and held her breath, staring at the ceiling but not seeing it. Then she turned over and went back to sleep, smiling.

At the altar the priest shot a terrified glance at Rory and Stephen, who were grinning at him in a particularly evil way. Dolores glared at the pair of them and they subsided, their shoulders shaking in silent laughter. Clare threw her eyes to heaven and from under her veil snapped, 'Oh, for God's sake, Father, get *on* with it.'

All in all, Dolores decided later, it was a pretty good wedding. Clare had been radiant, James aloof and dignified. He didn't seem to care what any of them thought of him. Well, good for him, thought Dolores. And Rory seemed grown-up for the first time in his life. He gave Clare away with a bearing that spoke of authentic generosity, with a gesture that said, 'Here's a million pounds. Mind how you go.'

To everyone's surprise and delight, the bride and groom got up to sing an old Austrian gypsy song, a bantering call-and-response tune that had Rory unconsciously gripping Dolores's hand and wondering at James's diligent homework, and his warm tenor voice. Gene hit the first plaintive notes on his violin and they began to sing:

> 'In the darkness of the wood,
> Free is the bird in the air,
> And the fish where the river flows.
> Free is the deer in the forest,
> And the Gypsy wherever he goes.
> And the Gypsy wherever he goes.'

James held her by the waist and continued, smiling:

> 'Girl, wilt thou live in my home?
> I will give thee a sable gown,
> And golden coins for a necklace,
> If thou wilt be my own.'

Clare put her arms around his neck and sang sweetly:

> 'No wild horse will leave the prairie
> For a harness with silver stars,
> Nor an eagle the crags of the mountain,
> For a cage with golden bars;
> Nor the Gypsy girl the forest,
> Or the meadow, though grey and cold,
> For garments made of sable,
> Or necklaces of gold.'

'Girl, wilt thou live in my dwelling,
For pearls and diamonds true?
I will give thee a bed of scarlet,
And a royal palace too.
My white teeth are my pearlins,
My diamonds my own black eyes,
My bed is the soft green meadow,
My palace the world as it lies.'

They kissed. And brought the house down. Clare turned and hugged Gene, who was looking incredibly pleased with himself. She'd been coaching the pair of them for a fortnight.

As they were about to leave, Rory shook James by the hand and said, 'Good luck, Jim.'

James hesitated for a tiny moment, then said, *'Dza devlesa.'*

Rory was impressed. It meant 'God go with you' in Romany.

The boy had promise.

To round off the night, and to huge, drunken applause, Rory and Stephen got up and sang an a capella version of 'Leaving on a Jet Plane' that broke everybody's hearts. It was Dolores's favourite.

As the last notes died away, a slender, sweating man in a Barbour jacket appeared by the door. He and Stephen looked at each other for as long as the applause lasted. Then Stephen jumped off the stage and fell, hoarse and bawling, into his arms.

After that, when most people had staggered off, there was only one thing left for Stephen to do. Pick a fight with the quiet twins.

So he did, and out of his love for John, he lost.

But they took him outside and handed him, not a beating you would give a grown man, but a soft introductory hammering, an almost friendly tattoo of patronising thumps.

They knew the rules. They were dignified about it. They even offered to buy him a drink. Well, they stole his wallet first, *then* they offered to buy him a drink.

He came back to the near-empty bar, gleaming in defeat, glowing and bleeding from a cut lip. John locked eyes with him and smiled, and got out a hanky. Dolores was dog-tired, but with a jumpy, clean kind of tiredness that she'd created herself, not the fatigue we take in through our pores, through a sort of choiceless social osmosis. She thought of how ferociously James had gripped Clare's hand throughout the ceremony. His knuckles had been white.

'Well, Toots, how does it feel to be a big, fat loser?'

'Pretty good, actually!' Stephen laughed.

He draped an arm across John's back. 'I think it's about time you and I went home, eh, kid?'

He hugged Dolores. 'Coming, girl?'

'No, you go ahead, pet. I think I'll hang around for a little while.'

After they'd gone, Dolores sat quietly, propping up the bar and listening to the voices of Rory and the twins. For a moment she imagined that she caught the smells of summer and the soft clanging of a sunlit outdoors. She closed her eyes and smiled.

She was content.

She was poised for flight.

BIG MOUTH

Aribatswa and Oubykh. As far as I know, each has only one speaker left, an old man and an old woman. They could both be dead now, I suppose. Aribatswa is (or was) a New Guinea language. Oubykh is (or was) a language of the Caucasus. There are 6,000 languages in the world. There have been half a million since we first started talking to each other. In the next hundred years, half of the 10,000 will die. Here in Australia, over 300 indigenous languages have died in the last hundred years. I know about these things. I know about languages. When I spotted what I thought was a familiar face in the mall three weeks ago, I wished I could've got close enough to hear him speak. But I didn't. I backed off and went home. It wasn't him anyway. It couldn't have been him.

I like Australia. It's a perky place. I've been here nine years and the energy of it still startles me. Since the Malaysians and Filipinos and Japanese moved in, it's become even more interesting. I don't have to work full-time. I still have plenty of money and I invested wisely. But I work anyway. When I'm not driving the cab, I read books. The kids don't bother me. She looks after them, keeps them out of my way, mostly. I still get angry when I remember those stupid taxi drivers in New York, where I was holed up for a while. Those stupid, dumb fucks couldn't even speak English! How can they get you to where you want to go if they don't even speak the language? Fucking Mexicans. And Lithuanians. Jesus. There are three things that are the same the world over: the taxi drivers, the big, balloon graffiti and the sound of couples fighting in the hotel room next door. I lost count of the number of hotels they put me in. Well, I'm settled these days and I've already done what the Japanese are doing now – I've assimilated. I've fitted in. And I keep my mouth shut. It is said that the serpent that seduced Eve spoke Arabic, the most persuasive of all languages, that Adam and Eve spoke Persian, the most poetic of all languages, and that the Angel Gabriel spoke Turkish, the most menacing of all languages. Well, that's probably what started all the trouble: what we had there, as Cool Hand Luke might have observed, was a failure to communicate. Me, I speak English and I speak Latin. Sometimes I speak Latin at the dinner table to her and the kids, just to piss them off. She's okay. Convict stock, with an addiction to prayer and girl-guide sensibilities. The kids, two boys, are eight and six, with lazy, soggy 'Strine' accents that drive me crazy. Why can't they speak properly? My Belfast accent may not be the prettiest sound in the world, but I've worked on it, softened it, and I've kept my grammar as tight as a drum.

Getting involved, for me, was an easy, snobby, slovenly business. I didn't believe. Not like the others – the lads, the missionaries, the Boys. Oh, they believed all right, they believed so hard it made my teeth hurt, that bunch of pained guignols, with their Gaelic classes and their unimpeachable Republicanism and their soothing folk pornography. Morons. But someone studying Linguistics and Latin at Queen's University was a trophy recruit and untrackable. It was only an academic poser for me. I just wanted to find out if I could do it and being regarded as a respectable, beloved parasite didn't bother me at all.

Not only could I do it, I was good at it. Lookout, mainly. Driver occasionally. I didn't see much but I always kept next day's newspapers. It was easy. Now and then it was even fun and I didn't have to share their simian enthusiasm to get away with it. Each death was an end-of-the-pier punchline. I was an antiseptic abstraction, an antidote to their cavalier, petulant cabaret. They knew I didn't believe but, for some reason, they trusted me anyway. They knew I could keep my mouth shut.

It was a pleasant two years: Latin during the day and the odd gig at night. There was no money in it, of course, but I enjoyed skimming with them, getting them to safety, listening to their vicious, beige tales afterwards. They were so proud of themselves. We divided our time between Lavery's and the Washington, drinking, plotting, holding industrious seminars in planned bloodshed. It was almost playful. I enjoyed Belfast back then, with its malicious accent and miraculous pubs. The pubs were the best thing about it. A Lorelei of towns. Pubs full of chesty rhetoric and a gallimaufry of weary menace and, occasionally, that brand of hatred so delicious I just knew it would cheer me up no end. I just didn't bury myself in the role. A friend, an actor who knew nothing of my life, got himself a job with the BBC, doing voice-overs for Gerry Adams. When he told me that, he couldn't understand why I laughed so hard. Then the ban was lifted and he couldn't afford to feed himself. That made me laugh even harder. But despite having to listen to the boys' flabby protestations of faith, and their Chaplinesque intentions towards some poor bastard or other, the pubs were fun. I didn't care; as long as I had my Latin and my pubs, and my extra-curricular night-time excitement, I was perfectly content.

Looking back, I think even their enthusiasm for language irritated me. The more windy and extravagant, the better they liked it. And Irish was just perfect. A language where 'to bury' and 'to plant' both employ the same verb. Perfect. A tongue of the air and the earth and the wind; so unlike

English, which is the language of castles, of steel, of man-made structures and of perfect, intelligible expression. Good for making plain, for giving instructions. But Latin – now that was a different matter. No bandying about there. Clear expression of thought and even clearer integrity of purpose. Stern, lapidary sentences, total functionality and a formal, divine polish that could express both the moody and the marketable in seconds flat. While everyone else was brushing up on their *Brúidiúlacht*, and their *Díograis*, and their *Creideamh*, I was amusing myself by translating modern terms into Latin; I got as far as *Exterioris paginae puella* for 'cover girl', *Ictus a metro undecimo* for 'penalty kick' and *Longior taenia cinematographica* for 'movie'. They thought I was making fun of them. I was. And I didn't give a shit. But when we went on a job, they knew that, despite my indolent indifference, I would not fuck up. And I never did. What happened on the Ormeau Road was not my fault.

The cops just got lucky. After the boys came running into Bradbury Place, I gunned the motor up and took off down Botanic Avenue, left, then right into Rugby Road, down Agincourt Avenue, through the Holy Land, up to seventy, no problem. Then that bastard in the Granada cut me off and we ended up crashing into the Ormeau Bridge. Well, they just took off, leaving me with whiplash and a broken ankle. Two minutes later the RUC arrived and, well, that was me. After four days my neck was okay, my ankle was strapped up and I was carted off to Castlereagh.

I told them nothing. For six days I remained completely silent. Not a word passed my lips and it drove them insane. They punched me, kicked me, slapped me, held a gun to my head, threatened to kill my parents, kept me awake for three days and then punched me some more, and I didn't say one fucking word. They screamed and hollered until they trembled. They flailed around the room, making hysterical, seismic threats. They even tried, in desperation, the nice-cop/nasty-cop routine. I almost began to feel sorry for them. Nothing like silence to send a cop gradually, caustically bonkers. I didn't care. It wasn't loyalty that kept me quiet. And I am not brave. I'm just choosy about the people I talk to. After that, there was nothing for them to do but half-heartedly thump me some more. *Qui tacet consentire videtur.* Silence gives consent. But, bruises or no, I won. I wore them out. My body hurt for a long while afterwards but I won because they had nothing on me they could prove and on the seventh day I was bailed.

As far as I remember, that's when things changed. Now, I am not a petulant man, nor a man who would expect to be lionised for his stoicism. But some things deserve an appropriate measure of recognition. Otherwise nothing makes any sense, and the things that we do and say are meaningless. I did not expect praise from my runaway comrades. They were too acutely aware that my participation was more academic than heartfelt, but even so, I wasn't prepared for the wall of silence in the pub two days after my release. No mention was made. They avoided my eyes. They shifted uneasily in their seats, downed their pints too quickly and discussed future projects with a childish earnestness that suddenly made me annoyed. All that gallant jabber. It was as if I wasn't there. They knew I hadn't talked, but it was as if the significance of what I had done had been consigned to some embarrassing kill-file. It wasn't what I had done that shamed them. It was the fact that it was me who had done it. Me, the one who didn't care and didn't believe. At that moment I made a decision. Oh – don't get me wrong, it wasn't petulance; loyalty was not the reason I protected them. And resentment was not the reason I betrayed them. It is simply that it was so easy. And communication is so important. I decided I wanted to be listened to. That would make a nice change.

The following morning I presented myself at the nearest

police station, discreetly, of course, and after various phone
calls and incredulous panics and breathed, ignored obscen-
ities, I was taken to see the very men who had kicked the shit
out of me the previous week. They were very jumpy and
amazed by my benign calm, my utter lack of belligerence and
even more amazed by my proposal.

For a fortnight I sang like a bird. I told them everything. I
talked so much they couldn't keep up. It was thoroughly
enjoyable. The money would be useful, of course, and I had
always wanted to travel, but it was the nattering I liked best.
I gave them names, addresses, physical descriptions, times,
places, sights, sounds, smells, idiosyncrasies, all in a deadpan
blah that I knew impressed the hell out of them. I was a
shiny one-man documentary, a walking karaoke, with lyrics
and sleeve notes to spare, a destroyer of silence. They bristled
with excitement as I drawled on, changing their cassette
tapes and sharpening their pencils and sucking on their biros,
not knowing that I couldn't have cared less whether they
used the information or not. I kept thinking about Dionysius,
Tyrant of Syracuse, who incarcerated suspects in a fifty-foot-
high prison, carved in channels into the rock in such a way as
to resemble the human ear. Even the slightest whisper by the
prisoner would waft its way upwards and, eventually, be used
against him. The Ear of Dionysius. Excellent idea. Mind you,
I made it a lot easier for them than that. A new identity and
£175,000 – I think that's fair.

I saw him again. Two weeks ago, in the mall. And there was
another man with him, with the kind of rounded shoulders I
hate, and remember. It's pretty funny, actually, the way
memories sneak up on you; ten years on and I still see their
faces, hear their adenoidal, Andytown rasps. And Belfast's
moody, playpen racket, a town oscillating between noisy
cod-fundamentalism and baggy, raving silliness. Sometimes I
miss it. The day before I left for good, in 1980, I was looking

out of the window of my hotel room on a grey, miserable November afternoon. And travelling slowly down the middle of Great Victoria Street was a huge transporter vehicle, carrying eight gleaming, sparkling silver DeLoreans from the plant. Cutting through the granite and the gloom, it was the most beautiful thing I'd ever seen. We saw that a lot but I never quite got used to it. And then, with the cocaine and whatnot, the plant went belly-up and that was that. I still miss the place. That's why I still see faces I think I recognise, and rounded shoulders and pigeon toes that just give me the creeps.

I go to the mall a lot during the day. I like it. Well, actually I hate it, but I can't stay away. Nothing cheers me up more than an afternoon spent marvelling at the orchestral stupidity of people, their gorgeous consumers' body language; the picking up and the putting down, the poking and prodding, the disdainful pretence that they're not really *shopping*, oh, no – they're just perusing, like beatific art collectors. Christ, they make me sick. And the teenagers are the worst, with their faux-funky lolling around, their vacuous vocab and their sunny hairdos. I blame television. No – I really do. I don't let my kids watch TV. I got rid of it three years ago. They probably hated me for that. I don't care. TV has no shame and these kids have no stories. They have answers to questions they never even asked and they think it makes them grown-up. They have adjusted to incoherence. TV allows no secrets and secrets are important. My kids didn't understand that and I was sick of their crying and whingeing, so I carried the damn set into the garden and took a sledgehammer to it. I didn't get any arguments after that.

You can tell a lot about someone from their clothes, too, and the mall is a good place to watch for that. Especially the women, with their bewildering squall of colours and styles. There are two women who meet outside the bookshop every lunchtime. They're deaf. One dresses like a cross between a beach bum and a construction worker, the other is always dollied up in a business suit, usually mauve. When they speak it's too fast to try to follow, their hands flutter about like pallid peacocks. Their fingers nibble and scrawl on the air so quickly it almost makes me dizzy. I like watching them. There's another guy who sits for hours eating rolls and drinking Coke and, I swear, one of these days I'm going to have to stop myself from punching him. He's disgusting. He must weigh at least 250 pounds. He's enormous, and he just sits there with his hideous rolls of fat and his too-tight T-shirt and his messy, pudgy fingers. I hate him. Because I can't read him. How can you read a body language that's buried, paralysed, imprisoned under all that? And I hate the assistant in the newsagent. He must've been in a fire or something. You can't tell *shit* from that shiny, immobile mask of a face. People like that, they don't play fair.

Something odd happened last week. A parcel arrived in the post. It smelled funny and the paper was greasy. I opened it. It contained a calf's tongue, fresh and quite bloody. The kids were at school but she wouldn't stop asking me about it. I didn't know. How was I supposed to know what it meant? It was probably a mistake, or a practical joke, or maybe our butcher's gone funny in the head. I gave it to the dog and told her just to shut up and stop going on about it. I didn't tell her about the note.

That night, I had a weird dream. I dreamed that I could speak every language on the planet, except English. I was impressive and redundant at the same time. It felt great. But I woke up feeling uneasy and I didn't know why. Ten years is too long a time. I'm on the other side of the world. It just wouldn't be practical. It wouldn't make any sense.

We sat around the dinner table last night. The three of them said grace, with hands clasped and eyes screwed shut, their faces a picture of mournful fervour. I held my breath, as usual, and just let them get on with it. Then the six-year-old announced that a man had approached him in the playground with a message for his father.

I froze in mid-swallow.

What was the message?

'"*Payback*."'

The kid began to laugh as if he found the word funny, but he stopped laughing when I grabbed him by the neck and screamed at him to tell me what the man looked like, what age he was, what kind of accent he had. Then he started to cry and stammer, and he couldn't talk, and she was belting me across the shoulders and squawking at me to put him down. What was wrong with me? she demanded, tears streaming down her face. Had I gone mad? I didn't tell her anything. I just walked out. I've never told her anything. She hasn't a clue. My past is an encyclopaedia of banished unwhisperables because that's the way I wanted it to be. So I walked out and after a while I couldn't hear the sonic whine of her weeping any more. I was a little frightened.

I have never understood passion, or even bumbling enthusiasm. What's the point? It simply broadcasts damage and wounds effortlessly wherever it goes. Their belief meant a bullet in the head. Her rapturous domesticity meant tears when she had to tell the kids Santa didn't exist. I wasn't on some kind of intestinal campaign. I just didn't care. In Japanese, the characters for 'busy' translate as 'mind dying'. I had no truck with their scruffy, unstable cannibalism. I had a new life and a cool new baptism. Okay, maybe they had a point about their lost land and their lost tongue, and the enforced translations that produced the ugliest aural geography in the world. But I knew that underneath their casual brutalism and forlorn whining was a big fucking gap, a huge hole, a hectoring emptiness that screamed the truth at them – that if they didn't have the Cause, they didn't exist. And they tried to convince themselves that the world is simply fascinated by what goes on there. Well, the world doesn't give a shit. The world's got more important things to think about. The world doesn't give a rat's arse and every time they looked at me they knew it was true. Cretins.

It's morning. I'm in the kitchen with the six-year-old. I'm chopping carrots. The back door opens and he's standing there. He is holding a gun. He looks a little older but not much. He's wearing a suit. He looks good. I don't know what to say. So I say, 'Why?'

He smiles at me.

And points the gun at my son's head.

'*Le díoltas.*' I don't understand. It's Irish. I don't understand the word. Then he says, '*Ultio.*' Latin for 'revenge'.

'*Maniae infinitae sunt species.*'

Fools are numberless. He's made an effort. Is it a tribute or is it scorn? I can't tell. He begins to talk and his gun hand never wavers. The child lets out a tiny chirrup of fear, then is silent and motionless. The man talks and his voice, older now, has a beauty that is venomous and pure, a timbre I have never forgotten. It is intolerably clear. He speaks of loyalty and I am hypnotised by the unimaginable depth of his conviction. He really means it. His smile is solicitous, almost kind, as if he feels sorry for me. Sorry for my lack of faith, for my poor, empty heart that has never belonged anywhere. He talks of courage. He tells me that I am dumb. That I have always been dumb.

And then he pulls the trigger and my son's blood is everywhere.

When he was small and babbling, his elder brother would translate for him.

His name was John.

I can't think of anything to say, so I don't bother saying anything. I keep thinking about how good he looks in that

suit. The old man and the old woman. Eighty-three conso-
nants and three vowels. And no one left to talk to. This
strikes me as funny. I don't know why, but I start to laugh. I
laugh uncontrollably, because I can't think of any words to
say. He is still softly speaking as he glides out of the door but
I am not listening. I am alone and walking in blood, swaying
and speechless.

TIE, COAT, HAT

Charlie's swaying a bit, but that's normal for Charlie I suppose, even at lunchtime. I'll let him have one more drink, then that's it. I've only ever had to bar Charlie from the pub once, but that was years ago and he was carrying a broken heart at the time. He doesn't have any real meanness in him and anyway, he suits the place.

I've been head barman here for fifteen years and, apart from the odd Friday night, there's never been what you could call real trouble. It's an old pub, panelled from top to bottom in mahogany. A couple of years ago there was talk of redevelopment, of ripping out the interiors and decking us out in chrome and plastic, but the talk fizzled out. I was glad about that. I mean, the trees have been dead for a hundred years and tearing up a handsome pub isn't going to help the rainforest, is it?

It's quiet at the minute. I'll get Charlie his vodka and see to this pair. They look alike. Father and daughter, I'll bet. Nice suit. Very expensive. Let's see; a gin and tonic, and a white wine. Nope. A gin and bitter lemon and a pineapple juice. Pretty close.

He handed her the pineapple juice and sat down opposite her. She took the glass by its rim, between thumb and forefinger, like a child, and thanked him. She did not look into his eyes; her gaze never rose above his tie. She had bought him that tie for his last birthday. They shared a birthday and, because they didn't want the rest of the family to feel excluded, only ever bought each other small, modest gifts. Ordinary things, like socks, or CDs. Two years ago, when she was almost sixteen, she'd got a Saturday job, so she had a little more money to spend on herself, or on good-quality ties, when the birthdays came around.

'The *abattoir*? You can't work in an abattoir, for Christ's sake!' he and her mother had both said. But they couldn't stop her. And anyway, it wasn't in the abattoir itself. It was in the office, doing administration and word processing. It was pleasant work and the other girls were friendly. Once, after a row with him, she went to work early and hung around the slaughter rooms for a while, hoping that the warm smell of dying would attach itself to her clothing, so that she could take it home and waft it around the house.

She sipped the pineapple juice and looked at her father's tie. She was nearly eighteen. She would be going to university in the autumn and she felt a hundred years old. The tie matched his suit very well. Why had he suggested coming here first? She just wanted to get it over with. It was a suit of beautiful, dull silver, the suit of a man who dislikes upsets and inconveniences. If he starts talking about Malcolm, she thought, I'll scream. He looked good, with his silver suit and greying temples. Like a man on his way to a business lunch, not at all like a man taking his daughter to the family planning clinic.

He looked at her bowed head for a moment, then adjusted his tie, sipped his gin and stared at the ceiling. This was such a beautiful pub. All that wood panelling. Pretty sinful, but so lovely. When he'd found out, he'd wanted to kill him. Malcolm was his best friend. He was a kind, funny man. They had grown up together, gone to college together, been best man at each other's weddings. And now that friendship was ruined for ever and his poor, damaged daughter . . . she had been calm and silent while a storm of bitterness and recrimination raged around her, as if getting pregnant by her father's best friend was an act of supreme modesty. It was only when he'd suggested an abortion that he caught the first flicker of genuine distress in her eyes. She was only eighteen, she couldn't go to university *and* look after a baby. She knew he was right and had loathed him for it.

He watched her swirling the juice in her glass, listlessly. He wanted to stroke her hair and tell her that this was for the best, that everything would be fine. But sometimes he just couldn't bear to touch her, and couldn't get the image of Malcolm and her together out of his head. Sometimes he thought of that, and the anger and embarrassment turned his mouth dry and almost stopped his heart. He suddenly felt absurdly overdressed. Why had he worn this suit? He had dressed this morning as if he was going to some gracious ceremony, like a baptism, for God's sake. He hadn't been sure what to wear and that annoyed him. He liked to look smart, or appropriately dressed, at least.

He and Malcolm had been the two sharpest, brightest lights in the clubs when they were young men. Northern Soul. That was their music. Sometimes they would dance until five in the morning. The girls didn't even matter very much. It was the dancing. Once they even weighed themselves before they went out, just to see how much weight they lost in sweat. Malcolm won. He lost six pounds. He was crazy back then. He thought Malcolm was like him. He thought Malcolm had grown up when he got married.

She looked at her father's face. He was miserable. '*Un ange passe,*' she said very softly.

'What?'

'An angel is passing. The French say it when there's a lull in the conversation.'

'Where do you *get* this stuff, pet?'

'I read a lot. You know that, Dad.'

She smiled at him. For some absurd reason she wanted to make him feel better. This was all his idea, this was what he wanted. Maybe it was what she wanted too, but she'd been happy to let him play the villain. She'd wanted to rub his nose in that, to win at least one fight, to get to play the martyr. He'd never asked her what she wanted to do about this; he'd just taken charge and assumed that she would disagree with him. She was stronger than him; he just didn't know it. And now he was miserable. Well dressed and helpless. She thought about Malcolm. They had made love only once. She had been curious more than anything. She certainly didn't love him. His wife didn't know, but some day she would. Some day it would all come out. It always comes out. Always. She looked at her father as he stared at his hands and she thought about how men together are at their best when they think they're unobserved. Without bravado and full of the still, small intimacies that women never share, and just have to take on trust, because as soon as they show up it disappears in a fragile shower of bluff and common sense and forward planning. Just then, a couple brushed past. He was in his thirties, with a brisk manner about him, a slightly hard face. She was younger and had a careless bounce in her stride, which the girl instinctively liked and knew her father hated. The corner of the man's expensive coat caught her glass of juice and spun it round a couple of times, without knocking it over. She and her father watched it twirl noisily and settle. There was no acknowledgement from the young man, although his lady glanced apologetically in their direction.

Her mother had said, 'I'll go with her,' but he had insisted. 'No, I'll go. I'll go.' Her mother had felt excluded, but secretly glad. So her poor, handsome dad was sitting there, being brave in a way that made no sense and did no good, toying with his gin. She felt sorry for him, so she reached over and took his hand, afraid that he might begin to weep for his lost friend, his lost armour . . .

I've seen some sad-looking bastards, but this one looks as if he's about to break down. Christ, he's only had one drink but then, that's gin for you. Never touch the stuff myself. There's only one thing worse than an aggressive drunk on vodka and that's a maudlin drunk on gin. I'd rather be thumped than have, say, Charlie cry all over me. He took off a while ago. He's in good shape. Charlie's steady. We know where we are with Charlie. But the strangers that come in, with shy partners and pained expressions, and clothes that don't quite fit in – they're intriguing. I don't want to get to know them, but they're like interesting props that come and go. Interactive wallpaper. Yeah. For example, that's a beautiful coat this guy is wearing. Is it cashmere? I think it's cashmere. Whatever it is, it's lovely. Davey would kill for a coat like that. He's sitting in the corner right now, staring at that coat. Poor Davey. He wishes he was bloody Quentin Crisp, but he's only thirty or thereabouts, so he just hasn't got the wrinkles for it. I think his main ambition is to die in bed at the age of forty, shot by a jealous wife. Anyway, he's a bright lad, a Fine Arts graduate, I think, or was it Textiles? He and his friend, the one with the camera, had a lovely routine going last year. Davey dressed up as tramps and loonies and all sorts of eccentrics – street furniture, only human – and his mate took these gritty black-and-white, 'social realism'-type snaps of him doing weird things. In the traffic, usually. One of the Sunday glossies paid him £600 for those. They ran a spread called 'Humanity on the Margins', or some such rubbish, and Davey took ten of us out to the Balti house. His latest project needs a gallery and a sponsor, he says. It's got something to do with him pretending to be a man who's dying from a thousand papercuts. From brand-new ten-pound notes. I'm not sure about this performance art. He once told me about a bank robbery in Stockholm. Three innocent people outside were blown away by shotgun blasts. While they bled to death on the pavement, a crowd gathered round and *applauded*. I thought that was quite sad. Davey laughed until he threw up. Here comes the Coat. Let's see, a whisky and a white wine spritzer. I'm half right. A Rusty Nail and a nice ugly pint of export for the little lady.

He noticed, as she took the pint with both hands, that she wasn't wearing the bracelet. Or the necklace. He didn't know why he bothered. He'd given her quite a few nice pieces of jewellery and she never wore any of them. She said they got in the way, that, in the florist's, her hands were in and out of water all the time, that she was always fiddling about with ferns and fronds and frills, and jewellery just got in the way. Still, it wouldn't have killed her to wear some of it when she was out with him. His wife adored jewellery. He'd had to think fast just to get here. She picked at one of her front teeth with a fingernail. He wished she wouldn't do that. She was gorgeous and it made her look like a gargoyle.

'The fight last night was unbelievable. You should've come,' she said.

'I couldn't make it. I told you. Besides, you know I hate boxing. It's barbaric.'

She gave him a sly smile and took a hefty swig from her pint. She was wearing her old sweatshirt. It wouldn't have killed her to wear the silk blouse he'd bought her. Boxing. Jesus. And Country music. He thought he'd seen it all, until she dragged him along to Wembley Arena for eight hours of steel guitars and cheatin' women and broken hearts and whining hoboes and God knows what else. But he made the effort, for her. He was crazy about her. She just had a few really annoying habits that, if he stayed around long enough, he could smooth away like sandpaper. He loved her so much it scared the hell out of him, but sometimes her accent got on his nerves. He could work on that. She had a good ear. Sometimes he felt like Professor Higgins. Give me six months, he thought, smiling inwardly. Six months and he could take her to the firm's Christmas Ball. God, she was so beautiful. He wanted to get a divorce and just show her off for a while.

'Whaddya mean, barbaric? It's just ballet with blood.'

Ballet with blood. And she made fun of his old movie collection. Well, she didn't exactly make fun of it, she just wasn't impressed. Especially the horror movies. 'Sorry, pet,' she'd said after they'd watched *The Bride of Frankenstein*. 'Face it. These things do have a sell-by date. That, frankly, was not scary.' But they'd only had one real argument; that was the night they'd emerged from the theatre. She was marching ahead of him. She was in a foul mood and he didn't know why. And then she stopped and gave twenty pounds to that beggar. He couldn't believe it. He'd never been so angry. He didn't want to think about that right now. He avoided her eyes and took a gulp of his whisky.

She watched him for a while. Poor baby. He's sweating in that damn coat, she thought, but he won't take it off. She thought about the boxing match last night. She knew this relationship was going to end soon. When two people, not having seen each other for nine days, can sit in a silence that isn't entirely comfortable yet neither can be bothered to break, well, it's time to call it a day. She wondered if it would just happen, like a slow puncture, or if she would have to say something. And what would she say? The match was fabulous. She loved boxing. He didn't understand. He thought she got some kind of sexual frisson out of watching two men make hamburger out of each other. But it was not what they could inflict that made her forget herself, and want to stand up and shout. It was what they could endure. They were brave. To have that kind of courage served up with a ticket delighted her.

Being around him was beginning to make her cautious. She found herself watching what she said and how she said it, and she knew that she was turning into a coward. He wanted to be good. But he wanted her to be better and it was wearing her down. She was beginning to foster false enthusiasms, just to annoy or embarrass him, to confirm his sense of organised superiority. He was a very kind man, but if he could lie to his wife and yet not understand how a Jimmy Webb song and Glen Campbell's voice could reduce grown men to tears, then to hell with it. It was all soul music, all of it. He pestered her to listen to Bach's Double Concerto without realising that was soul too. She had tried hard to let him in. She thought he was willing to understand, but the nicest compliment he could pay her was to tell her how beautiful she was. And the more he told her, the more she showed up looking like she'd been dragged through a ditch. And she loathed jewellery. She'd even told him that, but somehow her voice just wasn't as real as what he thought she was supposed to like. His job was everything to him. He was good at office politics. In a boyish way he actually enjoyed the mistrust and the back-stabbing, and the inefficiency. It didn't matter how shabby the game, just as long as he shone. Maybe that's how he could lie so easily. He was precisely the type of man who would send flowers, but when he found out she worked in a florist's shop he had probably decided that sending bouquets was redundant. She looked across the bar to where a young man was sitting alone at a table. His face was fine-boned, nervous, handsome. He was staring at the trilby hat he'd placed on the table. She suddenly felt sick and tired of the whole sad farce. The next tramp she saw was going to get fifty pounds.

'Did you know', she said suddenly and quite loudly, 'that when women live together for any length of time their periods synchronise?'

He stopped picking the fluff off his coat and went bright red.

Typical. Bloody typical.

Tomorrow she would go to work. She would find a way of saying goodbye that he wouldn't even understand. She would sneak into his office and leave her goodbye on his desk, in the language of flowers: a white rosebud for his heart ignorant of love, a foxglove for his insincerity, a leaf of evergreen clematis for the poverty he despised and, because she was not cruel, a white periwinkle for the pleasure of memory. It would all wither, unread, uninterpreted, and she didn't give a damn any more . . .

I'd better keep an eye on Christy. He's been sitting with his ugly mates, giggling at the guy with the hat. I don't want him starting trouble. Christy's odd. I mean, Davey's odd, but he's odd in a productive way. He's like, card-carrying odd. But Christy's just . . . weird. He was up in court a while back. He had been spending days on end travelling on the top deck of buses. And every time another one came alongside he would hold up these placards to the people on the other bus. Usually he picked on black women and held up cards that read 'Nigger bitch' or something like that. The judge didn't know what to make of him. Davey thinks he's a bigot who doesn't have the courage of his convictions, so he carries it on long-distance. I think he's just plain creepy, but he's usually quiet and he hasn't given me a reason to kick him out. Not yet. I like hats. I wish a man could wear a hat nowadays without feeling foolish. Not to look like Bogart, but to be able to tip his hat to a lady. That would be nice. A youngster with a sharp trilby.

Okay, I know it's a pint of Theakston's, but I wish it was a Martini.

He needed one pint. Just enough to calm his nerves. Any

more than that and he'd slouch through the audition with an artificial insouciance that he knew got on people's nerves. He knew he made an irritating drunk, when he'd had a few, which didn't happen too often. He became so nice, and so sweet, he could rot your teeth at a hundred paces. Well, he thought, it's better than throwing punches. Only the one, to settle himself. He wanted this part and he thought the hat might help. It might make him look older, for a start, or like a man who didn't mind looking foolish. It was the part of the best friend turned betrayer, in an adaptation of an American crime thriller. It was a cute idea. He could've gone for the part of the hero, the lead. Well, he was more of an anti-hero. Actually, he was a complete bastard, when you got right down to it, but the concept of an upright, modern knight would get laughed off the stage before half-time, so, flawed, cynical sadist it had to be. Which was pretty boring. No, he wanted to be the best friend who killed and maimed and betrayed because he honestly thought it was the right thing to do. Most of his colleagues and friends were brought up on the movies, as he had been, but he never seemed to be on the same big, blunt wavelength. He could never remember what the hero did, or said. He was always too busy watching the minor characters and how they managed to get out of the hero's way without knocking over the furniture. He loved their one-second reaction shots, before they were consigned to oblivion. He could remember what innocent bystanders wore, as they were shot, or punched, or shoved aside as they waited with shopping bags beside elevators. He adored the incidental people, the ones who conveniently died, providing the hero with a cause; the discarded people that the second-unit director got to dispose of noisily. He didn't want to be a hero. He wanted to be utterly without ego, a catalyst, a vessel, a big substantial nothing. He wanted to be a good actor. He wanted to be second banana. He wanted to be Robert Preston or a young Jeff Chandler.

If he got this part he could move out, rent his own flat and stop having to pretend that he was comfortable living in a house with five other people. One of them was a girl from County Fermanagh. Used to be very Republican-minded. She'd been arrested years ago for personation during the General Election. She told him, laughing, that the inside of the Sinn Fein van, which toured all the polling stations, was like a BBC make-up department. He liked her. They had dated a few times, but he needed his own place, where he didn't have to answer to anyone, or be politely energetic when all he wanted to do was lie on the floor and disappear. She was a terrific singer and would serenade him with Cole Porter tunes. She told him he was a Waldorf Salad, a Berlin Ballad, while he was shaving. Or when he was cooking, he was Romance, The Steppes of Russia, he was the pants of a Roxy Usher. When they made love he was an old Dutch master or Mrs Astor . . . She knew dozens of old show tunes, but they both knew she was just showing off. He liked that, but he wanted his own place.

At this audition he was going to have to pretend to be something he wasn't and that was before he even started to read. Maybe the hat was a bad idea. Even if he didn't get this job, he wasn't going back to the kill floor. He'd done the abattoir for nine months. The money was good, but the thing that had really scared him was that it had begun to seem like therapy. The air gun, and its three-inch rod of solid steel, had begun to feel as comfy as a microphone, so he'd got out. But those nine months were like a badge of honour to his fellow resting actors. Even the vegetarians thought he was pretty cool. The day he quit, he had a three-hour bath and then a shower, and then another shower, and then he went to the theatre. He hadn't been near a performance in nearly a year and the beauty of it made him almost cry and wish he hadn't given in so easily. He came out feeling revitalised and hurting, like near-dead flesh when the blood supply finally gets through. From now on he was going to act, or starve. Even the couple outside, rowing horribly about money, sounded like a comedy. From now on he was going to cultivate the emptiness we all carry with us until he became the best blank canvas around. He was going to disappear to the point where agents were hammering on his door. He was going to be the ultimate best friend. He was going to be crucially incidental; he was going to take loneliness and make it sweetly indispensable. He was going to be the best damn second banana anybody ever saw. And he was going to get this part.

He got up suddenly, leaving his pint half-finished, and strode out of the door, dropping the trilby in the bin as he went.

Davey is half-way out of his seat when he sees the look I'm giving him. Just leave it. I'm not having him lowering the tone, rummaging around in the bin like that. He subsides. I'll give it to him later, after I clear up. Well, your man took off in a hurry. This is the slowest lunchtime we've had in ages. Business hasn't been great over the last six months and I wouldn't be surprised if the breweries had another nibble soon. But this is one of the last independent bars left and it would be a pity if we were taken over. You don't have control over what you do. You have to take the beers they give you. You might as well be a McDonald's. There's a place for bad manners, for people who are inept, rather than vicious. We'd lose a lot of the interesting stuff if they took us over. I see the Coat and his girl are leaving. She looks a bit icy. Oh, that's priceless; he lets her walk ahead while he puts his wedding ring back on. And they looked married too. Sometimes I wish one of the breweries would lift the responsibility from me. We close at midnight but my head doesn't stop buzzing until 2 a.m. or 3 a.m. Still, I wouldn't do it if I didn't like it. If I wasn't good at it. All these folk, with their sad, miraculous yarns. The other couple are getting ready to go. Now there's a man with a problem and the young girl's no better. But she has the manners to bring the empty glasses to the bar, while he stands by the door, fiddling with his tie. Yes, they must be father and daughter, because when he takes her elbow to guide her, like a gentleman, she shrugs him off in that careless way that only relatives have. But at least now he's smiling.

Charlie's wandered back in. He has the good manners to know he's not going to get a drink, so he'll just sit and read the paper for a while. Or pretend to read it. I can't stop thinking about something my sister told me over the phone yesterday. She lives in Galway. A woman we both know, our old Geography teacher, was walking down the street last week when a swarm of bees settled on her. An entire swarm, covering her from scalp to toe. It must have been the queen, who got lost and alighted on her. Anyway, this old woman just stood there. She's crawling with bees, on her face, in her ears, up her sleeves, and she doesn't move an inch. Someone in the gathered crowd shouted at her to ask if she was all right and very slowly she nodded her bee-covered head. Are they stinging you? they shouted. She moved her head from side to side. After about fifteen minutes, apparently, they got hold of a guy from a couple of miles out on the road, who knows about bees. He located the queen and, when he took her away, the whole swarm just lifted. And this old woman never moved a muscle. She had to lie down afterwards, but she was fine. If that had been me, I would've gone berserk. Not a muscle, not a flinch. That's what I call self-control. I love that story and I'm glad it's true. True is better than anything. Here comes Charlie. No chance, mate. I'm not beating you over the head with a drink you don't need. I'm in charge. This is a Free House.

TRANSMISSION

The best way to trash a car is from decoration to chassis, from accessory down to frame, from light bulb down to skeleton. The opposite of the way it was built, in fact. It becomes progressively more difficult, of course, as the parts become bigger, tougher and apparently undentable. But that's the most satisfying way of doing it. A crusher is lazy, burning too flashy and neither involves much work or personal involvement. If a car can be hand-built, it can be hand-trashed.

Michael went to the counter and paid for his purchases; a length of rubber hose, a pack of cigarettes and a box of matches. He was in his mid-forties and immaculately dressed, his high forehead giving him a patrician look, that of a meticulous man who knows what he is about. He walked outside and sat in the driver's seat of his beautiful 1993 BMW 535i. Tracking it down had not been easy; he had decided to find it months after the trial, by which time it had been repaired, sold, sold again, given new papers and even resprayed. But he found it and was amazed that there was no sign whatsoever of either damage or repair. It was a lovely motor of dull, gun-metal grey.

He pulled out of the petrol station and drove south until he found the kind of small town he was looking for. He cruised around its run-down streets, came across a piece of waste ground and parked.

This car was not just a drive, it was a long, cool drink of water, a smooth, wondrous ride that eased a man's spine and focused his mind. He let the engine run idle for a long moment, then switched it off. He looked around. To the east was what looked like a big council estate, to the south, a derelict factory. It was a hot, sunny day and the air hummed. Michael felt calmer than he had in months and, at last, decisive. He got out, smoothed the lapels of his suit and combed his hair in the wing mirror. He wanted everything to be perfect. He stood back and looked at the car. There was a slight smear on the bonnet, which he carefully removed with a cloth handkerchief. Apart from that, the car was pristine.

He went to the boot, removed a heavy canvas bag and began to lay out the tools on the ground. Sledgehammer, hand mallets, various screwdrivers, hacksaw. In his beautiful suit and with his beautiful car, he had imagined that he would feel foolish, standing on a piece of waste ground in the middle of nowhere. But he didn't. He had a decent project here, a way to feel good again, and embarrassment had no place. It was around noon and beginning to get uncomfortably hot. Michael removed his jacket, carefully folded it and placed it on a clean clump of the destroyed, goulash grass. Then he removed his Rolex and his wedding ring, and put them both in his trouser pocket. A long way off a group of kids, shimmering in the heat, were kicking a football; their shouts carried to where he stood, again staring at the car. He wanted to begin but hesitated at the absurdity of the moment. Very slowly he picked up one of the smaller hammers and walked the length of the car, scrutinising every inch of its burnished, gleaming surfaces. Then he took a deep breath and, very gently, tapped the right-hand sidelight with the hammer. Nothing happened. He hit it harder. It cracked and Michael knew then that he had begun and could not now stop. He smashed it and moved on to the right front headlight and smashed that, then the left headlight: he broke all the lights, front, side and back, taking in the wing mirrors, and breaking off the centre grill valance and the wipers as he went. The glass made an almost musical sound. He was beginning to get into his stride. He took a tape from his pocket and slid it into the cassette player. He would leave that to last. Copland's Clarinet Concerto filled the air and Michael got himself a bigger hammer.

He had moved on to the windows and was shattering the back windscreen when he noticed that the group of kids had moved closer and were watching him warily. They were joined by a toddler, probably a younger sister. Michael ignored them and, wiping the sweat from his face, brought the hammer down on the front windscreen. It webbed and crackled but didn't shatter cleanly, so he took the sledgehammer to it. At first he tried a fairly timid blow, then, with a knotted, arctic calm, he swung the hammer high over his head and put every ounce of strength into it. The screen was noisily obliterated and Michael found himself grinning and staring, surprised, at his hands, with a kind of loveless relish. He was beginning to enjoy himself. He wasn't into physical exercise, or working out, but he felt, trembling slightly, that he could do this. It would take time but he could achieve this. A couple of the older boys moved closer and stood about twenty yards away, fascinated by the spectacle of a well-dressed businessman destroying his car. And on their patch, too. They sported shaven napes and cautious, wetback expressions.

Michael was contemplating the side door panels when one of shouted at him, 'Hey, mister! Is that your car?'

Michael, squinting in the sun, nodded.

'What's wrong with it?'

'Nothing. I just don't like it. You can give me a hand, if you want.'

The boys looked at each other, then sprinted forward and grabbed a hammer each. Michael directed them to the rear panels, while he tackled the driver's door and the bonnet. For ten minutes the three of them hammered and banged and whacked, creating a deafening cacophony, sending crumpled sheets of metal flying, whooping with exhilaration.

Michael was perfect management material; he enjoyed using his head, dealing with theories and abstractions, grappling with the ideology of business strategy. That was why repetitive, mechanical activities came as such a refreshing change. He had loved nothing more than cooking their weekend meals. Chinese food was perfect, since it involved hours of stripping, cleaning, peeling and chopping, a nicely mindless rota. And he was a good cook, too. She was proud of him for that, especially since she couldn't cook at all. As he finally sent the buckled bonnet flying, Michael thought of how Sundays were best. He would cook, sunlight would stream into the kitchen, and she would polish off a bottle of white and tell him her latest theories. He loved to listen to her talk; she could talk about anything and that simple arrangement made their days almost perfect. She talked, and he listened and chopped and laughed. She had decided to read the dictionary and had got as far as the 'G's. So, that last weekend, everything for her was gorgeous, great, gratuitous, grandiloquent, globular, geocentric and germinal. He used to laugh a lot at the weekends, he thought, as he brought the sledgehammer down on the roof as hard as he could. The boys were making good progress with the boot and rear doors and, taking a breather, they stood back to have a proper look. The car looked hideous. All the doors were gone, lying battered nearby. The roof was stove in, and the engine was exposed and naked to the world. Michael wasn't nearly finished. He was going to do this properly. He was going to dismantle this bastard completely. The boys looked at him expectantly.

'Take off the wheels,' he said, handing them the jack and wheel wrench.

'Cool!'

'Hang on a minute,' said Michael.

It took at least fifteen minutes of steady battering but eventually he got the driver's seat loose and dragged it to one side. The boys set to work on the wheels and Michael sat down heavily on the seat, lit a cigarette and closed his eyes.

'Be careful of the glass!' he shouted, keeping his eyes closed. The other kids, a young girl, a slightly older boy and the toddler, came closer, having decided that he might be mad but probably wasn't dangerous. Encouraged by the two apprentices, they picked up whatever tools were lying around and joined in.

Michael smoked his cigarette and listened to the livid, cheerful threnody, the combination of metal and giggle, the grating sounds of removal and childish squeals. She had been childish in her enthusiasms. 'The out-takes of humanity' she called them, the interesting, peripheral things that haven't yet been flattened by the tyranny of the mainstream. Sometimes he understood what she was on about, sometimes not. He liked her idea of shopping as being the only form of revolt we have left and when she'd said she wanted to firebomb Mothercare he had laughed until he cried. On discovering that she was pregnant, the first thing she said was, 'I think I'll teach myself Latin.' She showed him a piece of paper she had been carrying around for a little while. It was the Creed.

'*Et iterum venturus est cum gloria, judicare vivos et mortuos, cujus regni non erit finis*' – 'And he will come again in glory to judge the living and the dead, and his kingdom will have no end.' She was always bringing strangers home, tramps sometimes. 'The art of the dispossessed is the art of those who *are*, rather than those who *have*,' she would say. One time, she invited a twenty-year-old homeless punk to dinner. He had the most amazing mohican Michael had ever seen. He was blind. She announced that, if it was a boy, she wanted to christen him Theodore, after her hero, Theodor S. Geisel.

'Who?' asked Michael.

'Dr Seuss.'

She once went on a day trip to a nuclear power station, hoping to find something to scold about. She came home depressed and confused, because the absolute purity, stillness and utter immobility of the reactor rod cooling pond, the sheer perfection of that deadly water, was the most beautiful thing she had ever seen. It gave Michael a chance to pamper her for a week and to smother her with kisses every day.

Michael heard a noise beside him and opened his eyes. A young woman was standing looking at him, holding a child by the hand. He realised that he had tears in his eyes and looked away. The woman glanced at the swarm of children nibbling energetically and noisily at the shrinking, ruined motor, but didn't say anything. She wandered off to one side and sat down to watch. Michael stood up and took off his shirt. The sun beat down oppressively and he was afraid the heat might get to him. The children had stacked the wheels into a small tower and the girl was sitting on top, shouting proprietorially. The tubby toddler had produced a plastic hammer from somewhere and wobbled to the car, a breathless, tidy frame; as Robert approached, she tapped one bumper with it and ran off, shrieking with delight. They were all filthy.

Right, thought Michael. Down to business. Down to the M30, automatic guts of this beast. He contemplated the engine for a while, wondering if delicacy and patience, and a set of screwdrivers were what was required, or if the sledgehammer and his hurting muscles would be enough. For a moment he thought of a birthday cake he had been given as a child. It was in the shape of a car, and had been devoured in minutes. One of the older boys was sucking on a carton of Ribena.

Michael suddenly felt tired and thirsty. 'Can I have a drink?'

'Gimme a cigarette first.'

Michael blinked. The boy was about eleven. He tossed him the pack. It didn't matter. He got out the screwdrivers.

He worked all afternoon and into the evening. He unscrewed the valve cover and gave it to the boys, who fell upon it with hammers. Timing chains, sprockets, he removed them and flung them over his shoulder, and the children dismantled them even further. Intake and exhaust manifolds, camshaft, cylinder head and everything hiding beneath – he wanted to reach all of them. By now his hands were cut and blood trickled greasily down his forearms. He hadn't expected to get this far, to this degree of destruction, but having transformed things so much he had to finish it. He couldn't stop, but there were so many factors, what seemed like a million components, all bolted and clinging together. He felt soft and weak, but he kept going. He took a breather after getting to the pistons and connecting rods, and let the children have another go. After a few minutes of sitting in the sun he was restless again and could feel the woman's eyes on him.

He had unscrewed the drive plate and was grabbing for the oil pump when he thought of the expression on the defendant's face as sentence was passed. Twelve months for reckless driving. Suspended. Michael remembered the way the courtroom had gone very quiet, as if everyone knew that something had gone dreadfully wrong, but was too afraid to comment. Michael was expecting the man to be jubilant. Instead, he looked almost heartbroken and sat with tears pouring down his face, like someone who had been denied the punishment he felt he deserved. Only three months pregnant, but the baby managed to live for half an hour longer than she did.

Michael lost his patience trying to lever out the engine's rear plate, dropped the screwdriver and hammered insanely at the whole engine block. Shock waves vibrated up and down his arms, but he felt invincible. His sister had thought he was going mad. He didn't cry, or carry on, or *anything*; he simply worked and ate and slept, and refused to discuss his feelings, but inside he knew something would have to be done. He'd begun to have dreams in which he felt his hands around the man's throat, and he would wake up shaken and upset. If he could have identified with an inanimate object, it would've been the legally held shotgun that is always found nearby. He knew he had to do something. And that's when he'd decided. Since he could not destroy the man, he would destroy the car. He knew there wasn't any grand point to this wasteland circus. It was just something he desperately wanted to do.

There wasn't much more to be done. There are some things the human frame just cannot crack. The murderous impenetrability of the axles, the anti-roll bar, the driveshaft, the wheel-bearing housings' heartless iron stumps – no clever sophistication could deal with that. He was content with a draw. It had been reduced to a battered, ugly shell, but the kids were still howling, so Michael joined them in one final trash. They banged and thumped and clanged on every inch of what was left of the car until everybody became tired and quietened down a little. Michael was covered in bruises and cuts, and he had blood on his arms and on his back, and every muscle in his body hurt, but he felt exhilarated and young again. He had destroyed and in doing so, somehow he had wiped out the other act of destruction. He felt creative. He felt useful. This thing was his spinal, vulgar nutrition.

As the sun began to go down he organised his riotous crèche in a tidying-up exercise. They ran around collecting all the panels and largish pieces of metal into one crooked heap, components and iron, unbreakable pieces into a second pile, and every bolt, nut and screw into a third. Then Michael got out his length of rubber and, sucking on one end, he siphoned out as much petrol as possible from the fuel tank, into the toddler's plastic buckets. He poured the petrol all over the car, inside and out. One of the boys was rattling the box of matches and grinning at him. Michael hesitated for a moment, then rescued his Copland tape and said, 'Be my guest. But be careful, okay?'

They all settled and sat around for a couple of hours in the dying, corrosive warmth of the sun, just enjoying the sight of a burning car. In thrall to the conspiracy of fire. Staring into the flames, eyeing his blackened tyros and drinking a cold beer, which the young woman had unexpectedly and silently pushed into his hand, Michael remembered a news story from a few years ago. A motorist was trapped in a burning car in South Africa. And no one could get close because of the heat, so they were forced to stand around helplessly, listening to his screams. Then one man had walked up, taken out his pistol and shot the poor man in the head, before calmly walking away. Michael didn't know whether that was right or wrong. Maybe it wasn't a matter of right or wrong, but a question of what we permit ourselves, and others, to endure. At that moment he felt like weeping and decided to have his sister over for dinner on Sunday, just so that he could do some cooking. He was beginning to understand the necessity of crisis.

A few other people from the estate showed up with their children and threw old pieces of furniture on to the flames. No one asked whose car it was. One elderly woman arrived with a crate of bottled beer and, as more rubbish was added to the flames, it was transformed from a bitter pyre into a bonfire. People milled around, chatting quietly, while the children jumped up and down, and hamburgers appeared from somewhere. Infants yawned wetly. And that was how they spent that particular evening, long and warm, doing nothing in particular except watching a car die and the sun go down. Enjoying life's visible beginnings and obvious endings. The slow signals of recovery. Michael was surprised no one had called the authorities.

ABOUT LETTERS ABOUT LOVE, MOSTLY

The first letter arrived on the same day I found the body. It was addressed to her so I didn't open it. Not immediately. I put it on the mantelpiece. Then I took the dog for a walk. She was the former tenant but I didn't have a forwarding address. I could've found out but I didn't have the energy. So I just left it on the mantelpiece and took the dog for a walk. I used to write a lot of letters myself: letters, poetry, stories – I even started a screenplay once but it was clumsy and overpopulated, and then everything went wrong and I gave it up. It was months before I could summon the strength to write my own signature, but since I didn't have a chequebook any more I suppose it didn't make much difference. This was a bulky letter in a good-quality beige envelope. I propped it up beside a photograph frame and took the dog for a walk.

It was a fresh morning, quite cold. The dog automatically headed for the river, tugging nicely on the leash. We always walked by the river. Every morning. When we reached the river bank I let him off the leash. He ran ahead and skedaddled through the flusters of bracken, sniffing and snorting at twigs and pebbles, letting out the odd hefty yelp at nothing in particular, just glad to be off the leash and running. I distinctly remember the precise quality of ruffle on the water's skin. I was staring at it when I noticed the silence, that the dog had gone quiet and that, a hundred yards away, he was staring, snout pointed, at something on the river's edge. He was spooked and trembling. One paw hovered in mid-air.

I walked over and saw what he saw. It was a young man's body. A young black man whose face was half submerged in the water, whose head was closely shaven and whose right hand had all but buried itself in a useless grip on the bank's soft mud. The half of his face that I could see was broken and bloody. He was wearing a bright, baggy ski jacket and the lower half of his body swayed back and forth in the water, depending on what the wind was doing. He was definitely dead. He was the calmest, quietest thing I had ever seen.

I wasn't sure what to do, so I patted the dog on the head and sat down beside him on the grass, and we both looked at the body for a while. He shifted ever so slightly in the water, languidly back and forth, like a man asleep and dreaming that he was swimming. He was right in front of me but it was as if he was a fanciful and ghostly thing, as if I could reach out and touch his dead head, his chilly, tangled fingers, and feel no sloppy revulsion. I looked up. The raw sky was a suitable and splendid veil for this kind of morning. And then I got a nosebleed for no reason that I could think of. I stood up, fished out a hanky and decided that now would be a good time to walk to the town centre and inform the police. It was only afterwards that it occurred to me that I had become a cliché: the man who finds the dead body While Out Walking His Dog. It made me laugh, but not much. I didn't intend to be around long enough to acquire the peacock art of proper or ballistic mirth. I would not linger that long. I'm tired. I've had more than enough for one man. Being a cliché's a bonus.

When I told the police what I'd found, they put me in a squad car and we drove back to the river. I showed them the body and they very gently fished him out, rolling him over on to the grass. On his back, and dripping reddened water, he still gripped a fistful of mud, while the policemen stood around with radios squeaking and with their hands on their hips, looking sensibly sad and sucking their teeth. Twenty minutes later a reporter from the regional TV station showed up and wanted to ask me what had happened and how I had found the body. The policeman didn't seem bothered that I might say anything untoward or prejudicial, so I told him how I had found the body. How did I feel? I don't know. I didn't feel anything, really. I mean, I felt sorry for the poor cub, but I wasn't horrified or anything. I wasn't afraid. I wasn't frightened by what I saw. It was a quick interview. The police had no further use for me, so I went home.

When I got home, in the late afternoon, I had a cup of tea and I opened the letter. I don't know why. I knew it wasn't right, opening someone else's mail. But had been annoyed by the way the reporter looked at me and I wanted something interesting to think about. So I opened her letter. It was a love letter. From a man who signed himself simply as 'F'. It was a letter which spoke of the kind of love a man will carry around with him for the rest of his life, because to step aside and do otherwise would be pointless, and would kill him stone dead. It was a letter I might have written a long time ago. It held paragraphs of loss and tender aching, and mistakes shabbily regretted; it spoke of his life then, swiped by stupidity, and of his life now, a poem to ecstatic numbness because he was without her. But mostly it was about love. Just that. Love. Her every tic and idiosyncrasy, her eyes, her heart full of urgent bounce, her hair and her skin, her colour and feathery temper, a lassie rare and horribly involved, always ready to fight the good fight who had stunned him, perfectly, in the process. And so on. And so forth. Mostly about love. None of the banal and crusading mousiness that passes for love letters these days. This guy's love was full, true, rosy-cheeked and terrified. Just like it should be.

I read it several times. And I closed my eyes and tried to imagine what she looked like, what she sounded and smelled

and felt like. In my mind's eye, while my stomach flipped – I
don't know why – I saw a lurid smartass of a girl, clever, with
strawberry-blonde hair and metal glasses, and a full, lacerat-
ing smile. Shortish – five foot four – dressed in a bright,
tosspot cardigan, grey jeans and brilliant boots. A firefighter
on her day off. I read the letter again. And again. And with
every reading more of her became smackly visible – her eye
colour, her voice, now smoky, her weight and every ingeni-
ous pore – I had her completely after a while. She could've
been with me in the room. She felt that real. It could've been
her who turned on the TV set to listen to the sad report on
the young, dead man in the river. I looked weird on television
and my voice had no timbre. And they cut my line about my
not feeling anything. They probably thought I was a bit odd-
looking. I taped it anyway.

The second letter arrived five days after the first. I opened
it straight away and read it over breakfast. Then I walked
into town to collect my benefit. A few people looked at me as
if they knew me. They knew my face. I've been here for a
couple of years. But because I had been on television they
looked at me differently. I was silently, slightly famous. I felt
like the big, ever-present bald fellow on *EastEnders* who's
been given one or two lines over the last couple of years. It
surprised people. It was as if their wallpaper had come to life,
and they wanted to have a chat. I liked the soaps. I watched
all of them. So many interesting lives. So much life. I
especially liked the fact that I could drop out at any time.
And drop back in. And things would be pretty much the
same. Or I could drop out and stay out. The thread carried on
without me. I found that very reassuring. And I liked the
corrosive shambles of all those fake lives. So many problems.
La-di-da. So much pain. *How about a nice cuppa?* Death,
disfigurement and all the rest. *Beautiful weather!* For the
time of year. Yes, I loved my soaps. I could crowd-surf and
stage-dive and mosh impeccably, and know that I wouldn't

even suffer a sprain. Been there. A couple of older women in the butcher's looked at me as if I was some kind of villain, madder than most. As if by tripping over death I was now carrying its odour around with me. I stared at them. They looked away and went back to their bacon. *Ladies, you watch too much telly*, I thought to myself. Well, I thought, this is a nice, quiet, sucking publicity. I'm not too sure about this. *Not that it matters*, I thought to myself. *Not that it's going to matter*, I thought to myself. I didn't buy anything. I left and I went home.

That evening, after *Brookside*, I was reminded of the hospital and I read the letter again. Five days. He hadn't even waited for a reply. This one was shorter but no less full of worship, a beguilingly scrappy howl of adoration. The more I read it the harder I tried to imagine what it must be like to love so much. To love in that way. I had been in love once, but it didn't work out. No. It could've been perfect. It was me that didn't work out. Whatever. This letter spoke of specks of hope, his plans for their future, if only she would call him, if only she would take his calls. I'd had the phone disconnected as soon as I moved in. His handwriting was truly lovely. Old-fashioned and careful. He must've been a good ten years older than me to have had a hand as immaculate as that. I read it again. And then I read the first letter again and compared the two. I imagined him to be a reasonably presentable man in his early forties, with moderate tastes and a huge and shattered heart. What were they like when they were together? I placed myself in both camps. Outside, a car went by, but quietly so. I put on the tape of myself on the news. I was shivering by the river bank and saying how sorry I felt for the poor cub, then I was cut off in mid-syllable, before I could say that I felt nothing. Before I could embarrass anyone with words ripped out of context. I turned off the TV and read the letters again. And I disappeared into them. I just disappeared, like the minor celebrity who's been written out of the series.

The next person who says 'Get a life' within earshot of me I will kill. If I have the energy. If I give myself enough time. Some of us don't want to. Some people can't because it just hurts too much.

I was in and out of the ward for six years and, in the end, I guess they just got tired of me. Since I wasn't tuning into His Master's Voice or climbing the walls any more, I was deemed a safe enough bet for the outside. I was twenty-one when I first stood on the railings of the bridge, looking down. I went and stood there many times in that high and tall place, usually in the small hours, looking down, wanting any kind of ropy existence, any kind of life, just so that I could take it with me. On my twenty-third birthday I was there, on tiptoe in the dark, when a thin voice beside me said that he would take my place. He was pale and familiar; he had been two years above me at school. Everyone thought he was a nutter. I was numb and perfectly sane and sad, and barely listening but I heard him say that he would take my place.

His eyes were mad, mad with a celestial light, but for one moment I thought he was joking. He grabbed my waistband and I landed hard on the pavement. He said again that he would take my place because that's what Jesus wanted and when I looked up he was gone. I heard a dull thud but he himself made no sound beyond those words. He had promised to take my place and he did. He took my life. And I let him. I don't remember the week after that. I was told much later that I screamed and cried for the first two days on the ward, and was quite violent. But I don't really remember it. It was all a long time ago. But sometimes I feel as if I've never moved from that spot. As if I am still on tiptoe, hovering in the dark, with my legs getting weaker and the wind growing stronger. Wondering for ever and stoutly teetering, like a brave and stupid child who has traded his last card and has nothing left to bargain with.

The third letter arrived seven days after the second. While I was reading it, I turned on the local radio station. The news reports were still going on about the body. It was a gang thing. Or a drugs thing. Or both. And I heard my own voice, again and again, a nibbling, cut-off drone, leaking seamlessly into the sports and the weather. This letter was different. The handwriting was less handsome and the tone more desperate. I didn't feel bad about opening her letters any more. This letter was less about her and more about him. About his perplexed soul and collapsing faith. *F* was full of bruising apologies, jam-packed with icy sneers directed mostly at himself and sorry. He was so sorry. For everything. I felt as if I was holding a life in my hands, a watery thing as substantial as a mountain. His sorrow was real. And he was dealing with it as only a man who is truly gutsy can. Head-on and pissed off. The paper was not expensive this time. It was thin and cheap and, in my hands, it weighed a ton.

I didn't take the dog out for a week. I just opened the front door and let him go, and let him back in when I remembered. I didn't go out. I didn't go out at all. I had no energy to speak of. The fourth letter arrived six days after the third. This one was angry. He'd had enough. He was miserable and he was tired of being punished. He ploughed his way, on good-quality paper this time, through a self-made landscape of cryogenic composure and high-velocity threats, run through with dribbling tales of nights spent weeping and phone-grabbing. But all the time there was love. And he wrote well, with due care and attention. As if it would make a difference to her. If I had been her it would have made a huge difference. I spent the next few days reading and rereading those letters, tracing his forlorn journey and her disappearing independence, and learning about how a man's heart, so gob-smacked, can come within an inch of being nothing, being nothing at all. I forgot to eat. I didn't sleep. I just read the letters and watched myself on video, and drank whisky now and again. I wasn't hungry. I wasn't tired. I heard the dog scratching and whining. I just let him whine and scratch. I was skimming two lives, neither my own, and it was as easy as falling into a warm bath.

The fifth letter arrived two days after the fourth and it was just like the first. Full circle. Love and nothing but. It was so beautiful. I would have wept if I could. Full circle. He rambled and flirted like a happy man, like a man who would just keep on stumbling towards her because that's the only thing he was good at. A bright mascot who knew that he was right to hope. Her face was so clear to me now, I didn't even have to close my eyes to see it. I thought I was better. Not perfect. Just better than I was. But I was wrong. I'd slid and kept sliding. I had no life to lose. In my hands I had other people's lives, precious and oozing with a misplaced enthusiasm that was almost mythical in its common sense. And I didn't understand a bloody word of it any more. I had disappeared too far and the perpetual charmedness of other people's lives sank no deeper than the ink on my fingers and the sheaves on my lap. This bedlamite just could not understand. I was not afraid to. I couldn't. I had forgotten if I had forgotten. I didn't know and if swooning ignorance was all I had left then nothing had really changed. I kept reading, well into the night, reading and not crying, listening to the poor dog outside and knowing that there was nothing on earth I could do about any of it.

As soon as the sun rose I took the letters out to the back garden and burned them. I got down on my hands and knees, and breathed gently on the flames, just to make sure. The dog seemed to have disappeared altogether. Then I went back inside and lay down on the floor. I lay there for hours. I heard the knocking on the door but I didn't move. Not immediately. But the knocking continued. After five minutes, it was enough to drag me off the floor.

She was exactly how I had imagined her. Shortish and

strawberry-blonde, with terrifying Doc Martens. She smiled at me, then her eyes raked me up and down, and she gradually stopped smiling. I wasn't sure how I looked but I could imagine. She was so pretty. I just stared at her while she spoke, while she asked me, very politely, if any post had arrived for her. *You don't know me*, she said. *I used to live here*, she said, wavering and wishing, I'm sure, that I would say something. Anything. I shook my head dumbly. *No, no post. No. Sorry. Sorry. Not a thing.* I couldn't stop staring at her. How could I have been so right? She was a shadow-boxing copy of the wispy girl I had been carrying around in my head for a fortnight or more. Her smile returned, but it was a thing of habit and courtesy, rather than a smile felt, and I just knew that I, loitering and thieving, had broken her heart again. There had been something in the way she had reached out an open, expectant palm before she even spoke to me. She had been living, not with hope, but with a blistering and kind certainty that love was hers and that, this time, everything would work out just fine. Paper and the chunky, frightened love plastered on it. Or even just a beige envelope addressed with a hand wrenchingly familiar. That's all she needed. And that is all she did not get because when I began to close the door she did not protest. I closed the door and watched her disappear in a sliver of daylight out of the side of my eye. I tried to feel shame and I almost got there – almost. I felt like a chemical killer of dreams. I sat on the floor and I felt nothing, really. Not really. Just like some viral template upon which is written others' lines, others' songs and I felt like nothing. How could she have been so like my pictured pixie?

Then I felt sort of sick and like a decent robber might, in the middle of the night, maybe. She was so pretty and she was his. Or maybe not. Or maybe. Perhaps my puny vandalism changed nothing. Perhaps they would find each other again through other means. Perhaps. I lay down again on the floor. I still was not hungry and I still was not tired. I couldn't get her fraught, apologetic face out of my mind. She was loved, so. Loved greedily and remorsefully by a good and graceful man who wrote beautifully and whose one and best chance I had burned for ever. For the first time in my life I felt like a powerful and chunky predator who, having killed, just needed a good lie-down. I went to the bathroom and I threw up for a long time. I hadn't even eaten. It was nothing but bile and a little left-over Scotch, and a sore, sore belly. Beyond that, nothing much. I'm on my way out anyway. Better off. But what a lovely, excursive racket to think about. A love that could be a marvel and nothing to do with me. A love slightly soiled and nothing to do with me. By impeccable misunderstandings and hobbling cuffs, and nothing resembling the sweetly ordinary. It's not that I don't care any more. Jesus, I do. I really do. I'm just terrified and ticklish in that department. I rinsed my mouth and lay on the living-room floor again. I might have been hungry then. I'm not sure. I thought about the letters and about her face, her real face, on my doorstep. And about how I sent her away empty-handed, empty-hearted. I felt like screaming but I've done enough of that. So I've been told. I lay there until I was very, very calm. So stone-cold calm that I could no longer feel my own fingers, or my legs. Just my own heartbeat, which muttered inside my chest and was utterly, utterly slow.

When I could tell, even through closed eyelids, that sunset was on its way, I stood up, with difficulty, and looked out of the window. It was a perfect evening. I wanted to be clean and tidy. I had a shower. I dressed in a clean T-shirt and crisp chinos, and I went out of my front door for a walk. I think I may have left the door open. I walked to the park. It was easy. Now it was easy. The fairground people had moved in a month ago and business was good. People were everywhere, and the colours and lights were all around me. Couples in bright ski jackets, even though it was warm, their fingers entwined, wandered and kissed and ate and wandered. I was seeing without looking and hearing without listening, and nothing hurt any more. Nothing hurt. I was in the middle of harmless, ruffling crowds with ice cream and with small children, and nothing could touch me any more. They, and the cheerful, mechanical commotion of the hoopla stalls and the vivid rides, were beside me and all around me, and a million miles away from me. I looked up at the beautiful sunset and saw the Ferris wheel. I have always loved high and tall places. I felt very good and bought a ticket.

Twenty feet up, in a chair all to myself, the wheel stopped. And then I realised that they had stopped it to let other people on board. We shunted on and up, then stopped again. And more people climbed aboard, further below. At thirty feet up I could begin to see the town. Shunt and stop. And a moment of ringing, waiting focus. More people, their chatter thinner now. Shunt up and stop again. Forty feet and I could see all of the sky and all of the town. At sixty feet I could see cars heading towards the town centre and rooftops, too. I could see the miraculous sunset and when I stood up in the chair to get a better look at the town my legs were strong and the breeze was gentle. We were still waiting for others. I could see shop signs from three hundred yards away. Shop signs with letters missing. Important letters, missing and adorning a vandal's bedroom, in dead neon. I looked down at the crowds below and at the insect colours and, for a moment, I thought I saw my dog beside the hamburger stall. I closed my eyes and breathed in the high-silent air in this place of unfathomable height. Thoughts of a poor, wet, dead boy upon whose skin bruises showed less easily and of a poorer, paler and skinny bridge-jumper skittered across my mind, and it didn't bother me any more. Nothing could. She would be okay. And so would he.

And I knew what had happened. It was meant to happen, one way or the other. *Lettres de cachets.* A death sentence for the persons named within. The killer of love. It made perfect sense and although I did not inhabit those pages I knew then that the name was mine. And I did not mind any more. It was bound to happen. I would never write again. And I would never be lonely again. There would be no more doomed paraphernalia, no more imploding pain. We shunted up again and waited again. As I looked up at the blinding, frozen sunset I knew that I was at the top of the wheel, the very top, and that everyone was on board who was coming aboard and that I didn't have to wait any longer. I climbed out of the chair and stood, reaching up towards the sky, grabbing faint stars with my fists. At that moment I was supremely and perfectly sane.

I could hear voices faintly screaming at me to sit down. But I have always loved high and tall places.

THE OUTFIELDER,
THE INDIAN-GIVER

As they touched down at O'Hare, Fergal wondered how he'd got himself into this. Okay, Martin was charming and clever, and as persuasive as an upper-class rat with a gold tooth, but Fergal had only known him a month and now he was going to be spending the next week covering swathes of a country Fergal knew nothing about with this middle-aged man who was completely drunk two hours after take-off, and whose seduction technique involved roaring at a stewardess that 'Kafka was, in fact, sweetheart, a fucking *comedian*!'

They had met at a dinner party in Dublin. Martin was a sports writer for the *Telegraph*. Cricket commentator, mainly. Fergal was a research assistant to the Politics professor at Trinity College. He knew nothing about cricket, so when, in the middle of Martin's unintelligible gabble about front foot and middle stumps, cover point and deep mid-wicket, he quietly mentioned that he was going to America for a week or so he didn't expect him to be interested. He was wrong. Martin pounced, grabbing his hand and spilling gin on his lapel.

'America! *Really*? Why?'

'Well, ah, I'm just going to have a look at the original homelands of the, um, the Choctaw ... in Mississippi ...'

'The what?'

'The Choctaw.' Fergal felt a little embarrassed. He wasn't

sure if that was the real reason he was going, but he needed an excuse to get away and if he could do some research on the relocation of Native Americans in the 1830s, then that was as good an excuse as any. Research, hell – he just wanted to find himself driving through somewhere different.

Martin was bewildered. 'So what's the Choctaw, then?' he demanded.

Fergal sighed, then sat him down and explained all about the Choctaw tribe and their $710.

In 1847, sixteen years after their forcible removal to Oklahoma, their Trail of Tears, news reached the Choctaw of Skullyville about the Irish Famine. So they took up a collection. And in the midst of their own poverty and the memory of their 14,000 dead, they raised $710. A fortune. Two years later, 600 people died as they struggled across the Mayo mountains from Doolough to Louisburgh in search of food. The parallels made Fergal shiver, so he'd taken it upon himself to find out a little more about the Choctaw and the other mid-West tribes, about where and how they lived before they were squeezed out west of the Mississippi river. He was planning to start in Chicago and work his way south to New Orleans.

'Chicago!' spluttered Martin. 'That's where they're sending me! Well, to start with anyway . . . They're sending me to cover the first couple of weeks of the baseball season. My editor thinks it's a cute idea.'

He spat out the word baseball as if it was the most vulgar notion he'd ever encountered. 'The first game is on the first of April. Chicago Cubs versus the Anaheim Angels. If I screw this up, that's it – I'm out on my arse. This is my last chance, I think,' he said mournfully, staring at his gin.

Fergal looked at him for a while. He was pretty drunk. And he seemed to be in trouble, lost somehow. Then he suddenly clapped a heavy hand on Fergal's shoulder and almost shouted, 'Come with me! Really! I can cover games any-where along your route. We can travel together – and the paper will pay,' he added conspiratorially. 'The car hire, the expenses – the lot! Come on – it'll be great!'

When he thought about it afterwards, Fergal didn't remem-ber actually agreeing to anything, but he didn't remember saying no with any great conviction either. And Martin was a great talker. Before the evening was out he'd had the whole thing organised. Fergal remembered thinking, 'This is insane. I don't even know this guy. This is insane.' But he was pretty skint. And he had to get away. So he let Martin talk and plan, and nodded dumbly in all the right places. When Martin showed up on his doorstep a week later with a plane ticket and an itinerary he didn't even bother to argue. What the hell, he thought, it might be good. It might be fun. Besides, this clown needed looking after.

As the plane taxied to a halt, Fergal glanced at Martin's sleeping form and thought about Siofradh. If this trip stopped him from thinking about the past, about her, then that would be something and maybe he wouldn't feel like a bully any more. Maybe he could discover something new and breezy, a small thing to make him feel lightweight and glamorous once again. As they left the airport to pick up their hired Pontiac, Fergal noticed a *Sun–Times* headline on the news-paper stall – *'Appeal Rejected: La Salle to Die.'* After half an hour Fergal got the hang of driving the Pontiac and headed, very slowly, into downtown Chicago.

In their hotel Fergal tried to phone home.

Martin cleaned out the minibar and then started on his duty-free. He hated America and made no secret of it. This assignment scared the hell out of him. He would much rather have been at home, covering the cricket, and the drunker he became the more sour his rant. 'Multi-ethnicity, my arse! These people can't stand the thought that they're surrounded by shite, so they call it something else. Their theatre is vaudeville, their psychiatry is babble, their art is self-conscious tat and their whole fucking culture consists of giving enormous amounts of money to manicured gits who tell them it's okay to have the attention span of a fucking gnat!'

On his sixth whiskey, he was getting into his stride. 'Huxley was right,' he growled. 'We won't be corralled off and marched into oblivion – we will quite cheerfully dream and *dance* our way into it. Silence is mistaken for profundity, incompetent nonsense becomes "artful" kitsch and *Mr Ed* is hailed as seminal television!' He ranted on, becoming drunker all the while, not caring if Fergal was listening or not.

This guy's off his rocker, thought Fergal, as he tried Siofradh's number again. And again there was no answer. She'd told him not to call her. Ever. But somehow he thought that the novelty of his calling her from another continent would make a difference. After a while he gave up and persuaded Martin to get some sleep. He was still rambling angrily to himself when Fergal climbed into his own bed and turned out the light.

'And they're all so fucking cheerful too . . . my God, you could probably get arrested for having a depressing thought . . . they wouldn't recognise a thing of wit or grace if it jumped up screaming and bit them in the arse . . . well, I don't care what the revisionists say – *The Beverly Hillbillies* was talentless shite then and it's talentless shite now . . . baseball . . . Jesus H. Christ on a crutch.'

He fell asleep on his bed, still fully clothed.

In the dark, Fergal cursed silently. This was going to be a long trip. He knew little of America, but he liked the idea of it. And he'd come to be fascinated by its first inhabitants, the first true Americans. He thought about Sears Tower, built by the Mohawks, the Genawoggi to be specific, the legendary tribe with absolutely no fear of heights and therefore a talent for building skyscrapers, who would dance and shimmy on its steel skeleton at 1400 feet and do 200 sit-ups before breakfast, their torsos dangling over the abyss. As he drifted off to sleep, it occurred to Fergal that if a thing *belonged* to the men who worked on it, who built it, then London belonged to the Irish, America's railways belonged to the Chinese and all the grand, soaring towers belonged to the Mohawk.

How long will the noblest of God's creatures, honest men, be doomed to want food and to famish in the midst of plenty in their own nature-blessed but misruled country?
The Waterford Freeman, 9 June 1846

You ask me to plough the ground. Shall I take a knife and tear my mother's breast? Then when I die, she will not take me to her bosom to rest. You ask me to cut grass and make hay and sell it and be rich like a white man. But how shall I dare cut off my mother's hair?
Smohalla, of the Sokulk (Nez Perce) tribe, 1850

The next morning Martin awoke groaning and clutching his head. 'Oh, Christ, I feel like a pigeon caught in a badminton match – what the hell did I drink last night?'

Fergal laughed and pointed at the empty bottles on the floor. 'C'mon kid – you've got copy to file – up and at 'em!'

Martin's first game was over at Wrigley Field, home of the Cubs, and he had to e-mail his report to London by eight o'clock at the very latest. Still groaning, he headed for the bathroom while Fergal called Reception and asked them to arrange a hire car for him for the day. Preferably European. He was going for a drive. He just hoped Martin's expenses weren't going to be examined too closely when they got home. He was poring over a map of Illinois when Martin emerged from the bathroom.

Fergal said, 'So, Theresa's Lounge, nine o'clock, okay? It's on the south side, near the –'

'Hey!' Martin threw him a withering look. 'I've never failed to find a pub in my life and I'm not about to start now,' he said. 'See you later.'

Fergal tooled the Volkswagen down East Wacker Drive into Adams Street, then left into Franklin. The traffic was surprisingly civilised. He drove slowly out of town in what he hoped was a vaguely west-north-westerly direction, found Highway 20 and headed for what 200 years ago was the Peoria homeland. He wasn't sightseeing, he was just driving through. He drove for a couple of hours, through Elgin, Cherry Valley, Pecatonica, before hitting Dubuque, almost on the Wisconsin border. There was no real countryside, just flat expanses dotted with gas stations, motels, diners and suburbia's identikit presence, again and again. There was nothing much to look at, but Fergal enjoyed the simple fact that he was moving through it, simply travelling.

He turned north on to Highway 151, past Cuba City, on to Platteville and east on to Highway 18. He was enjoying himself. He loved the bizarre names – Mt Horeb, Verona, New Glarus – but after 100 miles of driving in a wide circle, he decided to head back to town. He was in another State, for God's sake, and the sheer hugeness of the place was beginning to scare him. He skirted Madison and, as the light began to fade, headed south on 1–51 towards Chicago, feeling quite brave at having negotiated these alien roads. But there was no trace left of the Peoria, nor of their lives before the whites came. He hadn't expected any. He just found it interesting to wonder, to guess about the intricacies of their daily existence in this giant parish where once had been only prairie, timber, buffalo and greenness as far as the eye could see. This part of Illinois had been home not only to the Peorias but also the Kickapoos, the Cahokia, the Sauk and Fox, the Kas-Kas-Ki-As, the Illinois themselves. Sophisticated farmers and vintners, they also cultivated square miles of plum trees, gooseberries, wild currants, prickly pears and, for the love of it, roses. Whiskey and smallpox did for the Kickapoos and the Kas-Kas-Ki-As, and by 1830 the inoffensive Peorias were down to 200 civilised members, under contract to move west of the Mississippi. Just like everybody else.

He dropped the keys at Reception and, outside, hailed a cab. When he got to Theresa's, Martin was already there. He'd filed his copy an hour ago and was sitting in a dim booth at the back, rewarding himself with a bottle of Black Bush.

'So, how was the game?' said Fergal as he sat down.

'Three hours of boredom, topped off with fifteen minutes of mild excitement I'd say. What did you do, anyway?'

'Oh, I just went for a spin around the county.' He knew that Martin wasn't remotely interested in either the landscape or the Indians. 'Really, though – tell me about the game.'

If I can keep him talking, thought Fergal, he might not get completely rat-arsed.

Martin looked at him for a moment and smiled slightly. 'Well, Sosa is on the injury roster, so the Cubs have got Jeff Reed, a fine defensive first baseman, who hits for a high average but without much power. Against that is the Angels' Mo Vaugh, the front runner in what is, admittedly, a pretty crowded left field. Okay, he doesn't have the highest ceiling of his group, but he's a .293 hitter over his career, a utility player and heir apparent to second base. Now, the first six innings were low scoring. The Cubs kept trying to steal second base before the pitcher got to the plate and Bengie Molina just picked 'em off one by one. Sloppy running as well, I noticed – too many fade-away slides; okay, it's effective because it gives the fielder nothing to tag, but not very interesting to watch, you know? Now in the bottom of the ninth it actually became quite exciting. Two bases were loaded, the score was close, Nieves batted to the infield after a couple of sacrifice bunks, Cline the catcher bounced up as first baseman and shortstop Liniak covered second. Morandini on third didn't stand a chance. Ball came back in from fair territory, he broke too early, catcher tagged his arse. Nieves should've bunted, given him a sacrifice fly. But there were less than two outs and it was a classic suicide squeeze. Hasegawa's split-finger knuckleball, that's some asset, believe me . . .'

Martin winked at him and sipped from his glass, pinky in the air.

Fergal stared at him. He'd barely understood a word. 'So who won?' he said through gritted teeth.

'The Cubs,' replied Martin, smiling sweetly.

'How did you get to be so knowledgeable about baseball?'

'I didn't. I lifted it straight from this afternoon's radio coverage. Why do you think I brought a tape recorder?'

And then he began to laugh. 'You think my editor knows the first damn thing about baseball? You think he's going to know the difference? Of course not. All he wants is jargon, a spiel, something that makes everybody feel as if they know what they're talking about. When they don't. To tell you the truth, it's not so different from my early cricket days. All I have to do is walk the walk, talk the talk, throw in some fancy verbiage and spell the fucking players' names correctly! Besides, when I get home, he's probably going to fire me anyway. Bastard. The man is not a writer. He doesn't know good coverage when he sees it, so how's he going to recognise a straight lift? Good writing? That swine couldn't write the word "FUCK" on a dusty Venetian blind. So why should I bother . . .? Hey! Just call me the Bubonic Plagiarist.' He laughed again and drained his glass.

This is not a happy man, thought Fergal. But even so, it was pretty funny. 'Fair play to you,' he said, smiling. 'Why not? It's a good plot.'

He wanted to talk about the Peorias, but he knew there was no point. As he went to the bar for another bottle of

Bush, he glanced up at the television. The news report was about James La Salle, the convicted killer on Death Row in Jackson, Georgia. He was due to go to the chair in six days. Behind him, Martin was staring intently at the screen. La Salle had been convicted eight years ago of murdering a gas station cashier. He was as high as a kite. But he did it. No question. The location TV reporter, a pretty brunette, was standing outside Georgia's Diagnostic and Classification Center, where La Salle and a hundred other Death Row inmates were being kept, most of them in H–5 block. The camera panned across the dozens of pro-capital punishment groupies as they waved banners and drank from their thermos flasks, and hollered for blood in the chilly night. Further along was a small group of La Salle's supporters, with candles and prayerful songs and no banners. They looked pretty pathetic. When it was announced that La Salle's latest application for a stay of execution had been turned down, there was a low murmur of approval from the other patrons, but apart from that no one was really interested.

Except Martin. As the night wore on, he became increasingly vocal in his disapproval. 'Fucking savages,' he snarled loudly.

'Please, Martin, shut up,' pleaded Fergal.

A few people looked round.

'No I won't shut up! It's barbaric and it makes me sick. And they call themselves civilised? Fucking Americans . . .'

At this, a large man stepped out of the next booth and, looming over their table, said, 'Well, I think the scumbag should fry and the sooner the better. I ain't got no problem with that, not one bit.'

He stared menacingly at Martin, who merely arched one snobby eyebrow.

'Well, sir,' he said pompously, 'as a guest in your fine country, my position does not permit me to argue with you.

However,' he hissed, narrowing his eyes, 'if it ever did come to a choice of weapons, mine would be *grammar*.'

For a long moment there was silence.

He didn't even see the punch coming and he was probably too drunk to feel it. Fergal spent the next ten minutes apologising for his friend's rudeness. When Martin had managed to haul himself off the floor and was steady enough to walk, they headed outside for a taxi. Fergal was furious. 'What's the matter with you? Why are you always looking for a fight? Jesus Christ, man, you want to get yourself killed – fine, but just don't drag me into it, okay?'

'I'm sorry,' Martin said thickly, holding a hanky to his nose. 'I'm just fed up with people dying all over the shop. Ah, fuck it, I need some kip. Let's go back to the hotel.'

This time, despite another whiskey, he managed to get his jacket and shoes off, before collapsing face down on his bed, mumbling to himself about fat comedians. 'What's that all about then, eh?' he drawled, his voice muffled. 'Oliver Hardy, Jackie Gleason, Zero Mostel, Jonathan Winters –'

'Martin, please be quiet. Go to sleep.'

'Alexei Sayle, Fatty Arbuckle, George Wendt, Mike McShane – what is it about big blokes and jokes? And why is it –'

'Martin, *please*.'

'– why is it that we got the best tragedy when times were good, y'know, like ancient Greece and Elizabethan England, and the best comedy –'

'I'm going to kill you in a minute.'

'– and the best comedy when times were tough – the Thirties, y'know, the Marx Brothers and that, eh? I wonder if Shakespeare could've come up with a decent comedy if he'd been writing in the 1980s, eh?'

Yeah, thought Fergal, he'd have written a blistering comedy about sleep deprivation and dead sports writers . . .

'And another thing –'

'Martin, SHUT UP!'

People dying all the over the shop. What had he meant by that? Something was eating this guy up, but Fergal was too tired to figure it out.

In the dark he wondered if she would ever speak to him again. God, Siofradh was so lovely. A placid, delicate woman with a breezy intelligence who was too nice to deny his anxiety, his fears for the future, a woman who had caved in so quietly he'd barely noticed. His decorative common sense had been too much for her; when she found she was pregnant, the whiplash dynamic of his logic, his financial nous, simply left her with nowhere to go, no space to stroll. The fresh, scrappy enchantment she'd felt in those first few days didn't stand a chance against him and his list of effortlessly worrying formulae, and gradually he'd whittled her precarious joy into a gloomy little problem that had to be solved. With his pessimistically steely chatter, he just wore her down until he had turned it into little more than a day trip without privileges. He never knew he could do that. He had never realised that fear could turn a good man into a kindly and nerveless lout. In the dark, Martin's phrase made a little more vile sense and Fergal forced himself to think of other things.

Fellow Countrymen – surely God is angry with this land. The potatoes would not have rotted unless He sent the rot into them; God can never be taken unawares; nothing can happen but as He orders it. God is good, and because He is, He never sends a scourge upon His creatures unless they deserve it – but He is so good that He often punishes people in mercy . . .

Rev. Edward Nangle, Achill Island *Missionary Herald*, 24 February 1847

When he first came over the wide waters, he was but a little man, very little ... But when the white man had warmed himself at the Indians' fire, he became very large. With a step he bestrode the mountains and his feet covered the plains and the valleys. His hand grasped the eastern and western sea, and his head rested on the moon. Then he became our Great Father. He loved his red children, and he said, 'Get a little further, lest I tread on thee ...' Brothers, I have listened to a great many talks from our great father. But they always began and ended in this – 'Get a little further; you are too near me ...'

Speckled Snake, Creek Indian, 1829

They paid up and set off very early the following morning for Indianapolis. And despite feeling about as lively as a galvanised corpse, Martin actually volunteered to do some of the driving. After a couple of hours and 150 miles they stopped off in Peoria, Illinois. In a shiny café that seemed to be constructed from plastic, Martin sucked on a beer and studied his new-found bible, *USA Today's* 'Baseball Weekly'. The Seattle Mariners were taking on the Milwaukee Brewers. In Peoria. Peoria, Arizona, that is. He sighed and looked at Fergal across the table. 'God knows how many Peorias there are. Jesus, sometimes the *size* of this place just does my head in.'

He went back to his paper, concentrating hard. He looked like a one-man slum. Talk about a fish out of water, thought Fergal. He studied Martin's furrowed brow.

'"Ken Cameron",' said Martin, reading from the paper, '"the best and most underrated five-tool prospect around," it says here.' He looked up and winked at Fergal, smiling evilly. '"This right-fielder's prospect ceiling is sky high; he flirted with a 30–30 season at Double-A Birmingham, falling two short in the homer department, but still leading the Southern

League with 39 steals, a great vertical leap and a good, solid work ethic."'

Fergal laughed gently. 'So a few more paragraphs nicked and that's today's copy sorted, is it?'

'Pretty much, yeah,' said Martin. 'Mind you,' he added, his nose still buried in the paper, 'this game's beginning to make a bit more sense . . .'

He read in silence for an hour, while Fergal stared out of the window at the people going by in the town plaza. Everything outside shone in the early-afternoon sun. Over to the left of the square there was a space in the throng, a gap around the edges of which shoppers veered, as if quietly avoiding something and yet not avoiding, just subconsciously veering, smoothly. And in the middle was a man, a preacher of sorts. Fergal shielded his eyes against the sun to have a better look at his livid mime. The man wore an ill-fitting suit and thrashed in circles, pointing accusingly at passers-by. Some smiled nervously, but most shied away from his mad eyes and windmill arms, and his yawning threnody, a silent rant of doom and condemnation. Fergal was mesmerised. The man was actually frothing, his pet faith, whatever it was, insanity's party line. Onlookers were scared and yet not scared, veering yet laughing and shaking their heads at this duff casualty. And the longer he sloshed around in his well-defined circle, the surer Fergal became that what he was screaming about was retribution and death, and days to come. He watched that mad, miserable flamenco until he realised that Martin was watching it too and that he also was dumbly hypnotised. His cigarette had burned through his bible's 'White Sox Spring Training Review' and he had noticed neither the smell of scorched paper nor his own trembling fingers.

Fergal took over the driving, south then east on to Interstate 36 through Normal, Bloomington, Decature and Tuscola. Finally, he thought, some of the open space he'd read about. Out here, at last, there existed a fine, big sky with ballpoint streaks of dirty cloud and all around a montage of sheer spring fields, growing little yet, but green and promising. An immense and orbiting version of home. He gathered speed, enjoying the Pontiac's power and the space he found himself in, and aimed the wheel at the goalposts of the road's distant horizon. At that moment he felt better than he had in two years and neither this place's metallic cities nor Martin's sulphuric, cavalier piffle could drag him down. He was tired of being held a twitching hostage to thoughts that mugged him in the night. He was just bloody fed up with it. After 250 miles, Martin hadn't said a word. In Indianapolis they checked into the Regal 8 Inn around seven o'clock. Martin headed for the nearest pub and Fergal settled on his bed with his books. This could get to be a routine.

Indiana. Shawnee territory. This powerful tribe had occupied grand tracts of Pennsylvania and New Jersey, and the Delaware and Chesapeake Bays before being shunted west into Ohio and Indiana, a long and disastrous pilgrimage, which reduced them to 1200 in number, poor, miserably dependent and without the nerve either to work or to hunt. Even Tecumseh, Shooting Star, their greatest orator and celebrated war chief, could not rescind the 1809 treaty whereby the Shawnee ceded most of their land to the government. They sold it because quite possibly they had never regarded themselves as its owners. Whatever prospects Tecumseh's great Indian Confederacy ever had died with him. There would be no Red uprising from Mexico to the Great Lakes, no mystery fire nor schemes of sacredness, nor battle frenzy to drive back the whites. Placid agriculturists, raising corn and beans, potatoes and hogs. By 1850, a small piece of land in promised perpetuity was all that remained.

Fergal threw the book aside. He was getting tired of sad stories about loss and plunder, true or otherwise. His earlier, buoyant mood had disappeared and offensive sorrow was crowding in on him. This trip was to have taken him out of himself, to have banished the past, yet that was all he could think about. Whole peoples shrinking and shivering into nothingness, his own vicious heart and a fellow traveller whose dedicated mockery spoke of something Fergal could not read. Christ, he needed a drink.

When Martin said 'the nearest pub' he'd obviously meant just that. Twenty yards from the hotel, Fergal found him perched precariously on a bar stool in a place called Gerry's. Unsurprisingly, he was pissed, but that didn't stop him talking. As Fergal approached he was expounding to a bemused coterie of locals his theory on heaven and hell. His accent had acquired an almost cartoonish Englishness. He sounded like Prince Charles stoned. The locals loved it. Nothing better than a drunk, talkative tourist. Cheaper than the juke box. Fergal parked himself with a lager at the far end of the bar, head down.

'You think heaven is some out-of-body experience, where everybody finds their own little psychic niche?' shouted Martin. 'Where everybody's happy and redeemed, and floats about like a fart in a blizzard in a place of great and infinite height? The ethereal, vaulted abode of God? Well, that's bullshit, okay?' Oh, this was going down well. A couple of drunk girls asked to check his wallet, just to see if he was for real. Martin handed it over. He didn't give a shit. Fergal swerved quietly into the noise and the giggles and, smiling the smile of the apologetic friend, retrieved the wallet, while Martin just carried right on. People were starting to laugh at him, but kindly so. He kept swigging and he kept blathering.

'The heaven we imagine, right? It's shite. The true heaven is the heaven we were taught when we were six years old. Heaven really *is* the pearly gates, choirs of angels, gleaming spires and an old, white-haired bloke who's been in a bad mood *for ever*. Except his son's a cripple. And it's the most boring place imaginable. Marginally worse than hell which, I might add, is also *exactly* how you remember it – fire, brimstone, screaming souls, guys with horns and pitchforks. The works. Great stuff,' he added happily and polished off another drink.

One of the girls draped an arm across his shoulder and said, 'Guys with horns, eh?'

Martin cocked a baleful eyebrow at her.

'You can buy me a drink if you like, sweetheart,' she cooed.

'Madam,' snapped Martin, recoiling, 'I strongly suspect that if *you* were in hell, Dante himself wouldn't piss on you.'

Her smile slipped.

'But being American, I imagine you already know what hell is like,' he added spitefully. That did it. After she'd slapped him across the face and kicked him in the kneecaps a couple of times, Fergal was obliged to bundle Martin out of the door before her burly friends did it for him. You just don't go around insulting women, that's all. Or America, for that matter.

As Fergal dragged him outside, Martin was still shouting over his shoulder: 'And if this place is so fucking great, how come the bald eagle, your national symbol for God's sake, is practically fucking *extinct*, eh? Answer that and stay fashionable, you bastards!'

I should've let them have his bloody wallet, thought Fergal, as he dragged Martin down the street by the scruff, still mouthing to himself.

He suddenly pulled up short and looked blearily at Fergal. 'I did it again, didn't I?' he said miserably.

'Yep. Martin – what exactly is your problem? These people haven't done you any harm. This place is okay. Why are you always trying to get yourself hurt?'

'That's what my wife used to ask. All the time,' Martin said, looking at the ground.

'Your wife? You never mentioned a wife.' Fergal was surprised.

'Ex-wife.'

'Ah.' Hardly surprising, really.

'Can't blame the girl, I must admit. When she found out what I was like she went through with the divorce faster than a dose of salts through a short grandmother. Nice girl,' he added sadly, swaying and rubbing his eyes. 'A very, very nice girl. Mind you, when she was annoyed about something she could have a tongue on her like a bee's bum . . . Poor cow.'

Fergal looked at him for a moment. He was too tired to be angry for long. 'Come on.' He sighed. 'Bedtime' and took him by the elbow.

Martin fell asleep sprawled on his bed, so Fergal took off his shoes and tie, and made an effort to cover him up and tuck him in. *Those guys would've killed him if I hadn't been there*, he thought and that thought made him, in an odd way, feel good.

At some point during the night he heard Martin's voice in the dark, a small child's voice, saying his name and asking him a question.

Fergal struggled to waken properly. 'What?'

'I said, do you know how many US soldiers died in Vietnam?'

'For God's sake – no, I don't know. I don't know. How many?' he asked wearily, blinking into the blackness.

'Just under 60,000.'

'So?' This was ridiculous.

'Almost 80,000 veterans have committed suicide since then.'

'Martin,' Fergal hissed, 'it's the middle of the night. Is there a point to this?'

'No. I'm sorry. It's just that some figures stick in the mind, that's all. Sorry.' His voice was barely more than a thin, grieving whisper. 'Go back to sleep . . .'

The Public Works have been a costly failure . . . the tide of Irish distress appears now to have completely overflowed the barriers we opposed to it. This is a real famine in which thousands and thousands of people are likely to die; none the less, if the Irish once find out there are any circumstances in which they can get free Government grants . . . we shall have a system of mendicancy such as the world never saw.

Charles Edward Trevelyan, Assistant-Secretary to the Treasury, 1 February 1847

I can remember when the bison were so many that they could not be counted, but more and more Wasichus came to kill them until there was only heaps of bones scattered where they used to be. The Wasichus did not kill them to eat; they killed them for the metal that makes them crazy, and they took only the hides to sell. Sometimes they did not even take the hides, only the tongues . . . Sometimes they did not take the tongues; they just killed and killed because they liked to do that. When we hunted bison, we killed only what we needed.

Hehaka Sapa (Black Elk), Sioux Chief, 1890

In the morning Fergal agreed to detour to St Louis so that Martin could take in the game between the Cardinals and the Minnesota Twins. Martin found it strange that a lot of teams weren't even based in their home town. 'The Atlanta Braves are based in Palm Beach, for God's sake – next year, they're moving to Disney World! And some of the best players are Cuban, or Puerto Rican or, these days, Japanese. It's strange,' he murmured, as he looked out of the car window. 'It doesn't seem to matter where they call home.'

He'd been reading more about the game. That morning before they set off he'd nipped out and bought a couple of books about the history and strategy of baseball, and buried his nose in them as Fergal eventually found Interstate 40 and headed south-west. They passed through a couple of medium-sized, compact towns – Brazil, Casey, Vandalia – before it started to rain. Sure, they all had the iconic pinnacles of McDonald's arches and out-of-town small malls, but Fergal loved each of them. He had trouble keeping his eyes on the road, he was so busy watching the kids and the late-afternoon matrons, the shops and the generally flat, two-storey, unambitious skylines. He'd seen this populated, concrete landscape a million times on TV and in the movies. It was ordinary and familiar to him and yet, because he was now in it, screamingly different. The rain kept up until they reached town, then lightened and stopped. The 630-foot steel Gateway Arch gleamed in the sudden sunshine; Martin swapped his books for a city map and they headed for the stadium. Flicking around the radio stations, Fergal alighted on a brief news report. La Salle had been granted a stay of execution. Martin stopped wrestling with the map for a moment and glanced at the radio, but he didn't say anything.

In the car park outside the stadium they agreed to meet back at the Ramada after the game. The Pontiac could stay there all night and to hell with the expense.

'Why don't you come on in and watch the game?' said Martin suddenly. A dull cheer went up from inside the grounds.

'No, thanks,' said Fergal. 'I'm not really interested. I think I'll just go for a wander, have a beer, do some reading . . .'

'Well, okay, but to be honest, I could get quite fond of baseball. Once you understand the rules, it's pretty interest-ing . . . well, anyway. See you later.' Martin looked disap-pointed.

'Yeah.'

A thought occurred to Fergal as he walked away. 'The Choctaw played ball, you know,' he called. 'A hundred years ago. Great ball players. Nothing like baseball. Or cricket, either. But they played a massive, big bloody game of ball.'

Martin looked at him, baffled.

Fergal laughed. 'I'll tell you about it another time.'

He walked around the city for a couple of hours, poking about in second-hand bookshops and coffee houses, visiting the Old Cathedral Museum, learning about the fur trade and the tobacco trade and the cotton trade, the selling and the buying, the loading and the shifting and the unloading, the slaves and the free men, the lives lost and the fortunes won. He learned a lot in one afternoon but, after a while, his head began to spin and he needed to sit down somewhere quiet with a cold beer and no one for company. In a small, graceful bar on Chestnut Street he flicked through the books he'd bought – local history mainly – and sipped his Miller.

He hadn't attempted to phone her in two days. There was no point. And there was no point in wittering on internally about the possibility of getting her back. At the bar no one bothered him. No one spoke to him. Fergal had always liked that. In public places he had a knack for creating around him an impenetrable shield which, while not making him appear unfriendly or odd, simply put people off. But if he did feel like talking he just had to smile or raise an eyebrow, the invisible barrier dissolved and after ten minutes most people thought he was a pretty nice guy. Maybe it wasn't a knack. Maybe it was dumb strategy. But he had never done that with Siofradh. No, she had marched right in like some fearsome pixie and nibbled on his heart until he felt bright and chuffed, and madly in love. He could not understand why he had been so afraid, so anxious, why this little snippet, barely a life, had sent him into that bullying freefall. She went to the clinic by herself and, after that, he wasn't brilliant any more. After that he was a care-beaten chicken who'd won his argument.

He was the clever, steroidal boy whose touch she could no longer bear. He was the man with all the wrong jokes. A month later she'd packed and moved out, crying and empty still.

Martin showed up in the Ramada bar around ten o'clock, looking flushed and pleased with himself. He'd finished his report earlier in another bar; the owner, an ex-pat Brummie, had let him plug in his laptop and send it there and then. 'And it's good stuff too – you missed a really good game! Wanna hear about it?'

'Oh, sure,' said Fergal drily. 'Do I have time to run out and get hit by a bus first?'

Martin laughed and talked enthusiastically for ten minutes about the outfielders' balleticism, about McGuire's miraculous hitting (in spite of a shoulder injury), about how the Cardinals' second- and third-base runners almost accidentally flattened each other, about the Twins' three homers from David Ortiz, about how the crowd went crazy and did the cleanest Mexican wave ever ... Martin stopped and looked at Fergal. He laughed, almost sheepishly. 'I think it's that thing about the rules. Once you understand the rules, everything else just automatically makes sense. Sort of. And I didn't even swipe the copy. Wrote it myself.'

'I understand that, I think,' said Fergal.

They talked for a while about St Louis and tried to ignore the TV report on La Salle. The flickering background candles, people in thick jackets, the pseudo-urgency of the reporter's voice, mike in hand – it was becoming as familiar as *Panorama*. La Salle's stay of execution had been withdrawn and a few banner-waving rednecks were having a satisfying whoop. Martin ordered another whiskey, downed it in one and covered his ears with his hands. This case was getting on his nerves. Fergal didn't mind it so much. He patted him briefly on the head. Poor Martin. It was sad, but what can you do? Why, scientists in Moscow and Atlanta were currently arguing the toss about whether or not to kill off the world's last two remaining stocks of the smallpox virus, kept in secure laboratories. Kill it and keep us all safe in our beds, or let it live and study it? Fergal didn't fancy the idea of a life without risk, or even the desire for a life without risk. Otherwise we'd all end up like the moron he'd read about who got half fried in Yellowstone Park and sued the authorities for not advising her on where lightning was likely to strike. And won. As for risk – well, thought Fergal, if Martin was too tired to start another fight, then he'd be happy enough with that particular result.

Martin had uncovered his ears and was listening to the news. The way they mangled the English language seemed to hold for him a kind of horrified fascination. 'My God,' he said at last, 'it's like watching a monkey with a Ming vase . . . Christ, I need some kip.'

As he drifted off he was mumbling about TV shows and their 'chickenshit 5–5–5. You don't get that at home, I'll tell you. I bet our lot give out *real* phone numbers. I'll bet we've got thousands of little old ladies being tormented twenty-four hours a day, up and down the country . . .'

There was no real venom in it, though. He was simply talking for the quiet joy of hearing the sound of his own voice. It was his own personal lullaby, a thing to keep a man company when nothing else seemed to work any more.

In the dark Fergal found his thoughts drawn to La Salle and his three days of life left. What a thing that must be. To know. I'd rather be sitting in a Chinese restaurant with my friends, he thought, after a good meal, plenty of wine and beer, and just have some total stranger sneak up behind me with a double-barrelled shotgun. I wouldn't know a thing. Perfect. The chair. Jesus, that must be like some modern equivalent of being burned at the stake. Fergal had read stories of prisoners' eyeballs popping out and their hair catching fire, of how the brain reaches sixty degrees Centigrade, about how, when the autopsy is performed, the liver is still so hot it cannot be touched by human hands, about how one guy took six jolts and forty minutes to die, whimpering for his life most of the way.

Fergal shuddered and turned over in his bed. He didn't want to feel sympathy for La Salle. What he did feel wasn't sympathy, exactly. It was more like what a soft, shrinking child feels when scolded. The feeling that rebounds, antiquely, saying, 'You should have known better.' La Salle should've known better. Fergal should've known better. Better than to have trusted the interior colony of his own scared common sense. Martin's distressedly quiet snoring drifted across the room, a trademark of wincing bliss. Wondrous affliction.

The general feeling is one of despair. The subjection of the masses in Westport is extraordinary. A large crowd marched to Westport House and asked to see Lord Sligo. When his lordship appeared, someone cried 'kneel, kneel', and the crowd dropped on its knees before him.
Commissariat Officer, Westport, October 1846

In the life of the Indian there was only one inevitable duty – the duty of prayer – the daily recognition of the Unseen and Eternal . . . His mate may precede him or follow him in his devotions, but never accompanies him. Each soul must meet the morning sun, the new sweet earth and the Great Silence, alone . . . He sees no need for setting apart one day in seven as a holy day, since to him all days are God's.
Ohiyesa, Santee Dakota Physician, 1911

Martin, despite his hangover, drove most of the 300 miles from St Louis to Memphis, where he wanted to drop in on a small game between the Knoxville Smokies and the Memphis Chicks. Neither team was major league but that was okay. Besides, Fergal wanted to be able to say he'd at least driven past Graceland. In filthy hail, they caught Highway 45, east through Cairo, Clinton and Greenfield. After stopping off for a quick beer in Milan – Martin wanted to commemorate the fact that he'd just driven through a town called Martin and Fergal had just about persuaded him that pissing on the town's name post was neither a grand nor a wise gesture – they headed south-west on 70 through Humboldt and Bells. Fergal remembered vaguely that this had once been Chickasaw country, along with the Quapaw slightly to the north-west and their eastern neighbours, the Koasati. The Chickasaws and Choctaws were amiable enough neighbours, sharing cultural idiosyncrasies such as head-flattening, which they seemed to have borrowed from the Chinooks. Fergal read aloud from one of his books, '"This process was done in earliest infancy, with an inclined piece of wood strapped against the child's forehead, and drawn down a little more tightly each day. While seemingly cruel, it probably caused little pain since, at that age, the bones of the skull are soft and cartilaginous, and easily pressed into that distorted shape. By this process, the brain was changed from its natural dimensions, but not in the least diminished or injured in its natural functions."'

'They probably ended up looking like some of the guys I went to school with,' snorted Martin. 'Flatheads, to a man.'

Despite the dirty noon weather Martin was determined to catch at least some of the game. He dropped Fergal off near Elvis Presley Boulevard, agreeing to meet at the same spot at five o'clock. They had to get to Atlanta, over 400 miles away, before their hotel gave the room away. Fergal thought he might go for a wander around town, see a few things.

In the end he saw nothing of Memphis and nothing of Graceland. He spent all afternoon in the gift shop. It was the most mind-boggling shop he'd ever been in and he wasn't even a fan. He pored over the velveteen paintings of the King in heaven, the mugs, embossed with the lyrics of 'Love me Tender' in the shape of Elvis's head, the twenty-four-piece dinner sets emblazoned with images of the mansion. He was mesmerised by the sheer imagination required to come up with something like a white jump-suit teacosy. Who drank tea, anyway? Eventually, he caved in and bought himself a small pouch of dirt in a special folder, officially certified to be taken from Graceland's flower beds. It even came with a stamped gold seal of authenticity. A snip at four and a half dollars.

It was almost dark when Martin rolled up. He'd filled the tank so they made straight for I-78 and south-east.

Just after New Albany, Fergal took over the driving. 'So, what was the game like?' he said.

'Oh, the Chicks got hammered, but it was good. Lots of families. Lots of kids. Guess what I did?'

'Punched a linesman?'

'Sod off. No. I had a hotdog. And a Coke.'

'Oh, Jesus,' said Fergal, 'that's it. There's no hope for you now. You've gone the Way of all Flesh.'

'With mustard and onions.'

'Well, I might as well just take you out and shoot you right now, eh?'

Martin smiled to himself and got out his copy of 'Baseball Weekly'.

They drove through the evening gloom for a couple of hours in a silence that was almost comradely. Forty minutes after crossing the Alabama State Line, Martin shouted, 'Stop! I've got to see this!'

'What? Jesus . . .' said Fergal anxiously.

'Turn left here.'

'We can bypass Birmingham.'

'No, I want to see it. It'll only take a minute.'

'See what?'

'The stadium. Rickwood Field. It's the oldest baseball stadium in America, according to this,' Martin said, jabbing a finger at his paper. 'Come on, please. I want to see it.'

'Well, gee whiz . . .' muttered Fergal sarcastically as he found the next exit.

Outside the stadium Martin produced a bottle from his pocket, took a swig, replaced it and began to climb over the fence. He rolled over the top and landed with an audible thump.

'Martin, this is fucking insane! We're gonna get arrested!'

'By whom, pray tell?' came Martin's voice, grunting, from the other side.

He had a point. There was no one around. It was dark.

Oh, fuck it, thought Fergal and climbed over. Sitting smack in the centre of the pitcher's mound, in complete and frosty darkness, Martin took out his pen-torch and his bottle, and offered it to Fergal.

Fergal took it and sat down. This was surreal.

'Eighteenth of August 1910,' said Martin, shining the light in Fergal's face.

'Don't do that.' Fergal took a large swig.

'Sorry. Ty Cobb, Babe Ruth, Satchel Paige, Josh Gibson, Frank Thomas, Walt Dropo, Cool Papa Bell. They say Papa Bell was so fast he could turn off the light switch and be in bed before it got dark.'

Martin flopped on to his back and laughed gently to himself. Then he stopped laughing, grabbed the bottle and finished it off. 'The White Sox shouldn't have been crucified for taking the easy option,' he drawled. 'That wasn't right. Nobody should be crucified for doing the only thing they can do. For just looking after themselves. Everybody would go crazy otherwise, wouldn't they? That's why I left. I left and *then* she divorced me. And I don't blame her one bit. No sirree Bob – hey, I'm even picking up the language!'

He started to laugh again and a crusty, bitter sound it was. Fergal shone the torch at him for a long time. 'Why did you leave?'

The stadium seemed to him like a giant grave. The blackness and the deserted space were tangible things, swallowing up Martin's cracked laughter, dissolving blackly the torchlight, the feel of cold grass, sucking their very breathing into funky silence. They lay on their backs for a while, freezing and thinking about people who leave and people who are driven away, freezing and staring at the stars, the only light, cold and considering their options.

Martin didn't answer.

Eventually, Fergal decided he was still sober enough to drive, so he hauled Martin off the grass and they searched blindly for an exit. With the thin torch they found a tunnel leading out on to the street. The place wasn't even locked . . .

Fergal drove through the chilly night, through Leeds and Bremen and Tallapoosa, while Martin slept on the back seat, and he remembered that this was Cherokee country. He couldn't get out his books but he recollected, as cars thundered past him in the dark, that in the 1830s they numbered about 22,000 members. Skilled agriculturists and well advanced in the arts. Their chief, John Ross, was a man known for the 'rigid temperance of his habits and the purity of his language', a man who opposed the treaty obliging the Cherokee to move. West of the Mississippi again. The river seemed to be a totemic benchmark, the watery line of banishment. Even Ross couldn't fight it and they moved. West of the Mississippi. Fergal looked out of the side window into the dark at the orange, distant chimera of towns he had no wish to visit, and tried to imagine their obliteration and a green ancient daylight, filled with quiet colour and underpopulated industry, without exotic whites, shorn of grimly flashy incomers. They never stood a chance. Neither the Cherokee nor their good North Carolina neighbours, the Yuchi, nor any of the rest. Moving west was the ultimate, unbeatable virtue. Trying to imagine a flipside history, with eternal stasis and no one having to leave, simply made Fergal's head hurt. And besides, the notorious Atlanta Bypass was coming up. He had to concentrate on what he was doing if he wasn't going to get blown away by the Indy–500 boy racers. Even at 10.30 p.m. it was packed and furious. Once in town, Fergal stopped dead in a side street and asked for directions to the Red Roof Inn. In the back Martin began to talk softly to himself.

In the hotel room neither of them wanted to turn on the radio. Martin laid his clothes out neatly. He didn't touch the minibar. He sat silently for an hour, typing out his copy on the small, unimportant game between the Chicks and the Smokies. It was going to be late but he wanted to take his time with it. He wanted it to be good. He wanted it to be poetic. Fergal swiped a mini-gin, read his book and said nothing. Just after they turned out the light, Martin slotted a tape into his cassette, pressed 'play' and turned the volume almost completely down. Fergal could just barely hear it, a sweet, forlorn horn, so familiar yet now a strange, fine sound. He smiled to himself as he drifted off. The tune played all night on a soft continuous loop. It was the theme from *Coronation Street*.

I often think of betaking myself to some other country, rather than see with my eyes and hear with my ears the melancholy spectacle and dismal wailing of the gaunt spectres that persecute and crowd about me from morning until night, imploring for some assistance.
          Archdeacon John O'Sullivan, Kenmore, Co. Kerry,
                                                    January 1847

Had our forefathers spurned you when the French were thundering . . . to drive you into the sea, whatever has been the fate of other Indians, the Iroquois might still have been a nation; and I – instead of pleading for the

privilege of living within your borders – I might have had
a country!
Wa-owo-wa-no-onk, Cayuga Chief, May 1847

In the late morning, Martin sat in the lobby, boning up on the
Braves who that afternoon were making an infrequent trip
home to take on the New York Yankees. He was actually
pretty excited about this game. He'd learned a lot in less than
a week.

Fergal took himself off for a wander and some lunch. He
mooched around the art gallery, or rather the High Museum of
Art, on Peachtree, with its great Le Witt and Stella rooms, and
then decided to try out some Southern cooking in a nearby
restaurant. After an astonishing plateful of fried chicken,
baked squash, turnip greens and corn muffins, he settled back
in his chair with his books. The waitress didn't seem to mind.
The sun streamed in the window. There were only three other
diners. It was very quiet. He skimmed over the pages and
wondered if Martin was okay. In the last five days Fergal had
spoken to virtually no one else; he wasn't a great one for
getting in with the locals. Hotel receptionists, gas station
attendants, waiters, dog-walkers – with fingers pointing
vaguely and garbled directions – that was it. That suited him.
His books spoke of authentic tongues, of Mak-pi-ha Lu-ta and
of Tatanka Yotanka – Red Cloud and Sitting Bull – but Fergal
felt too full and sleepy and warmed by the sunshine to think
about anything very deeply. He knew he wasn't adventurous
or a great and good talker. He could do it, but he preferred to
watch and to indulge himself in the wisdom of idleness and
observation. Well, that's how he liked to think of it. If he was
honest, it was probably laziness as much as anything. He
leaned further back in his chair and closed his eyes, and hoped
Martin was getting a good take on the game.

He kept his eyes closed and allowed the sun to warm his
face, and decided that he might make a phone call home. And

then he decided that he wouldn't. He could not compete with the niceties of justified hatred. And that's what it was. No getting away from it. She hated him. It was a hatred so tangible, distantly, that it felt like reassurance. He could hang on to that. There were to be neither sophisticated pleas, nor hot sympathy, only a taut acceptance. His stomach heaved every time he thought about it. He couldn't help it, but no amount of haywire, hurtful gut-rumbling was going to make him pick up a phone. No point in being a sheer fool about it. Sometimes he wished for Martin's syncretic blather, a small turn at being aloof, at playing the bristling fancyman who could advise earnestly and with real love. Instead of leaning with a cool and heavy kindness, and a fear that spoke of no love at all, a fear that spoke of solutions, of cares and of a grieving commonwealth. Fergal leaned further back in his chair, knowing, even with his eyes closed, that the waitress was watching him and waiting for him to fall over backwards. No chance. He teetered in the sun's rays for a long while, head back and filled with nothing very much.

'Let's go to Jackson!'

Fergal opened his eyes. It was Martin. The sun had begun to set. 'How did you know I was here?'

'I didn't,' said Martin. 'I was just looking for a drink. I walk in and here you are. Amazing, eh? Anyway c'mon, let's go to Jackson.'

'Isn't that a song?'

'Yes. No. I don't know. Never mind. I want to go to the Center.'

'La Salle?'

'Yeah. C'mon, let's go.'

'Why? I mean, *why*? Martin, you hate all this La Salle stuff. You *hate* it.'

'I know. That's why I have to go.'

Martin swiped him over the head with his 'Baseball Weekly'. 'It's only thirty or forty miles south of here. I just want to see it. Please. I'm half pissed. I can't drive. I have to see it. Come on, Fergal, be a good boy and do the driving. C'mon, Fergal, we at least have to see it. Just to stand outside for a while.'

That was the first time in a month and a week that Martin had used his name.

'What was the game like?' asked Fergal, trying to calm him down.

'Never mind that. It was wonderful. It was sublime. It was fantastic. Never mind. I'll tell you later. Never mind that now. C'mon. Now!'

The man seemed to be raving. But he wasn't. He wasn't even that drunk. Fergal decided – what the hell. They might as well. But if Martin started anything, Fergal was going to throttle him.

They found the prison easily. It glowed from a mile away in the late dusk, and the approaching roads were jammed with TV vans and parked cars and pedestrians all heading in the same direction. Fergal parked on the side of the road several hundred yards from the prison walls and walked towards the gathered crowd. It was like a quiet circus. On one side the eerie, almost blinding glow of the high prison lights picked up every shiny surface, reflecting them back until it seemed almost like daylight. Outside the walls, dozens of TV crews had rigged up their own light shows. The place was a metallic jungle of cameras, cables, aerials, sound booms and of the tinny, continuous babbling from the reporters, each more sincerely urgent than the next. The anti-death-penalty protesters numbered a couple of dozen at most, separated from the other lot by a line of policemen. They stamped their feet and hugged themselves against the cold, and tried in vain to keep candles lit against the nippy breeze. There was no shouting from either side. It was all very placid. There were to be no more appeals. La Salle would fry either tomorrow or the day after. Fergal and Martin backed off a hundred yards or so, and sat down on a grassy patch, observing the scene. Martin produced a half-bottle and took a long, mean swig, never once taking his eyes off the prison walls.

'Martin, what are we doing here?'

'Same as everyone else,' replied Martin quietly. 'Nothing. We're just here to watch. We're just here for the sake of being here.'

Fergal studied the quiet, milling, glare-lit crowd outside the walls, all bundled up in their thick jackets, trailing wires around, pointing, patting their dogs, smoking. He felt strange. He scanned the building, wondering where La Salle was, what he might be doing, thinking, eating. His dull, mean-featured face popped up periodically on the TV crews' monitors, an ugly cathode poltergeist, accompanied by the familiar drone of his crime recounted. Oh, he was a brutal bastard all right, a plundering, vicious life-grabber. The steam from thermos flasks rose through the cold air like a sugar-spun, thin textile. Fergal couldn't take his eyes off it. He felt as if he would not be able to haul himself off the grass, to turn away, to stop looking at what was in front of him. He felt calm and transfixed at the same time. Marooned in the strangest place, with a man whose inexplicable and drunken concern made no sense. He looked at Martin.

He had finished the bottle, still staring beyond, then dropped his head into his hands. He sighed a hard, jittery sigh. 'It was such a beautiful game today,' he said softly. 'All that energy. All that skill. The Braves were so good. It was almost like being at Headingley. Maddux pitched like some kind of lovely, short-arsed android. The Yankees couldn't touch him. The last time I saw a thrower as saucy as that was Patterson in the 1986 One-Day International in Jamaica.'

Martin kept his eyes closed tightly and his head bowed, as if he was praying for a miracle, or a refuge from disaster.

'Martin, are you okay?' Fergal was beginning to feel a little worried.

'And Jones, my God, that youngster's a bloody marvel. He hit three homers in twenty minutes. Big, soaring bastards, too. He still needs to work on his switch-hitting, but maybe he should forget that and concentrate on his fastball – he can hit the low nineties on a good day, y'know, and today could've been a good day. Today could've been such a good day. Now Perry a couple of years ago, he could've shown us the shiftiest, most subterranean pitches you've ever seen; I know all about *his* plays. After *that* trade, the Braves couldn't find room for him on the forty-man roster. So they've gotta trade or release, trade or release –'

Martin's eyes were still screwed shut and he was balling his fists spasmodically.

'Martin, come on, let's go.' This babble was beginning to unnerve Fergal.

'– trade or release, or send to the Minors. Trade or release. Trade or release . . .'

'Martin. Stop it. Come on. Let's go back.'

Suddenly Martin opened his eyes and looked at the crowd. He could barely focus. He was breathing in soft, ragged gulps. 'It was so beautiful.'

Fergal laid a tentative hand on his shoulder. 'Come on. Let's go.' He couldn't think of anything else to say.

Martin stood up, wobbling slightly. 'I'm just fed up with bastards dying everywhere,' he said and weaved away towards the car.

Fergal stared after him. He suddenly felt very tired. The candle-wavers had started to sing an anthemic song, but softly so, marred by a yelping dog and the damn lights. Fergal looked at the ruined skyline, at the devout cameras and the steamy, well-behaved people, and for a moment he felt that he might never be able to walk away. The sound of Martin falling over in the dark twenty yards away brought him up short. He turned his back and walked.

In the middle of the night a noise wakened him. It was a near-inaudible crying, the kind of shuddering, silent-type crying that tears out your heart and against which you must, for the sake of decency, turn your back.

There should be no question of supporting a government that will not fling its wretched blighted theories to the winds when the people are starving – open the ports, establish depots for the sale of food to the poor at moderate prices, and employ the destitute.

Father Bernard Duncan, Kilconduff, Co. Mayo,
December 1846

We did not think of the great open plains, the beautiful rolling hills and winding streams with tangled growth as 'wild'. Only to the white man was nature a wilderness . . . To us it was tame. When the hairy man from the east came and . . . the very animals of the forest began fleeing from his approach – then it was that for us the 'Wild West' began.

Chief Luther Standing Bear, Ogala Sioux

In the morning, Martin was listless and quiet. 'Where are we going now?' he asked, sitting on the edge of his bed like an obedient, debauched child. 'I've forgotten.'

'Jackson,' said Fergal, putting on his coat. It was 6 a.m. They had ground to cover.

We've *been* to Jackson.'

'Jackson, Mississippi, you clown. It's almost five hundred miles west. We'd better get going.'

'And what's in Jackson, *Mississippi*, then?' He was still barely awake.

'My Choctaw turf. Your baseball game. Whatever. Let's go.'

He wasn't drinking, but nevertheless, Martin slept the sleep of the dead in the back seat as they headed south-west on I–29 through La Grange and into Alabama. He woke up briefly, struggled upright and stared gloomily out of the window at the dainty, tidy towns of Opelika and Auburn, before falling asleep again just as they reached Montgomery. Fergal pitched an almost perfectly western route through Uniontown and Demopolis, then, after briefly getting lost looking for I–180, made pretty good time across the Mississippi State Line, through Meridian, Forest and Pelahatchie. He was dog-tired and the lowish, springtime, sidelong sun was baking the right side of his face and making one eye water.

They got to Jackson around two o'clock in the afternoon. Fergal booked them both into the Friendship Inn International. Budget, but at least it was clean. Martin collapsed on to his bed and Fergal freshened up, as best he could. His back was beginning to ache from all this driving.

'Aren't you going to cover the game?' he said, emerging from the bathroom.

Martin sat up slowly, rubbing his chin. He needed a shave. 'A *college* game? What's the point? Memphis State versus South Alabama University? Jesus Christ, I doubt if either team could pour piss out of a shoe if the instructions were written on the heel. I've seen footage of this college crap. They're babies. They're fat. And they're lazy. Lazy, lazy! Give 'em a cocktail mixer and most of these fuckers would stand around and wait for an earthquake. I don't want to see that game. I've already seen the best game. I saw the best game I've ever seen in my *life* and I'm too tired and too fucked up to describe it. I couldn't type one word. Not a word. I'm not even going to try. Because I'm fired already. He's got it in for me. I know it.' He put his head in his hands. I'm dead meat.

Where am I going to get another job? I'm dead meat. I'm dead. She's dead. I'm dead.'

Fergal stared at him. 'What do you mean "She's dead"?' he asked as softly as he could.

Martin's head snapped back. He smiled warmly. 'Nothing. Nobody. Figure of speech,' he said and, without even taking off his coat, reclined gracefully back on his bed. Within a minute he was snoring.

Fergal sat by the window, looking out at a delirious sunset. He was 160 miles from New Orleans. Everything that happened to him seemed to be happening at dusk. *That's early spring for you*, he thought. At home everything would be growing, a fête of greasy particles and green things whose names he didn't even know. He looked at Martin's prone form, twisted up in his glossy overcoat. He was just hanging around for contrast's fun, a baseball tyro whose wet arrogance hid very little these days. *If he doesn't watch himself*, thought Fergal, *this bossy dazzle-dragon is going to plug himself into the mains. He's going to skedaddle from one crisis to another until he's hobbled for good.* And Fergal wasn't entirely certain what those crises were. Suddenly, and without knowing why, he was almost overwhelmed by a protective tenderness for this dodgy messer, this mournful jackass who genuinely needed looking after.

He stood up, walked over and kicked him on the shin. 'Come on, get up. If you're not going to the game, then we're going for a drive. I want to show you something.'

Martin snorted, grunted almost angelically and pulled himself off his cot. 'What? Show me what?' he demanded querulously, eyes still closed against the light.

'Nothing very much. In fact, nothing at all, really. But let's go for a spin anyway. Better than sitting around here.'

They drove south for about thirty miles. There was still a good deal of light in the sky. Fergal wasn't looking for anywhere. He was looking for nowhere; or more specifically, the middle of nowhere. Just past Crystal Springs he found it. An out-of-town, mall-free, open and empty field. Grass and nothing else. Some farmer's big, fallow patch. He parked by the road, got out and looked around at the landscape. This had been Choctaw territory. Sainted Mississippi, virtually a third of it, had been their home since God knows when. Not because they owned it but because they moved through it, up and down, following the food, north and south. Of course, he knew that 200 years ago there had probably been forests and scabrous beasts, but just being in that place, looking at a modern, clean patch of grass, made it easier for him to close his eyes and grab some vicarious memory.

'Fergal, why am I standing in the middle of a field, in the middle of the night, in the middle of fucking Mississippi?' said Martin politely.

Fergal looked at him and laughed aloud, spreading his arms wide. 'I don't know. I just wanted to show you where the Choctaw used to live. Anyway, there's a little light left. It's not dark yet. Remember their ball game I told you about? Remember the seven hundred and ten dollars?'

Martin leaned against the car, extracted his bottle, took a civilised nip, folded his arms and said, 'Yes. I remember. Carry on. Show me.'

Fergal should have felt self-conscious but he didn't. He wanted to teach Martin *something* about the Choctaw. He marched into the middle of the field and whirled around, arms outstretched. The light was fading fast. 'Well, for a start there would be two narrow goals and one ball. And anywhere between six hundred and a thousand players.'

Martin almost choked on his whiskey.

'Yeah! And the whole tribe would gather and there would be five or six thousand people watching.'

Fergal's voice grew louder in the gloom. 'And the players were all naked, except for a breech-cloth with a beaded belt, and a mane of dyed horsehair on their heads.'

'And then what happened?' called Martin across the field, as he leaned in and switched on the car's headlights. Fergal found himself bathed in light, centre-stage, and he felt like shouting and hollering.

'These games started at sunrise and ended at sundown, Martin! A thousand guys, all going *mad*!' He gesticulated wildly, trying to describe the beribboned, thronged sticks every player carried, the throw-up, the instant scrambles, the insane dust and the kicking, the jokes and the water-breaks, the tripping and throwing and howling, and the women gambling on the sidelines, gambling with pots and kettles, dogs and knives, blankets and guns.

'Can you imagine the noise, the *commotion*?' shouted Fergal. 'A thousand players, all going after one ball on a pitch the size of two acres? Mad! And when their ball-sticks were all broken, they used their hands, their feet, their heads, *anything* to keep the game going until new ones were brought on. And this went on for twelve hours without a break! Can you imagine it, Martin? Can you imagine it?'

He was getting hoarse and the headlights blinded him, but he didn't care. He whirled and whooped and ranted on about the Choctaw, imagining hysterically, until it felt as real as remembering. 'Sometimes, when the ball got to the ground, a hundred guys would pounce and for fifteen minutes there would be nothing but a man-high cloud of dust, with no one even able to *see* the damn ball! Sometimes it would be two hundred yards away, and these guys would still be whacking and scuffling and barking and eating dust like madmen! God, it must have been something to see . . . And when the game was over, ten thousand people had a party, danced the Eagle Dance in their finery and drank for two days. Christ, it must have been something to see. A game of a thousand players . . .'

His voice trailed off. He put his hands on top of his head and walked around in small circles, trying to imagine, in this quiet carlamp-lit field, a scene of such nourishing chaos. Such fun. He looked over at Martin's silhouette, black against the headlights. And he still wasn't embarrassed. 'Better than baseball any day, eh?' he called. His voice now seemed unbearably loud in the near-dark.

'Better than cricket, too.' Martin's voice was barely audible. The bombast seemed to have leaked out of his throat, and in Fergal's beam-wounded sights Martin's outline suddenly looked hunched and smallish.

'And on the twenty-seventh of September 1830 it all ended,' Martin whispered, and his words zoomed the distance between them. Fergal stared at his outline.

'The Treaty of Dancing Rabbit Creek. The Choctaw gave up their last acre in Mississippi, and twenty thousand of them moved west, in steamboats and wagons. The government paid for it. Sixteenth Article. The government pays. I've been reading some of your books.'

Fergal just gazed at him. He couldn't even see his face but when he looked up at the starry sky, because he didn't know what else to do, Martin's voice carried on floating across to where Fergal stood and, against the washing cascade of stars, it was a shy and playpen sound, a sound of hardness abandoned and efforts made. His voice was that of a holy academic.

'But the Choctaw believed that the spirits of the dead lived in a future state, that they had a great distance to travel after death, across a dreadful, high river. And that while they crossed, those spirits who had gone before separated the good from the bad by throwing rocks at them as they crossed over a slippery pine-log bridge. The bad people succumbed and drowned. But the good people walked on safely, to the good hunting grounds, where there is one continual day, where the trees are always green, where there are fine breezes and the sky has no clouds, where food is plentiful for ever, and where there is no pain or trouble and people never grow old but live, young, forever, where ...' Martin's voice cracked in the dark. His silhouette shrank from the shoulders down and, as Fergal ran towards him, he sank to his knees and began to weep.

Fergal grabbed him and looked directly into his eyes. 'What was her name?'

'Hannah. Her name is Hannah,' Martin croaked, head bent.

'You said she was dead. You said, "She's dead." I heard you.'

'She's not dead yet. She will be. Three or four months, tops. Cancer. Breast cancer. I have to go and see her. I have to. But I can't. I'm afraid. I haven't spoken to her in four years, for God's sake.' Martin covered his face and sobbed silently, his whole frame shuddering. 'All I ever did was hurt her,' he whispered wetly. 'When I found out, all I wanted to do was run. That's why I didn't tell them to stuff this bloody assignment.'

Fergal sat down heavily beside him in the dirt and leaned against a tyre, eyes closed. He patted Martin on the shoulder, and gently on the back of his clenched hand until he'd stopped crying and sniffing, and his breathing became more stable.

'Ah, Christ.' Martin sighed.

'Martin. Why did you leave? It wasn't just the booze, was it?' Fergal was terrified of asking but he had to.

'No, it wasn't just the booze. The booze was the least of it,' Martin said quietly. 'Let's just say I turned out not to be the man she married.'

There was a sardonic condescension in his voice that was not entirely unkind. And with that he took Fergal's hand and looked into his eyes with the look of a man who was no longer scared of being crucified one more time, a man who had travelled the scant distance between fear and fearful fun, a man who had once tried to be brave and got it half right. He patted Fergal's frozen hand and said, 'Hell's teeth, pet, precisely how thick *are* you?'

Fergal stared at him. He didn't exactly recoil. He remembered how Martin's flinching disdain had exquisitely clobbered that poor cow in Indianapolis and he felt like the stupidest man on the planet. Oh, Christ, he thought, withdrawing his hand and covering his eyes – I've been *stripping* in front of this guy for a week . . . And for some reason the thought made him smile and then laugh to himself. He was only embarrassed and, if he was honest about it, he wasn't really that surprised. He was just embarrassed and sorry.

'Don't panic,' said Martin almost brightly. 'And stop flattering yourself, for God's sake – you're not my type. Besides, haven't you heard? Celibacy is the new rock'n'roll . . . and I should know, believe me.'

Fergal stared at the ground and felt insulted. Almost. He was too tired to care, really. Slightly sheepish and couldn't-care-less. He felt just like that. And more.

'Nothing more tiresome than a cowardly old queen, eh, kid?'

'You should go and see her,' said Fergal quietly. 'You really should. Listen, I know it's none of my business, but it would be . . . the gentlemanly thing to do.'

'I know. Oh, God, I know. But that's me – every other inch a gentleman. Oh, Christ, I hate hospitals . . .'

They sat on the grass at the field's edge for a while. The wind picked up a little and the cold began to set in. But neither of them felt like moving just yet. Martin blew his nose loudly, took a comforting swig and sighed a sigh that lasted for a frosty age. Fergal took the bottle and finished it in two swallows. The damp of the grass was beginning to soak the arse of his trousers. The night darkness was complete, now, and the blackish sky a hand-tinted thing so huge it could have been a terror. A few cars passed by on the main road, a hundred yards away, their noise and light scared into needle-thin redundancy by the darkness. Fergal thought of Siofradh and felt his gorge rise. But he knew for a fact that it was the whiskey. He knew for a fact. Whatever twists of distress were going on in his gut were no longer for himself but for this poor, bereft bastard beside him, whose loss had happened once and would happen soon again.

He looked out over the black field, whereof only a sliver existed in the narrow, jealous headlight. It was so quiet. Martin sat beside him, still with his head in his hands. So anxious. So quiet. Whatever hybrid sympathy Fergal felt was for him. Fergal needed someone to take care of. He was filled with a need to rummage through the debris and find a one that he could look after, a one whom he could drag, priceless, from the mire and look after. He'd had his chance once. And he blew it. He had worn his common sense like a girdle of chastity and he had lost her because of it. The thought of his own foolishness made him clench his fists and fling away the bottle, and feel dressed in violence. But then Martin, head still down, coughed and sniffled like a sick baby, so Fergal again patted his head in the dark and made a soothing sound and thought, again, about the Choctaw and their $710. What a thing that was. What a thing that was. Wherever loss and the pain of banishment existed, he could still hang on to that. He leaned his head back against the car's cold metal and comforted himself with the ringing focus of that particular piece of generosity. The rest of us could fashionably slum, but there was no subtracting from that $710.

It was getting really cold now and he could feel Martin begin to shiver. Troublesome, muddy swine that he was, a dim and pained poor sod. Well, Siofradh was gone and Fergal didn't know where to put himself any more, so he stood up and took off his coat, and wrapped it round Martin's shoulders. He didn't get as much as a thank you but that was okay. He looked around this now ridiculous patch of blacked-out green and wondered what the farmer grew in this place. Not spuds, anyway, that's for sure. Behind him Martin very slowly keeled over and curled up on the ground, drawing Fergal's coat around him with a polished smoothness that spoke of many, many nights on other people's sofas.

Fergal looked up again at the sky. He couldn't help it. It was a fine and mesmerising sky. The kind he could only see at home, with no light pollution, no street lights to get in his way, no delta of spots or the becurtained, sneaky blue of TV sets. There was nothing out here, just one dilapidated set of headlights, his famished heart and a gently purring heap who called himself a sports writer. Fergal sat down again and wished he had another bottle, even though he felt pretty drunk already. He thought of hunger although he was not himself hungry. He was very cold. He was beginning to freeze. But the thought of hunger hit him in his gut like some rebel, historical strand of DNA kicking in, and for a nanosecond he felt starving and perished in the night, with pictures of gleaming and bony stretched skin thieving and shifting around his head, and for a longer moment he felt the archivist's malice creep up on him.

Fergal leaned across and, just the once, stroked Martin's head. He was dead to the world and snoring still. Whatever dented skill in denying the past Fergal had left, dribbled away from him just then. He kept patting Martin's sleeping head and, looking upwards at the sheen and stranded sky, he was stunned by a tiny vision of scrawny, needful hordes and a killer killed, and a nice girl's hatred, and if he hadn't been flattering himself on being tougher than that he would've laid his head down next to Martin's and wept. He was freezing and he wanted to go home. He was hungry and he wanted to go home, and in this difficult place he could find no compensation. No compensation at all. He was tired, and sick of being touched by memory and by Martin's ailing warmth. He wanted some cool distance and he knew that, if only he was selfish enough he might, some day, get it before he died. Even if she didn't take him back, and he knew she wouldn't, he still might get that thing before he died. So he hauled himself up again in the frosty air, and struggled with a limp and annoying Martin. And he bundled him exhausted into the car because he wanted to feel responsible, and to feel good, and to feel like a man who had once known how to be kind without thinking about it first.

We are told that we have a large number of our own poor and destitute to take care of, that the charity we dispense should be bestowed in this quarter, that the peculiar position of ourselves and our co-religionists demands it at our hands, that justice is a higher virtue than generosity, that self-preservation is a law and principle of our nature . . . It is true that there is but one connecting link between us and the sufferers . . . That link is humanity.
Rabbi Jacques Judah Lyons, Famine Relief fund-raiser, New York, February 1847

Brother, my voice is become weak – you can scarcely hear me. It is not the shout of a warrior but the wail of an infant. I have lost it in mourning over the desolation and injuries of my people . . . Our warriors are nearly all gone to the West, but here are our dead. Will you compel us to go too, and give their bones to the wolves? Our people's tears fell like drops of rain, their lamentations were borne away by the passing winds. The palefaces heeded them not and our land was taken from us. Brother! You speak the words of a mighty nation. I am a shadow . . . my people are scattered and gone. When I shout, I hear my voice in the depths of the forest, but no answering voice comes back to me – all is silent around me. My words therefore must be few. I can now say no more.
Colonel Cobb, Choctaw Chief, 1831

It was their last day. Their flight home from New Orleans airport was due to take off at 9.15 p.m. Fergal and Martin were sitting in a bar on Decatur Street, on the river front. They'd delivered the Pontiac to Hertz as soon as they'd arrived in the early afternoon and Martin, between beers, was sorting out his expenses. The table was covered with invoices, receipts and a hundred other scraps of paper rescued from various trouser pockets. When he'd totted it all up, after much head-scratching and mumbling, he winced. 'Jesus,' he said, 'if they believe this figure, I'll be getting away with it by the skin of my rosy, red, royal, English arse. Luckily, they never check. Well, hardly ever. To tell you the truth, I'm past caring. I don't care what they do to me.'

He looked pretty rough. But to Fergal he seemed calmer, as if he'd made a decision. Fergal decided not to bring up the subject. It would only upset him. And since he had never mentioned Siofradh, he wasn't going to bring up that subject either. He didn't really feel like talking much, so the pair of them just sleepily sat and looked out over the Mississippi. It was such a beautiful day, warm and comforting. Even the steamboat chugging along looked, not like something for the tourists, but like a real working craft, a boat with a heavy purpose and crucial cargo. The bar's background nattering was a nice watery sound, a quiet buzz-saw, and the waitress was under instructions just to keep the beers coming.

Fergal reached into his pocket and took out an A4 page, ragged and crumpled. He'd been carrying it around for months. 'Martin. *Sa-ga-nosh.*'

Martin opened his eyes.

'I want to show you something. I made it myself. I'm thinking of getting it printed up and framed.' Now he felt embarrassed.

Martin held out his hand, puzzled, and studied it. It was a calendar. A Lakota Moon Calendar, in which every fourteen days of all our months Fergal had translated into an Indian Moon. Martin stared at it. 'Where are we now?' he whispered.

'The seventh of April.'

'The seventh of April – "Big Leaf Moon".' He read out others – 'Silk Corn Moon, Flying Ants Moon, Moon of the Deer Pawing the Earth, Geese Going Moon, Moon of Popping Trees, Moon of the Snowblind, Moon when Wolves Run Together, Moon of Making Fat . . .' He looked up. 'How long did this take you?'

'Oh – months of research!' Fergal laughed. It was closer to two years. 'I dunno – I kept reading all this stuff and it just struck me as a nice idea. Something to do.'

Martin trailed his finger along those Moons which represented June, and July, and August, and was struck by their optimism and beauty. July or August. Tops. No chance for her beyond that. Not seriously. Strawberry Moon, Ripe Cherries Moon, Moon of the Red Blooming Lilies, Hot Weather Begins Moon. He was miserable but he smiled to himself anyway and Fergal looked out of the window. To Martin this made it seem a tiny bit less painful somehow, as if by stepping outside our own notions of time we could make the history to come bounce off us in a different way. 'What does *Sa-ga-nosh* mean, by the way?'

'"Englishman". Sounds like "*Sassenach*", doesn't it . . . ?'

'Oh – I thought it might have meant "faggot".' He smiled before Fergal could protest.

Behind the bar someone turned on the TV.

'Fergal?' said Martin.

Fergal turned to look at him. Martin had tears in his eyes but looked less of a mess now. Stronger, more nailed down, somehow.

'I just want to thank you for letting me tag along. It's been . . . interesting. And I'm sorry for being a pain in the arse sometimes.' He really meant it.

Fergal smiled warmly. *You silly sod*, he thought. 'Hey –

don't worry about it. Thanks for the car hire. And listen – when we get home, I'll come with you.'

Martin flinched slightly.

'I'll come with you. You won't have to go to the hospital by yourself. It'll be okay. It really will. I'll come with you. That kind of thing doesn't bother me at all.'

Martin looked at him seriously. 'Thank you. I'd like that.' He reached out his hand. Fergal took it and as they grasped each other's palms, the TV reporter's astringent voice pierced the cool and placid air: *'James La Salle, convicted killer, died today at fourteen minutes past two, in the electric chair at Georgia's Diagnostic and Classification Center. Officials at the Center report that it was a clean and standard execution. About twenty anti-death-penalty advocates remained outside the prison right up to the end. At this stage, we do not yet know if La Salle had any last words, but it is rumored that . . .'*

Behind the bar someone turned off the TV. A disinterested murmur moved around the lounge.

Fergal and Martin gripped each other's hands still and stared into each other's eyes. Martin was trembling. Fergal tried to transmit calmness through his pores. Martin looked quietly transfixed for a moment and Fergal's knuckles were beginning to hurt. After a long moment, Martin took a deep breath, very slowly let go of Fergal's hand and sat back in his chair, staring at the table. Then he looked up and smiled the saddest smile Fergal had ever seen. 'It's okay. Really.'

Then he poured himself another beer, got out his paper and began to read. It wasn't okay. But it might be. Good enough to be going on with.

Fergal gazed out again at the river. He felt calm. Misplaced tenderness. That was okay. Nourishment for the guilty. A slap on the wrist for the despairing. A little plundering mirth for the hungry. He glanced at the phone and away again. Had La Salle asked for forgiveness in his last moments?

The sun began to go down west of the Mississippi and a piece of sweet and anxious blues leaked from the jukebox, like some eighth harmony of the rainbow. He lazily looked at the bar staff moving around and the waitresses, the essence of caution, with their trays balanced and balancing, themselves, over tables like shy apprentices. He watched Martin put down his paper and pick up a pen, and take a piece of blank paper from his inside pocket and begin to write in careful longhand. He was writing his last piece of copy. He didn't even know if he had a job any more, but he was going to get the Braves down on paper if it killed him. Without asking, Fergal knew what he was writing and he knew that it would be good. He was writing and oblivious, brow furrowed, tongue protruding, and it would be a wonderful story of guts and skill, and the broken hearts of some players who have to lose because they are scared of winning. Fergal settled back in his chair. He had never felt so sleepily comfortable in his life. He looked again at the phone. He would go with him and perhaps look after him a little, and he would try to be an impeccable friend. There was always hope. There must be. Because if there wasn't, then he and others would lie down and simply die. So there was always hope. It was common sense. He hoped that La Salle had asked for forgiveness. That would be a good and clean thing, if he had. A clean moment for all our charlatans' hearts. Charity from a wounded and disappearing wife, from a stunning and reasonable girl, forgiveness from a small life barely started. It was not a possibility. It was a necessity.

The sun went down and the bar filled up, and Fergal spent the late, lazy afternoon simply watching. Watching, and glancing now and again at the phone, and listening to the jukebox and the muffled crinkle of pen on paper.

What is life? It is the flash of a firefly in the night. It is the breath of a buffalo in the winter time. It is the little shadow which runs across the grass and loses itself in the sunset.

Crowfoot, Spokesman for the Blackfoot Confederacy,
April 1890